THE ROOM WAS EMPTY EXCEPT FOR BARBARELLA STRETCHED OUT, STILL ASLEEP, THIS TIME ON A WIG BOX.

The cold tingle at the back of Anna's neck subsided. Her own face, looking back from the mirror, wore a strained, worried expression. There were circles under her eyes.

As she turned to go her sleeve caught a glass and sent it rolling off the edge of the dressing-table. She stooped automatically to pick it up.

As she looked up, she saw something was wrong. The cat's eyes were open. The mouth was open too. It seemed to be laughing.

Anna stared. A tiny drop of blood hung like a scarlet tear from one sharp tooth. It gathered weight, stretched, and dropped to the floor.

She straightened abruptly, and reached out an unwilling hand to touch the creamy fur. Her hands were clammy.

She ran her fingers down the little cat's side. There was no sign of life but she found the hard circle of a nail head hidden deep in the fur. The point had been driven through Barbarella's chest pinning her to the lid of the box.

Bantam Crime Line Books offer the finest in classic and modern British murder mysteries
Ask your bookseller for the books you have missed

UNDER CONTRACT

Liza Cody

BANTAM BOOKS

NEW YORK · TORONTO · LONDON · SYDNEY · AUCKLAND

This edition contains the complete text
of the original hardcover edition.
NOT ONE WORD HAS BEEN OMITTED.

UNDER CONTRACT

A Bantam Book / published by arrangement with
Charles Scribner's Sons

PRINTING HISTORY

First published in Great Britain by William Collins Sons
& Co. Ltd 1986
Bantam edition / August 1990

ISBN 0-553-28345-6

Published simultaneously in the United States and Canada

Bantam Books are published by Bantam Books, a division of Bantam
Doubleday Dell Publishing Group, Inc. Its trademark, consisting of
the words "Bantam Books" and the portrayal of a rooster, is Regis-
tered in U.S. Patent and Trademark Office and in other countries.
Marca Registrada. Bantam Books, 666 Fifth Avenue, New York, New
York 10103.

PRINTED IN THE UNITED STATES OF AMERICA

RAD   0 9 8 7 6 5 4 3 2 1

UNDER CONTRACT

Chapter 1

A top-heavy pile of bagged debris blocked the entrance to the office. Bernie took a deep breath and sucked in his stomach as he sidled past it. But he was a bulky man and his thick winter coat became smeared with cement and mortar. Anna, skipping up stairs behind him, had no such trouble.

'I'll have to lose some weight,' Bernie said sadly as he banged the dust out of his coat. 'We should change places. You live with Syl for a month and let her feed you up. I'll take over your gaff and live off apples and tinned soup like you do. We'd both feel the benefit.'

'Starting when?' Anna asked eagerly. They both laughed and turned towards the rec-room to make coffee.

Change was in the air. It hung like the dust. Martin Brierly had the builders in.

A month ago Martin Brierly had bought the lease on the language school next door, and now a newly plastered gap in the wall linked the Brierly Security office with its mirror image on the other side.

Typically, the first change was to his office. He now had a larger, grander one, a small waiting-room for clients, a bathroom all to himself, and a private entrance.

'Expansion!' Beryl cried in tones of equally mixed pride and funk. 'More room for my office. The Commander says I shall have to take on a girl.' The word 'girl' was said with a pucker of distaste that creased her crimson lipstick.

'Not a *girl*!' Anna sounded aghast.

'Well, not just anyone.' Beryl ignored her sarcasm.

'I've got a system here and I don't want anyone interfering. Good systems don't grow on trees.'

At the moment work was about to begin on the rec-room and this was causing problems. The five Brierly Security agents came in as usual at half past eight to find their meagre furniture cleared away from the wall. They huddled uncomfortably in one corner while the rest of the space was taken up with equipment, cables for power tools, and a ten-foot I-beam which Phil Maitland and Johnny Crocker had already fallen over.

Worst of all, when the builders themselves filtered in at nine, there was nowhere for them to sit. Both Anna and Bernie offered to make coffee for them but they preferred to drink from their Thermos flasks while they stood in a defensive ring around their tool bags.

Tension had been building up for several days. It was caused by too many jokes about gumshoes and keyhole peepers, and by the agents' habit of falling silent whenever one of the builders came near.

Even Beryl was bitter. A week ago the youngest of the builders in a clumsy attempt to chat up Anna had said, 'Is this all the crumpet? Just you and that bossy-boots secretary?'

Remarks like that never went unheard. Beryl would have overlooked 'crumpet,' she might even have forgiven 'bossy-boots,' but 'secretary' was a fatal insult. Beryl could be Office Manager or Head of Administration, but never, never a secretary. Her methods of revenge were small but she made them felt.

Now, as she was issuing the day's instructions, she called each of the agents by their titles – Mr Schiller, Mr Baker, Mr Crocker, Mr Maitland, Miss Lee, but as she swept out she fixed the foreman with a spiteful glare and said sweetly, 'Oh, Alf, be in my office in ten minutes, won't you? If you've *quite* finished your tea, that is.'

'Snotty cow,' Alf replied, when she was well out of ear-shot. And Anna who would normally have agreed found her-self stiffening. The temperature between the two camps fell another degree. Only Bernie Schiller, Brierly Security's el-der statesman, seemed immune. He spoke in his normal tone of voice and not the self-conscious whisper the others adopted. Without him relations between builders and agents would have broken down completely.

A few minutes later the builders screwed the tops on their flasks and attacked the wall.

'They might've waited till we'd gone,' Tim Baker shouted above the din. Johnny ducked a flying lump of masonry as he made for the door.

'Sorry about that,' Alf said innocently. 'But some of us can't sit on our bums gossiping all day.'

First strike to the away team Anna thought as she hid herself in the washroom. The rest of the home team dispersed to their various tasks. She had an appointment with Martin Brierly himself in a few minutes and didn't want to appear covered in brick dust.

'Sit!' he ordered when she came in. He sounded like a dog-handler. She crossed the new tough carpet and sat on one of his new tough steel and plastic chairs. He did not look up but spent the next five minutes signing letters and cheques. He examined each cheque minutely, wearing an expression of acute discomfort. The hair on his perfectly round head was thinning as if the nap had worn off a tennis ball.

At length he said, 'Well, Miss Lee, interesting circumstances have arisen, I'm sending you on attachment to J. W. Protection. We haven't dealt with them before so I will accompany you myself.'

'J.W.?' Anna said, startled. 'What do they want with us? They don't need stringers – they've got all the personnel they can handle.'

'Industrial security requires numbers,' Brierly said airily. 'Van drivers, couriers, night watchmen. They are highly organized, I grant you, but their complement of specialized agents is relatively small, as is always the case when quantity rather than quality is the order of the day.' He leaned back, looking pleased with himself. 'Besides,' he added with a quick glance at his watch, 'for some reason they need an extra woman.'

'What for?' Anna began, but she was interrupted by the buzzer on his desk. Brierly flicked a switch and Beryl's voice said, 'Your driver has arrived.'

'Driver?' Anna smothered a grin, but Mr Brierly was

already out of his chair and shrugging on his raincoat. She followed his soldierly back out of the door and down the stairs on to Kensington High Street. Light cold rain sprinkled the pavement. A waxy black Rover waited by the kerb. The driver, collar turned up, peaked cap pulled down, stood miserably beside it. Brierly tapped the ground once with his furled umbrella and the driver opened the door. Brierly got in without a word of greeting.

"Morning," Anna mumbled. She was embarrassed. The driver ignored her and took his place behind the wheel. They set off at a stately pace. If Martin Brierly had overcome his miserly instincts enough to spend money on the hire of a car, it meant he was seriously trying to impress the competition.

J. W. Protection certainly had a reputation in the trade. There were three partners with backgrounds in the Army and Security Services, and they had recruited mainly from the forces. Anna could not imagine what they would want or need from a small, personal firm like Brierly Security. It was as if a supermarket chain had gone to the local family butcher for a lamb chop.

J.W.'s headquarters was in the commercial section of Chiswick. It was surrounded by a steel mesh fence. A uniformed guard stood by the gate and checked their identities from a list on a clipboard. He then waved them through a large car park which held ranks of armoured vans and patrol cars. The mechanics working there wore overalls designed to look like army fatigues.

The atmosphere was one of extreme efficiency, but appearances could be misleading. Anna knew at least two men who had joined J.W. one particularly hard winter for the sole purpose of acquiring the good pair of boots and heavy greatcoat which were part of the uniform. They had resigned in the spring, having slept their way through their nightwatch duties and avoided any of the perimeter patrols which J.W. guaranteed their clients.

She was grinning when they reached the main doors. Their names were checked again before they were escorted up to the first floor, along a corridor, and through a door with 'Executive and VIP Division' stencilled on the glass.

Grey steel filing cabinets and desks were squared off

with military precision. Each desk had a grey plastic waste-bin on the right-hand side of it which made Anna wonder if J.W. agents were selected for right-handedness.

A door to an inner office opened and an athletic-looking man with suit and hair to match the filing cabinets emerged. He looked at his watch and said, 'Ah, Brierly, good of you to come.' Martin Brierly was whisked out of sight and the door closed, leaving Anna alone with the regiment of desks.

Chapter 2

She read a list of instructions telling J.W. agents about use of the shredder, number of copies allowed from the photocopier, what not to do in the darkroom. A postscript mentioned that in order to avoid abuse of company phones outgoing calls would be randomly monitored.

Two men came in from the corridor so she left the noticeboard and leaned nonchalantly against a desk.

One of them said, 'Bandits at four o'clock,' and they paused in the doorway surveying her as if she were a horse on its way to the starting gate. They were both dressed like young businessmen.

'What's she doing here?' the taller one asked. The other one said, 'Must be the spare skirt from Smallfry Security.' They both laughed.

'I'm from the Equal Opportunities Action Squad,' Anna said. 'I see you haven't filled your quota of fifty per cent left-handers. Tut-tut.'

'No minority groups allowed in here,' the tall one said. 'Fancy a cup of coffee?' He went away to get one. The other man said, 'I'm Dave McPhee, Exec and VIP Div. You can call me darling.'

'Anna Lee, Brierly Security,' she countered. 'Call me irresponsible.'

They stared at each other. He was so broad in the shoulder that he looked like an upside down pyramid. The heavy muscles of his neck made his ears seem as if they were hiding behind pillars. He said, 'Anyone tell you what's going down?'

'No.'

'Your governor in with Colonel Bogey?' Her jerked a thumb at the inner office door. Anna nodded. He said, 'Better let the brass tell you, then. Security begins at home.'

'Give the girl a break,' the tall one said, coming back with three cups on a plastic tray. 'We're going to be on the same account.'

'So long as she knows who's boss,' Dave said, taking a cup and passing one to Anna. She accepted it, muttering, 'Yessir, thank you, sir.' J.W. coffee, she noted, was just as bad as Brierly Security's.

'This here's Kevin,' Dave said. 'Just don't think you can give me the old eyelash treatment like you can him. Some of us don't just roll over for a pretty face.'

'Is this personal?' Anna asked. 'Or are you practising for your Charm Test?'

'Don't mind him,' Kevin put in. 'Like I said, we don't allow minority groups in here. He doesn't know how to behave with the fair sex.'

'The what?' Anna put her cup down. 'Are there really no women working here?'

'Apart from the clericals, in this division there's only Julie,' Kevin told her. 'And she's on sick leave.'

'Sick, my eye!' Dave snorted. 'She couldn't stand the heat. I hope you're tougher than you look.'

'Probably tougher than *you* look, too.' She glared at him. He snorted again. The door to the inner office opened and the grey-haired man came out followed by Martin Brierly. Dave and Kevin put their cups down and stood up straight. Martin Brierly frowned at Anna who remained perched on the edge of a desk.

The grey-haired man said, 'Well, it seems as if Miss Lee's already acquainted with Mr McPhee. I'll leave the briefing up to you, Brierly, old chap.' He turned to Anna and said, 'Glad to have you under contract, young lady.' He shook hands with Brierly.

'Goodbye,' Dave and Kevin said in a polite chorus.

'*Ciao*,' Anna called as she followed Brierly out. He said nothing until they were back in the Rover and passing through the main gate. Then he turned to her irritably and said, 'Do you have to be so casual, Miss Lee? That's a tight ship they run there, a tight ship. I didn't take you along to have you show me up like that.'

'Why did you take me along?' Anna was irritable too. 'All I did was hang around like a goldfish in a shark tank and take insults. Spare skirt! I'll give him spare skirt on the end of a cricket bat!'

'Well, that, of course, is their problem,' Mr Brierly said. He leaned back against the leather upholstery and looked smug. 'They may have all the manpower they need, but they simply don't have a balanced team.' He looked so smug that Anna was convinced money must already have changed hands. 'What they don't consider is that some of their VIPs are going to be ladies who don't welcome round-the-clock protection from a man.'

'Is that what the job is?' Anna asked. 'Minding?'

'Basically, yes. But I gather there are complications. The client is Daniel Horowitz Management. Now *his* client, the lady who requires our services, is someone I've never heard of. But I'm sure she's well enough known to your generation – a lady rejoicing in the name of Shona Una.'

'I've heard of her,' Anna said thoughtfully. 'She's quite new, though. Is this a PR exercise or is there a reason?'

'According to Colonel Beamish, it's a bit of both.' Brierly put on his patronizing smile. 'He says that J.W. are doing quite well out of pop stars who like to turn up at concerts escorted by bodyguards. But apparently Mr Horowitz has some worries which he thinks ought to be taken seriously. Colonel Beamish assigned two of his agents to the case – one of whom you've met – and their initial reports suggest that there's no cause for concern.'

'The woman they had on the job,' Anna began carefully. 'Julie something – I was told she couldn't stand the pace. What does that mean?'

'She has 'flu or something.' Mr Brierly looked out of the window. He seemed reassured by the sight of Hammersmith rolling past his window, glad to get back to his own territory. He shrugged and went on, 'There was some suggestion of generation gap, though. The young lady she was assigned to is several years her junior. Perhaps she felt out of place among that generation. Different values, you know.' He shrugged again and added tartly, 'Of course you should find no such difficulty.' And then, because the case itself did not interest him much while the fact that J.W. had been forced to coopt him obviously did, he said, 'Balance, Miss Lee, I cannot overstress the value of a balanced team.'

Nothing more was said till the Rover pulled up outside the office, when Anna punctured his well-being by asking, 'Who am I supposed to report to? Where exactly am I working from?'

'We'll talk about the details upstairs, if you don't mind,' he said, hurriedly getting out of the car and making for the stairs. It was still raining and Anna, following more slowly, thought they had better weather in Chiswick.

Chapter 3

Upstairs, everything was covered with a fine layer of dust. The builders had punched their way through the rec-room wall. The ceiling and I-beam were supported by two Acrow-jacks and the men were beginning to sweep up the debris. Beryl, rosy with annoyance, was sneezing and complaining of grit between her teeth.

Anna glanced at the mess and for once decided against a cup of tea. She went straight to Mr Brierly's office where she found him dabbing at his desk with a handkerchief. She brushed the dust off a chair and sat down. She would not mind working away from the dirt and noise for a while.

She said as much to Mr Brierly, who looked up sharply from the contents of his briefcase. He seemed about to say something but stopped himself. Instead he handed her a slim plastic folder and another difference between J.W. and Brierly Security became immediately apparent. The folder looked more like a holiday brochure than a functional client file.

The contents, however, were brief and to the point: Subject – security for the Shona Una UK tour; Required manpower – two permanent officers, others as required; Dates of concerts; Venues – which of them had security staff of their own and who to liaise with; Hotels; Tour personnel; Travel arrangements; and so on. So far there had been only one concert. The tour had opened without incident in Birmingham and there was a short report to that effect at the back of the file.

Mr Brierly said, 'Copy that. There are a lot of useful names and numbers there. Meanwhile, you have an appointment with Mr Horowitz at one o'clock in Greek Street. You are to take two passport photographs.' He leaned back in his chair and laced his fingers across his waistcoat. 'Now, procedure,' he said thoughtfully, fixing his eyes on a point a few inches behind Anna's left ear. 'This is J. W. Protection's account – there should be no doubt about that. You should at all times show yourself to be willing, helpful, and polite. However, there should be no doubt either that you are a Brierly Security operative. It might transpire – I hope not, but it might – that action is required of you that would not be countenanced by this firm. In such an eventuality I would expect you to act with discretion and inform me immediately. I would, in any case, like regular progress reports.'

'That would be all right with J.W., I take it?' Anna asked innocently. Mr Brierly swung his chair away to face the window. She smiled at the back of his head. 'I would not anticipate any conflict of loyalty, Miss Lee,' he said to the double glazing, 'and I would not like J.W. to get the impression that there was any. That being so, your communications with this office should be private.' He swung his chair round again and Anna met his gaze with a straight look of her own. He smiled stiffly and went on, 'For your own safety, Miss Lee, I want to know at all times where you are and what you're doing.'

'Of course,' Anna said. 'Thank you.'

He relaxed. 'Well then, perhaps you should be on your way to Greek Street.' She turned to go but he stopped her by the door. 'You might like to know, Miss Lee, that, along with all the other changes we are undergoing, we may very soon be re-evaluating the salary structures. That'll be something to look forward to when all the alterations are complete.'

Anna nearly laughed out loud. Instead, she said seriously, 'That's great, Mr Brierly,' and put a suitably grateful expression on her face. She hesitated and then added, 'That reminds me. Since I'm going on the road, I wonder if you'd have a word with Beryl for me. Travelling with a rock star might be expensive, and Beryl's very, er, careful about floats.'

'Rightly so,' he replied sourly. 'But I agree, these are exceptional circumstances. Don't worry, I'll sort something out.'

In the back of a taxi she gave way to the giggles. There was nothing like a nervous boss for making life suddenly and unexpectedly easy. The taxi was proof. Beryl herself, with bad grace to be sure, had suggested Anna take one. However poorly Brierly estimated her services, he did not want any competition for them. Exceptional circumstances indeed!

Chapter 4

Horowitz Management had its home on the top two floors of a narrow building tightly wedged between cutting-rooms and a porno cinema. The chaos and overcrowding of Soho was reproduced upstairs in the reception area where girls, their make-up as thick as winter woollies, dealt with scores of importuning punters, clamorous telephones and untidy piles of paper.

Anna was rescued from the mêlée by a man in his fifties wearing a pink-striped shirt. 'Anna Lee?' he said, anxiously regarding her with watery blue eyes. 'Yes, good, did you bring the photos? Yes? Sadie, my sweet, take these down to Whatsisname and get him to run us off another thingy. Anna Lee. That's right. She's joining the tour. And a couple of the sweatshirts. Medium? Yes, medium. I want everything ready when we get back. Joanie darling, what day is it?'

'Chez Angelo,' Joanie darling said without looking up. 'But, Mr. Horowitz . . .'

'Later, darling.' He set off through the crush and down the stairs like the White Rabbit. Anna trotted after him. In the street he struggled into a squeaky new leather coat, still moving at a brisk pace and remarking breathlessly, 'It never ends, it never ends, and what for, I ask you? They've no idea, simply no idea.' He veered sharply across the road into a side street and then dived into a basement restaurant. Down the steps he went, now struggling out of the coat that had been hardly worth putting on. 'Ah, Angelo,' he said, out of breath, 'nice to see you. My usual! Thank you, and a bottle of your . . . Over here, Anna, you can just squeeze through, can't you, darling? Sit, do sit, oh your coat, yes, Angelo, the young lady's coat.'

He collapsed into a chair at a cramped corner table and let out his breath. '*Oi veh*, what a life,' he sighed, handing her a menu. 'White meat, I recommend white meat and white wine here. Red inflames, you know. I wanted to get you on your own because what I've got to say is absolutely confidential and gossip runs round that office like a greyhound. You like music? What about Shona Una, have you heard of her?'

The sudden break in his conversation caught Anna unprepared. She cleared her throat and began, 'She's pretty new, isn't she? I think *Bitterness* is great, but . . .'

'Well, that's something.' He ran his hand over his sparse hair and looked at her closely for the first time. 'Maybe you'll do. The last one they sent thought music began and ended with the Hallelujah Chorus and made no bones about it. Rubbed poor Roz up the wrong way. You've got to get along with Roz or we're wasting our time.'

'Roz?' Anna asked, ducking as a waiter rushed and deposited a bottle of white wine on the table as he went. Mr Horowitz poured a splash into two glasses. 'Roz, Shona Una, what difference? Look, I'm worried about that girl. She's been on my books going on four years and she's been there or thereabouts club-wise ever since. Not a bad following. Nothing to write home about, but not bad. *Bitterness* was the big one, the lucky one, the one you pray at night for. Now we've got the LP and the tour and I don't want it all spoiled. You understand? We could be talking mega-mega. I'm not saying it *will* happen, but it might if nothing screws it up.'

The waiter hovered over them, pencil poised. Anna, who had not had time to look at the menu, said, 'The same,' when Mr Horowitz ordered. He smiled his approval. In spite of not having time to look at him properly either, Anna thought he was rather nice. The tired pouchy face managed to look quirky and kindly when it smiled. She said, 'What might spoil it, Mr Horowitz? What are you worried about?'

He sighed. 'I can talk to you, can't I? You're young, but you know how to listen, don't you?' Anna nodded. She didn't have much choice. 'You've got to be tolerant in this game,' he went on with scarcely a pause. 'They lead a strange life, these artists. Lots of pressure – image and so on. You may think it's superficial, but it's life and death in their business. And they're children, you know. Don't know fire burns. You read the music press? No? Well, who does? But there was a bit in *Sounds* about the gig in Birmingham. "Shona Una – Will Bitterness Go Sour?" They could kill her, you know. She was late out. Kept the kids waiting. They don't like that, you know. There was the usual announcement about technical difficulties but it didn't wash.'

'What happened.'

'She was locked in the dressing-room. All ready. But she just wouldn't come out. It was lucky I was there. I don't usually go – my ears, you know. But I drove up specially, this being the tour opening. Well, she let me in finally, but she was shaking and carrying on like Judy Garland. I don't know how we got her out there, but thank God, we did.'

'And was she okay? What did she do out there?'

'What does a fish do in water? It swims. She was fine. She's a pro. But it did my heart no good at all. All that money, the record company, the promoter, sponsors. You wouldn't believe the money depending on that poor girl. Word gets round she's unreliable and she's dead, believe you me, she's one dead girl.'

The waiter came with the food. Anna looked round while he served it. The restaurant was packed, mainly with men hunched over the tiny tables talking nineteen to the dozen. Forks flashed, glasses emptied, but everyone seemed to concentrate on talk rather than lunch.

While Mr Horowitz had his fork in his mouth, she said, 'This wasn't just nerves, was it? You wouldn't want my help with stage fright, would you? What happened before Birmingham?'

'Good girl.' He chewed rapidly. 'After *Bitterness* began to take off and before Birmingham things were beginning to roll. You know it's happening – the people you want to talk to are always in when you call, the money comes sniffing instead of the other way round. Success just round the corner. You can smell it. Wonderful. And Roz was loving it – interviews, photo calls. A girl like Roz, well, all those years begging for a mention somewhere, knocking on all those doors, and now they're knocking on hers. And then, suddenly, she shuts up. Doesn't answer the phone. When she does, it's 'Oh Danny, I'm not sure. Perhaps the timing's wrong. I'm not ready.' Not ready! What's she been doing all these years? Knitting mittens? And the deals! If she'd pulled out, it'd've been like Centre Point falling down. You've no idea what it takes to put a thing like this together.'

The fork hung suspended in mid-air and sweat broke out on his upper lip. He suddenly looked quite unwell. Anna hurriedly poured him some more wine. He patted her hand. 'Don't worry about me. I want you to look after Roz. I want to know what's wrong. That other one they sent suggested drugs. I'm not saying it isn't, but Roz's been a long time in this business. It wouldn't happen overnight. But anyway, if someone's giving her something she can't handle I want to be told. Or if it's a lover I don't know about, whatever. If I know what it is, I can sort it out. If I don't, I can't.'

'You must've asked her yourself, Mr Horowitz.' Anna leaned forward. 'What does she say?'

'She doesn't say anything. I won't say we're close, because we're not. Well, not particularly, but I always thought she trusted me. Now she treats me like the enemy. I say, "What's up, Roz, tell Danny," and she accuses me of interrogating her, sapping her confidence. You'd think I was trying to wreck her career. Me! So when the question of security for the tour came up I thought I'd put someone next to her, keep an eye on her, you know. Only they sent me this klutz in support stockings who doesn't know rock from reggae even.

'Roz isn't hard to get along with, or she wasn't till a few weeks ago, so what I'm asking is for you to get close to her, make yourself useful, find out what's on her mind.'

Anna had only a hazy picture of Roz, and listening to Daniel Horowitz, she couldn't make up her mind whether he cared for her as a person or as a property. When she asked him about her, he gave the impression that either he did not know her individually or he was unwilling to describe her. He drifted too easily into trade descriptions. 'Oh, she's creative all right,' he said, over pudding. 'She writes some of her own material – I know what you're thinking, but she does. She's not really in the singer-songwriter category, though.'

He had talked about her so often in those terms, attempted to sell her so many times, Anna thought, he was quite unable to think about her personally. At other times, though, she thought she saw an almost paternal anxiety. 'She should see her family more often, make new friends away from the business. There are too many dogs around the bone here. Sincerity's a rare commodity, never mind what you read in interviews.'

By the time coffee arrived Anna had decided she would just have to make up her own mind when she met her. Some warning notes were sounded here too. He fingered his saucer and looked a little evasive. 'I'll call her later on and break the ice for you,' he said. 'She's staying at a friend's place for now. Don't go round there till I give the say-so, will you? And listen, as far as she's concerned you're part of general security, all right? I'll check with the tour manager too, so he'll be expecting you. And another thing: like I said, there's a lot of interests represented, Dog Records, Vanguard Promotions, etcetera. Now they're the people who want everything like clockwork. I wouldn't want anyone to know I'm concerned. Confidence – that's the name of the game. So watch who you talk to, all right? Anything wrong – you tell me, no-one else, not even the guys you work with. Anything iffy that gets out finds its way straight into the media, and then kaput!'

Back at the Horowitz office, Anna discovered that the 'thingy' was a large white identification badge with her picture on it. 'White's for security,' Joanie darling said, handing it to Anna. 'That's right, isn't it, Danny?'

'That'll get you in anywhere,' Mr Horowitz told her.

'I put in two T-shirts as well as the sweatshirts.' Joanie darling produced a plastic carrier bag. She was more efficient than she looked. Anna took the bag.

'Okay.' Mr Horowitz drew her out of everyone's hearing. 'You've got my private numbers, right? And I've got yours. Don't do anything till you hear from me. And . . .'

'Don't talk to anyone but you,' Anna finished for him.

Chapter 5

The design on the sweatshirts was a silver-winged snake spitting out the words, 'Shona Una UK Tour.' It was the same on the T-shirts. The basic colour was black, and it looked as if one good wash would finish them for ever. Anna sighed and put them back in the bag.

The taxi stopped at her door. As she got out she saw Selwyn Price, a ludicrous figure in a green waterproof poncho and hat, pedalling his bike towards her. There was something wrong with his brakes. He took his feet off the pedals and tried to stop himself. His shoes slipped on the wet road so he tried to get off with the bike still moving.

Anna squatted on the kerb to untangle his left leg from the chain. His shoelace had come undone and was jammed in the links. She said, 'You'll have to take your shoe off.'

Selwyn stopped cursing and did as he was told. The taxi-driver said, 'Do I get my money now or do we wait for the rest of the circus?' Anna paid him. Selwyn picked himself up and hopped over to the front door. Anna followed with the bicycle. Chain and shoe dragged noisily behind.

'What you want is a "Just Married" sign,' the taxi-driver called as he pulled away. 'Or better yet – get the comic a pushchair.'

Selwyn turned round to reply and put his unshod foot down in a puddle. As homecomings went, this was a little worse than usual. Anna bundled Selwyn, bike, and shoe into the hall. He found the key and opened the door to his flat. 'What're you doing home so early?' He wrung out his sock into Bea's carefully nurtured begonia. 'And a taxi. Did someone die and leave you the cab fare? Where are you going?'

'Upstairs,' Anna told him. 'I'm going to get my tool kit. And then I'm going to fix your bike. You're a public nuisance, Selwyn Price. What's more you're a bloody danger to yourself and anyone who comes within a half a mile of you. You've no sodding coordination.'

'Well, nobody's perfect,' Selwyn relied in a huff.

'Just average would be a big improvement.' She ran up the stairs and let herself into her own flat. The air felt damp and chilly. She lit the gas fire and went to the kitchen to sort out some tools. If she had any sense of responsibility to mankind, she thought, she'd take the bike to bits and bury each one separately in the garden. The only thing that stopped her was the alarming thought that Selwyn might retaliate by taking driving lessons.

She had replaced Selwyn's chain so many times she could almost do it blindfolded. Grumbling and insulting him at the same time was part of the ritual. Selwyn expected it – he even enjoyed it. 'I don't care what you say,' he had admitted once, 'so long as it's *me* you're talking about.'

Today, however, he was oddly contrite. He even made her a cup of tea, which was completely out of character for him. Normally, his idea of hospitality was to point at the wine bottle and tell her to help herself – and while she was on her feet how about refilling *his* glass?

Now he hovered behind her, unusually subdued and offering to help. The offer aroused her suspicions. After a while he sat down on the stairs and said, 'What do you do with your money, Leo?'

'What money?' Anna was surprised. Selwyn was simply not interested in money. That was Bea's responsibility. It came and it went. And so long as he had enough for the odd bottle, his paper and typewriter ribbons he didn't care where it came from or went to or in what quantities.

'Well, er, just money,' he replied awkwardly. 'I mean, haven't you got some put by . . . in a building society or something? Like candles. I mean, you've always got candles when there's a power cut, haven't you? You're a very practical person, Leo.'

In fact she did have a small emergency fund. It was for the time when Martin Brierly either fired her or went broke himself. When thought about rationally, neither event was likely, but Anna was no more rational about her fears than anyone else. It wasn't much, just enough to last for a couple of weeks while she looked for another job.

'Is there an emergency?' she asked. Selwyn looked away, embarrassed. Anna turned back to the bike and rubbed at the rust which was causing the brakes to lock. Selwyn coughed and fidgeted. Finally he said, 'Leo . . . you know Foolscap Press . . . ?'

'The one's who're publishing *Whole and Corners*?'

This was to be Selwyn's second collection of poems and he was very proud of it.

'Yes, and they've stolen my books,' Selwyn said dramatically. 'Well, held them hostage actually. And I can't raise the ransom.'

'What on earth are you talking about?' She turned to look at him. He had his head in his hands. He groaned and said, 'Foolscap's gone bust. They've got the liquidator in.'

'What rotten luck,' she said sympathetically. But there was worse to come, and by and by the story came out. In the first place, Selwyn had agreed to take his payment after publication and it was well past that date now. His books were printed and ready, but because Foolscap was in liquidation there was no money for him.

In the second place, the receiver had written to Selwyn asking if he had any claim on the company. But Selwyn, with his mind on loftier things, had stuffed the unopened letter in his dressing-gown pocket. Bea had only found it this morning, when she was about to take the dressing-gown to the launderette. After Selwyn read it, he panicked.

'It was like finding a scorpion in the lucky dip,' he told Anna glumly. 'I was expecting a cheque, you see.' In the letter the receiver told him that if he had a claim he must register it immediately. The deadline had expired last week.

Selwyn sweated and dithered over the phone all morning. Then, feeling he should tackle the receiver in person, he had pedalled in a frenzy over to Camden Lock to see him. There he was told that, since he had not registered as a creditor, he would lose not only the money Foolscap owed him but also his books. All fifteen hundred of them were now part of the company's assets. They would be sold and the proceeds would go to pay off other creditors.

'And that's robbery,' Selwyn cried. 'It's my work, isn't it? But all the profits will go to the printers and solicitors and I shan't see a penny.'

Privately, Anna did not think there would be much by way of profits if his previous royalties were anything to go by. But she said, 'So you thought you could buy the books back?'

'And sell them myself,' Selwyn said. 'But *Wholes and Corners* wouldn've gone for £1.50 a copy. And if you multiply that by fifteen hundred it comes to . . . well, I worked it out on the way home and it's too much. Where will I get an amount like that? Unless you've got it Leo . . . ?'

She did the sums in her head. She hadn't – nothing like it. She said, 'I'm sorry, love. I haven't got that much.' He hung his head. 'But look,' Anna went on, 'usually, when a company goes broke, the assets are sold off at a cheaper price, aren't they? Maybe they won't want the face value.'

'No?' Selwyn looked suddenly hopeful. 'If you could lend me what you've got . . . and I could go round to all my friends, take up a collection . . .'

'Oh Lord.' Anna's heart sank. She could imagine several people willing to lose their small savings on Selwyn's behalf. 'Wait a minute. First you must talk to the receiver again. Find out what he's prepared to accept. It's no good borrowing till you know how much you're got to raise.'

Selwyn's face fell. 'I don't know if the receiver'll talk to me again.' He shook his head dismally. 'I was a bit upset when I saw him today. I called him "an official receiver of stolen goods, thief, scoundrel, vulture pecking at the corpse of British Art, carrion eater". I don't think he likes me.' Anna had to laugh. It was so like Selwyn to leap before he looked. 'Well, then you'll have to get Bea to represent you,' she suggested. 'She has a calm responsible approach. Officials like women like Bea.'

Selwyn exploded. 'You're not to tell Bea,' he shouted. 'She's not to know. She gave me a terrible earful when she found out about my not getting any money up front. Cruel, it was. She said a Foolscap was what I should wear and I was incompetent anyway. She said I'd do anything to get in print and it'd be vanity publishing next. Now she'll say I told you so and I'll do anything to avoid that!' He heaved himself off the stairs and disappeared into his living-room. From her position, stooped over the bicycle in the hall, Anna heard the muffled screech of a cork as it twisted out of a bottle. Selwyn, once more, had been driven to drink. Usually he didn't need much driving but today Anna had to admit there had been some provocation.

She tested the brakes, and when she was satisfied she wiped her hands and joined Selwyn. His pint beer mug was filled to the brim with red wine and he stared dolefully at her from his armchair. Traitor, his look seemed to say. Anna ignored it.

'If you want your books, you'll have to find out how much they'll cost,' she said reasonably. 'And to find that out you'll have to get someone to deal with the receiver. Bea's involved in accounting and bookkeeping. She knows how to talk to people like that. So what if she says I told you so? She's only human, after all.'

Selwyn poured wine down his throat and looked mutinous. Anna tried again, 'If you could swallow your pride the way you swallow that plonk . . . Come on, Selwyn, be your age – you know it makes sense for Bea to handle this for you.'

'No!' he shouted. 'I'm not having her tell me what an idiot I am. She's always at it, and so are you. I'll handle this myself.'

Chapter 6

'Dave McPhee,' the wiry voice said. 'What're you driving?'

'Pardon?' Anna said stupidly.

'Wheels, small fry, wheels. What you got?'

'Oh.' She adjusted the receiver more comfortably to her ear and began to concentrate. What she had actually been thinking about before the phone rang was clothes. It had suddenly dawned on her while cleaning the grease from under her nails that she was about to enter a world where image was all important, where your credibility depended more on your clothes than on your competence. To get it wrong was to invite derision. Dave's question about her car made her realize that J. W. Protection had its own sense of style too.

Now he hooted with contempt. 'A Renault Five? Wow! I'll have to stop calling you small fry, won't I . . . Tiddler?'

'From little tiddlers big fish grow,' she said smartly.

He changed tack. 'Have you met Superbitch yet?'

'Not yet. The client's arranging something.'

'Well, don't hang about. We're shifting the whole circus up to Luton tomorrow p.m. and you'll be driving her. Done any security driving?'

'Some,' Anna said cautiously. He sighed with exaggerated patience. 'Well, not to worry, Tiddler. I'll explain procedure before we leave. And I suppose I'll have to draw a motor from the pool for you. Renault Five! Jeezus!'

'Gosh, thanks,' she said sweetly. 'But nothing vulgar, mind.' She hung up, annoyed. She had never expected to use her own car. On a job like this a car to suit the client was always provided. She knew it, and she knew Dave was simply finding ways to make her look silly. She went back to thinking about clothes.

The only time she had seen Shona Una was in the *Bitterness* video on TV. All she could remember was a witch-like figure, dressed in what looked like black silk cobwebs, posed by a moonlit pool. A skeletal hand had emerged from the water making a slow oily ripple which spread until it touched Shona Una's bare feet. It was no help. Nobody could guess from that what she was really like.

Anna tried to think of the witch-like figure as Roz. But that didn't help either. She went into her bedroom and peered anxiously into her wardrobe. It was a fact of life, she thought, that there was nothing like the sight of your own clothes hanging deflated from a rail to make you feel inadequate. How could she possibly enter a world dominated by style wearing anything in there? People in that world dressed to attract attention. Anna dressed to avoid it.

She shut the cupboard door with a bang, thinking that even if she had a garment remotely suitable there would then be the problem of hair. Hers was uncoloured, unpermed, and altogether unremarkable when compared to what was fashionable. She wasn't going to do anything to alter it.

There was only one answer and that was to do nothing at all. A half-hearted attempt at trendiness was always a pitiful sight.

With nothing else to do she went back to the kitchen to make a pot of tea. Then she settled in the corner of the sofa with J.W.'s plastic file and tried to get familiar with the lists of names and tour dates.

At half past five she heard Bea come in from work, and

about an hour later she came up for a chat, looking tired and cold. Anna made some more tea.

Bea said, 'Selwyn's like a sick bear this evening. He's reading *Les Misérables* – in French, mark you. It's a fine thing to come home to, I must say!'

'He fell off his bike again,' Anna told her. She didn't like keeping Selwyn's secrets from Bea. But sometimes she had to keep Bea's secrets from Selwyn too, so she supposed it worked out evenly. Bea launched into a story about a minor outrage at work. It was what she would have told Selwyn if he had been in a better mood: not very interesting, but the sort of story she had to get off her chest.

Anna listened patiently. It was dark outside and rainy wind spattered like gravel on the window. She felt suspended in time.

Release came when the telephone rang. Daniel Horowitz said, 'Anna, sweetie? Good, listen . . . I've told Roz about you. She wasn't too pleased but she says she'll see you nowish. So look, darling, a low profile, please . . . nothing pushy, know what I mean? She's a tiny bit prickly. Tell her . . . no . . . tell her I've had some letters, crank letters. She'll think I'm an old woman, but she does anyway.'

'And have you?' Anna managed to interrupt.

'What?'

'Had crank letters.'

'Anna, darling, of course. Cranks write to famous people. That's how it goes.'

Chapter 7

She stood for long minutes in the rain. The shutters were closed and the house seemed deserted. It was a very big house on Addison Road, not far from where Anna lived, but with one of those abrupt social changes you get in London just by crossing a road, the area south of Holland Park Road was several cuts above the area north of it. The streets were wider, the houses detached. There were front gardens, more trees, and wide stone steps which led up to freshly painted front doors.

Anna rang the bell again and waited, shivering.

At last the door opened. The chain was on and a suspicious face looked through the crack. Anna held up her security badge and said, 'Anna Lee. Mr Horowitz sent me.'

'No-one told me,' the face complained. A pale hand emerged from the gap allowed by the chain, fingers snapping impatiently. Anna put the badge into it. The hand withdrew and the door shut. Anna waited, still shivering. As far as she could see, Shona Una's security was quite adequate as it was.

After a while the door opened again. The woman who let her in was frail and tiny. A stark white face hid behind enormous tinted goggles. The hair was jet black and severely cropped. She was wearing a curious garment which looked like liquid steel and fitted like fish scales to the thin body. She said, 'This way. You can wait in the kitchen. She's watching the show-jumping.'

Anna followed the dully gleaming scales to the back of the house, unbuttoning her coat as she went. Inside it was as hot as the tropical aviary at the zoo.

The kitchen was immense, red and white tiles on the floor, oiled black slate on the work surfaces, oak cupboards on the walls. A Siamese cat perched among the dirty plates on the drainer licking an oozing pat of butter. At the table a cadaverous man tucked into a huge platter of spaghetti hoops on toast.

'Gross,' the frail woman said. The thin man stared at her and forked more food into his mouth. Tomato sauce stained his chin. The frail women left, slamming the door behind her. The man transferred his blank stare to Anna and went on chewing, lips apart, so that she could see the contents of his mouth.

'Hot in here,' she said brightly. 'Who was that?' The

man looked down at his plate. When he had filled his mouth again he said, 'Who?' and a gob of tomato sauce sailed across the table and landed at Anna's feet.

'Her,' she said, ignoring the gob and gesturing with her thumb at the closed door.

'Oh, her,' he mumbled. He shovelled more spaghetti hoops into his face and, long after Anna thought he had forgotten the question, said, 'Lena.' He got up and went over to a tall fridge and took out a pint of milk. He pressed his thumb down on the top. Milk sprayed on to the floor. He chucked the top over his shoulder and made for the door, walking like an old man, heels dragging loudly on the tiles. The fridge door hung open. When he had gone, Anna crossed the kitchen and closed it.

She looked around with an amazed eye. Basically the kitchen was very clean. There was no dust, no accumulation of crumbs in the corners. Whoever had brought about the mess had done it very quickly and so thoroughly that it looked quite deliberate. The jam wiped on the curtains was still fresh and sticky, the mangled banana in the soapdish had not yet turned black, the beer spilt on the floor was frothing. The hot air stank of burnt toast.

She pulled a cord that worked the ventilator. The fan started up with a whoosh, and the cat, startled, leaped from the draining-board, dislodged a glass which smashed in the sink.

Anna turned away and continued her inspection. One interesting find was a chopping board with a razor blade on it. Traces of white powder clung to both blade and board. She wet a finger and wiped the powder up. When she rubbed it on her gums they tingled. She grimaced and went back to the table.

The Siamese cat had both its front paws in the platter and was delicately nuzzling up the spaghetti hoops. It raised its head and looked at her. The look was not unfriendly so she stretched out a hand and stroked. The sandy back arched under her touch while the chocolate face dipped into the plate again.

She sat down and got J.W.'s personal list out of her bag. No-one called Lena appeared on the list, but there was a Marlene Pecci, wardrobe.

Quiet – just the whirr of the fan, the hum of the fridge and the cat's hoarse purr. She wondered if she had been forgotten. Had everyone gone out, or was she being deliberately ignored?

A few minutes later the door opened and a woman came in. She looked surprised to see Anna but made no comment except to say, 'They want coffee.' Anna watched her go to the sink to look for the percolator. It was full of old grounds and orange peel. The woman searched for somewhere to put the mess but the bin was overflowing. Anna caught a tiny unguarded expression of disgust and she was encouraged enough to introduce herself. The woman laughed. 'Oh well, security,' she said. 'You never know round here.' She had, as far as Anna could see under some bizarre make-up, a plump ordinary face. Her black satin trousers were cut to conceal comfortably wide hips. 'I'm Avis,' she went on. 'PR. Well, really PA to A and R Dog Records. Have you seen any clean cups?'

They started opening cupboards. There were dozens of cups but they were all dirty. Anna even looked in the dishwasher but everything in that was dirty too. 'We'll have to start from scratch,' she said. 'What's PA to A and R?'

'Well, Dick is the Artists and Repertoire man, sort of talent scout if you like, and I'm his assistant,' Avis said. She found a plastic bag and dumped the coffee grounds and orange peel into it. 'Which means I get heaps of practice making coffee.' She laughed again. Anna collected broken glass from the sink.

Avis made the coffee. Anna washed cups. Together they assembled milk, sugar, and spoons. They failed to find a tray but settled on a large breadboard instead. In this simple way an alliance was formed – two practical people in an atmosphere where menial service was taken for granted but despised.

The cat weaved perilously between their ankles as they crossed a wide carpeted hall where Avis opened a door for Anna who carried the loaded breadboard. The air was so thick and hot it could be cut up and buttered. Anna had to put the board on the floor because there was no other space free enough from mugs, glasses, bottles, and ashtrays to hold it.

Apart from herself and Avis there were five other people in the room. Lena and the messy feeder she had seen already. But there were also two more men and one woman. They were sprawled across sofas and chairs and on the floor gazing at a quiz game on TV.

Anna watched Avis pour one cup of coffee, milk and no sugar, and hand it to the woman who wasn't Lena. Lena produced a brandy bottle and added some to the coffee. Without taking her eyes from the screen the woman said, 'Who's she?'

Lena said, 'Just another set of trotters in the trough.' And Avis said, 'It's Anna Lee. Security.'

'Not Snoopy Two?' the woman drawled. 'Well, stone me! These Snoopies come up like weeds. Shut that crap off, someone – I want to meet Snoopy Two.' The cat jumped on to the arm of her chair and, with its front paws planted on her shoulder, sneezed into her ear. Everyone laughed. 'Barbarella, Barbarella,' the woman purred at the cat. 'You love me, don't you?'

She had a sheet twisted around her like a sari. Her pale hair was shorter than the cat's fur. She was colourless and quite beautiful. The light eyes fixed on Anna. She said, 'Step forward, Snoopy Two.'

'You talking to me?' Anna inquired politely. She stayed where she was, leaning against the door.

'Yes, you,' Shona Una said. 'Aren't you going to check the windows and take down our particulars like Snoopy One?'

'Do they need taking down?' Anna asked. Avis lowered her eyes. One of the men tittered. Shona Una's long, thick eyelids twitched. She said in a thin voice, 'You can tell Danny Darling he's paid to keep me solvent, not to fuck with my private life.'

'Well, I expect he knows that already,' Anna said, still very polite. 'Only he's had some very weird letters.'

'What letters?' One of the men looked up, interested. He wore rainbow-coloured braces to hold up a pair of running shorts, and nothing else.

'There's always some nutter,' Shona Una said scornfully. The man with the braces got up. A doormat of bronzy hair sprouted from his chest and shoulders. He came over and sat on a hard chair close to Anna. 'Go on, Snoopy Two,' he wheedled childishly, 'tell us about nutters you have known. Go on. I bet you've known ever so many.' He crossed his eyes and let his tongue hang out. Suddenly his arms snaked out and he caught Anna by the waist. She found herself dragged towards him. His knees clamped like nutcrackers round her thighs.

Everyone laughed except Avis, who began to look anxious.

'Glob-lob-lob,' the man slobbered into Anna's chest. 'Snoopy Two going to tell us about glob-lob-nutters, ain't she-wee-wee-wee?' He gripped harder. He was very strong. Everyone watched expectantly. Anna relaxed.

'Nutters,' she began musingly. 'Nutters have the strength of devils. They are cloven-hoofed and have pink piggy eyes.' The man raised his head from her breasts to look at her. Instantly she clapped the palms of her hands on his temples and stuck her thumbs in his eyes. Her nails dug into the corners nearest his nose.

'Nutters cannot see without their eyeballs,' she went on in the same conversational way. 'I could have yours out and in the palms of my hands before you could say sorry, so stay very still. I wouldn't like to blind you by accident. I want to do it on purpose.' She increased the pressure. His grip slackened.

'Hands behind your back,' she said quietly. When he obeyed, she stepped quickly out of reach.

'Oh, very tough,' Lena drawled admiringly. Shona Una relaxed and said, 'Not bad. I never saw that one before. You want some coffee, Snoopy?'

'Not now, thanks,' Anna said, very friendly. 'I just came round to say hello. I'll pick you up here tomorrow. OK?'

'Going anywhere near Gloucester Road?' Avis asked, standing up.

Chapter 8

'You're shaking,' accused Avis when they got outside.
'You weren't scared, were you? You didn't look scared.'

'I'm just angry,' Anna told her, unlocking the car. 'Who
was that poxy lump of meat anyway?'

'Christ, Anna, that was Van Vritski, Shona's drummer.
Didn't you recognize him?' Avis climbed in and clicked her
seat-belt in place. 'He started out with Bugle and then went
on to Third Leg. Remember?'

'I've never seen any of them live,' Anna said, starting
the car.

'He's brilliant.'

'That's no excuse.'

'The thing is,' Avis said slowly, as if speaking to a child,
'they're artists. They have funny little ways. They're not like
you or I.'

'That's what *they* think,' Anna said, 'but it isn't true.
I've known people with twice the talent who behaved like
normal human beings.'

'So've I,' Avis said, and they both laughed. 'Trouble is,'
she went on, 'this lot are Dog artists and I can't be critical in
public.'

'Well, never mind critical,' Anna said. 'I got the hump,
that's all. Just tell me who everyone was. Who was the tall
thin geezer, for instance?'

'Oh, that's Porky Wall. He basically makes things work.
He used to be an ordinary electrician but somehow he got
attached to Shona as a sort of sparks cum gofer. Been with
her for ages.'

'And Lena?'

'She's more recent. Clothes, costume – very *avant
garde*. Shona won't go out now unless Lena tells her what to

wear. The other guy makes wigs. Ducks, they call him.'

They drove in silence for a while and then Avis said, almost apologetically, 'It's very cliquey. There's an inner circle, thick as thieves. Sometimes you're in for no apparent reason. You can be out just as easily. Then there's an outer circle – people who're useful but not important, and not a threat either, if you see what I mean. I don't mean just Shona Una: most bands are like that. Me, I'm usually in the outer circle. Occasionally I get promoted – which is fun for a while. Occasionally I get dropped – which is miserable, because you never know why.'

'No business like show business,' Anna said lightly.

'With knobs on,' Avis agreed. 'I'm only telling you because otherwise you might've taken what happened tonight personally.'

'I might've,' Anna said, straight-faced. Avis gave a glum giggle and went on, 'Actually, I left when you did because I was afraid when you'd gone they'd start picking on me. Everyone's awfully ratty lately. It's tour yips, you know. Happens all the time.'

'No worse than usual?'

'Shona's never been on a big tour before, so I don't know. But I hate getting picked on. Besides, they're clubbing later, which is a drag, and I have to be at work tomorrow.'

Anna dropped her off soon afterwards and went home.

Chapter 9

She broke out of Van Vritski's rude embrace, and finding her hands furry with his bronze hair, let out a yell as she went falling, falling, falling.

She woke, sweating and bolt upright in bed. It was five in the morning. She lay down again and closed her eyes, but her mind stayed obstinately awake. After a while she gave up, dressed carelessly in a thick pullover and jeans, and crept downstairs.

The Renault stood under a street lamp, dripping with the chilly drizzle, its mid-blue stained greeny-orange by the sulphur light.

The night in London is never quite dark, never quite still. There are always a few with somewhere to go or work to do. And there are always a few who can't sleep. The city at night is like a big animal, groaning and twitching when it should be unconscious – the restless fleas on its back giving it no peace even at the smallest hours. No wonder the old thing is dirty, worn, and sometimes bad-tempered.

In Addison Road topaz raindrops fell from the bare branches of trees and dropped on to the shiny paving stones. Anna slowed the car to a crawl as she approached Shona Una's house. It looked as dead and empty as it had earlier.

But as she passed, she saw a figure in a pale raincoat leaning against one of the gateposts. She stopped the car and opened the window. The figure seemed to be gazing intently up at the house. Warned by the sound of her handbrake, he turned to look at her, and she caught a momentary glimpse of a pale face under a peaked cap before he hurried away in the direction from which she had come.

She turned the car, and as she did so saw him break into a run. She put her foot down but by the time she got to the end of the road he had gone. He could have slipped into any of the front gardens. One of the cars parked by the kerb could have been his. Anna cruised slowly round the block but saw no-one on foot.

She came back to the house and stopped. Nothing stirred. She got out and crossed the road to where the man had stood. Not a trace of his presence remained. The house was still dark and shuttered.

Shivering, she went back to the car and waited for a while to see if someone else would start up and drive away. But nobody did, so she took another slow tour of the neighbourhood and then went home.

* * *

There were two phone calls in the morning. The first was from Dave McPhee who was going to Luton early for a 'quick liaise with the Warehouse team'. He and Kevin would drop by her place first with a 'suitable motor'.

The next was from Lena who opened the conversation by saying, 'Got any black leather?' Anna told her she hadn't.

'No leather?' Lena said, incredulous. 'Well, I suppose I can fix you up. You've got to fit in with the general design of things. I couldn't do anything with Snoopy One. She was past redemption – like a Stalag wardress, know what I mean? But you I could do something with.'

'Hang about,' Anna interrupted. 'I'm security – not part of a bleeding designer set . . .'

'You're telling me,' Lena cut in frostily. 'Look, if you want to fit in you've got to get a bit more in the mood.'

'Yeah, but I can't be got up like you lot are,' Anna said. She was in a quandary. 'I shouldn't stand out in a crowd and I have to be able to move freely. And besides, I tend to look a right Herbert in anything fancy.'

'I wasn't thinking fancy,' Lena said. 'We've met, remember? I know what you'd look good in.'

'Black leather,' Anna said in resignation.

'Tell you what – the sound check's about five, right? So you'll be picking us up about three-thirty, right? So if you come a bit early, say, two-thirty, we'll have time to dress you. All right?'

'Well, I'll have a look anyway,' Anna agreed reluctantly.

'Don't worry.' Lena sounded bored and languid. 'You'll look great. It wouldn't do *my* rep any good if you didn't, would it? What you look like reflects on us, doesn't it?'

There was a warning implied. Anna certainly didn't want to go the way Julie went but she didn't want to look like a King's Road freak either.

She flipped through the J.W. folder and found Julie's full name and home phone number. After a moment's hesitation she dialled the number. A woman answered. Anna asked for Julie Ibbotson and a few seconds later another woman came on the line.

'I'm Anna Lee. We haven't met, and I'm very sorry to

bother you when you're on sick leave,' Anna started, sounding rather young and anxious. 'Only I've been seconded to J.W. for a while and been assigned to the Shona Una job . . .'

'Don't talk to me about them. They're disgusting.' It was a forty cigarettes a day voice and it sounded angry. 'They live like animals – if I'd brought up children to behave like that I'd be ashamed, downright ashamed.'

'It's just that they don't seem to understand I'm there for their own protection,' Anna put in when Julie paused for breath.

'You don't have to tell me that,' Julie said. 'I never met a more ungrateful lot of so-and-sos. They obstructed me at every turn. It's all a game to them. And the way they talk about that nice Mr Horowitz, anyone'd think he'd put me in there to steal from them. "Acting strange," he told me. "That's good," I told him at the end. "If any one of them had acted halfway normal they'd've been acting strange." Acting strange! I ask you, how can anyone tell?'

'One of them – Van Vritski . . .' Anna began, but Julie interrupted, 'Don't talk to me about him. You won't believe this, but do you know what he did? It was after the concert in Birmingham and I'd already had the lot of them up to here. We were all stopping the night at a hotel up there, and I was doing the rounds checking who was where, and I got to his room, and he came to the door – this is a five star hotel, mind – and he came to the door stark naked, and he came out in the corridor – a public corridor, mind – and he stood there and waggled his – his thing at me. Shouted abuse too. You never heard such language. And she, that Shona Una, well, *she* wasn't in her room. If you ask me, she was in that animal's room. But I never got in to see. I told Colonel Beamish I wouldn't stand for that sort of treatment. It was making me ill.'

'That's awful,' Anna murmured, her teeth clenched against an unworthy urge to laugh. 'Mr Horowitz said something went wrong at the Birmingham concert.'

'Oh, nothing went wrong. That stupid girl had hysterics – or pretended to. If you ask me, she was just getting as much attention as she could. She's got no consideration – keeping everyone waiting like that.'

'But why? Did anything happen?'

'How would I know? They never let me in the dressing-room. I had to stand in that freezing passage like some sort of servant. If you want my advice, you'll leave everything to Dave McPhee. He's an ex-para, you know. He won't take any nonsense.' Julie, having vented her indignation, was beginning to sound patronizing. If she had failed, she was suggesting, there wasn't the slightest possibility of another woman succeeding. Anna could sympathize: she had seen immediately that if they decided to take against her, Shona Una and her friends could make life unbearable.

She asked, 'Wasn't there anyone who was at all cooperative?'

'No-one. Well, that designer girl – she's a sarcastic little bitch and she looks a fright, but at least she's clean. Look, dear,' Julie went on, the experienced agent soothing the ingenue, 'don't waste your time and trouble on those creatures. They won't thank you. The opposite in fact. Just put in an appearance and leave the sharp end to Dave. He's used to it. I don't suppose you've been on a big job like this before, so just keep your head down – you'll only get in the way otherwise.'

Chapter 10

He arrived with Kevin about half an hour later. 'Hello,' he said when she opened the door. 'We've brought a jam-jar for our Tiddler.' And laughed uproariously at his own joke. Behind him, double parked, stood a gleaming white BMW with darkened glass windows. It dominated the street like a cheetah among alley cats.

'I don't suppose you've driven anything like this before,' he said haughtily. 'Come and have a look. I'll go over the finer points.'

'Well, I have, as a matter of fact,' Anna told him just as

haughtily. She followed him over to the car. Kevin leaned against the door looking a little embarrassed. Net curtains all the way up the street were twitching violently. Anna sighed and said, 'Oh well, it might've been a pink Roller. People would've noticed that.'

'Pop stars like to be noticed,' Dave informed her. 'Get in. I want to show you how to use the RT.'

'I already know,' Anna said. But he wasn't listening so she got in and waited patiently while he unfolded the mysteries of the radio telephone and its procedure. After that he explained the route she was to take to the Warehouse on the outskirts of Luton. Then he turned to the alarm and locking systems. 'Shatterproof glass,' he said, knocking on the window with his signet ring. 'But you never know. Hit this one and the alarm starts. Want to try it?'

'No,' she said firmly. She could see Selwyn peering cautiously at her from behind his curtains. But he was only doing what the rest of the neighbours were doing too. 'Want to come up for a coffee?' she asked. She was anxious to get them all off the street.

'No time for that,' Dave said. 'I want to make sure you know the SOP.'

'Oh, I think she'll manage,' Kevin said awkwardly. 'And we ought to get on our way. They'll be doing their cobblers up in Luton if we're late.'

'I hope you're right,' Dave said. And turning to Anna: 'This is an expensive piece of machinery so don't fuck it up.' Reluctantly he handed her the keys. 'And don't exceed the speed limit and don't for Gawd's sake stop for passing hitchhikers, no matter what Superbitch says. Got it?'

'Oh yessir. I gottit, sir,' Anna said.

'You may laugh,' Kevin said, 'but she only wanted to bring some stray fans down from Brum with her. That's just what we don't want.'

Finally, to Anna's relief, they drove off, leaving her to park the elegant lump of metal. Selwyn came out to offer advice. 'Not too close, Leo, not too close,' he implored. 'Mr Chatterjee might see it and put the rent up. Tell you what, though – ' his eyes lit up – 'what we could do, see, is sell it to one of those dealers who change number plates and all that. You could report it stolen and the proceeds'd be just the capital I need to get *Wholes and Corners* back.'

'You know,' Anna said, following him into the house, 'I think this money thing has poached your egg for you.'

'I had another idea.' He stopped in the doorway. 'This pop star you're working for. She's bound to be interested in a good lyricist. You could put in a word for me. That's where the money is.'

'Lyricist? You?' She edged round him to get to the bottom of the stairs. 'Selwyn, do us all a favour – tell Bea, and get it sorted properly. Fantasizing about nicked motors and pop music isn't your style at all.'

'What is my style?' Selwyn cried. 'I'm stony broke, I'm the victim of capitalist greed and I don't know which way to turn.'

'Turn to Bea,' Anna said callously and started upstairs.

'Insensitive, hard-hearted, uncaring, may you break out in boils . . .' followed her up.

Safe in her own flat everything looked peaceful and under control. She put the kettle on for tea and made a thick cheese and pickle sandwich. She was just sitting down to eat it when the phone rang. It was Lena again. She said, 'What size shoes do you take?'

Anna told her, and with a muttered comment of, 'Kipper clogs,' Lena rang off.

Anna had just taken the first bite of her sandwich when Lena rang again. 'Porky wants a favour,' she said. 'The combo footswitch went. She'll probably want to practise when she gets up so we need another. I said you'd go.'

'Oh, did you?'

'I might've gone myself but I've got your daisies to see about.' Lena left an accusatory pause. Anna said, 'What is it Porky wants?'

'An FSE2 reverb footswitch. They've got one at Rose Morris, Denmark Street. They're holding it for you. Got that?'

'Sort of.'

'Better give it some wellie,' Lena advised. 'She'll be getting up any time now.'

If the price for being included in Shona Una's circle was to be taken advantage of, Anna thought on her grum-

bling way to the West End, she had better accept it grace-
fully. It wasn't going to be easy.

Rose Morris was a man's world. A small group in one
corner had a Fender bass hooked to an amplifier and one of
them was picking out a riff which he repeated over and over
while the others listened attentively. A pimply boffin who
looked as if he'd only just reached puberty was explaining
about low and low-mid frequencies being dependent on
soundhole radiation. Someone was pestering someone
about the fuses always blowing in his PA amp and someone
else was extolling the virtues of a distortion pedal with a
second-trigger feedback function. Phrases like 'chain programme mode' and 'high frequency digital ovetones' were
reeled off like football scores. Nobody looked as if they
didn't understand.

At the counter Anna managed to catch a salesman's
eye, and in a low voice told him her business. 'For Shona
Una?' he said loudly. 'Got it right here.' He reached under
the counter for a plastic bag.

The man standing next to her turned to Anna and
asked, 'You with Shona Una, then?'

The salesman said, 'FSE2 reverb footswitch,' and the
man next to Anna said, 'She still using the Sherwood
combo, then?'

'I'll do the usual with the invoice, shall I?' the salesman
asked, and Anna, who hadn't the slightest idea what the
usual was, agreed. She grabbed the plastic bag and escaped
into Denmark Street.

The man who had stood beside her followed her out
and hovered behind her while she unlocked the car. At last
he said, 'She used to sing with my band, you know.'

'Oh yeah?' Anna said, turning to look at him. He had a
long thin face with deeply scored lines that made him look
as if he'd recently been very ill. His bristly hair receded
into an M-shape over a high forehead. In spite of this he still
seemed quite young, and he dressed with jumble sale chic.

'It's true,' he said, as if he hardly believed it himself.
She did all the sha-la-la, oo-wah stuff. 'Course she was plain
Hilary Simpson then.'

'Must've been a long time ago,' Anna said sceptically.

Her eye was caught by a brace of policemen coming over from the Charing Cross Road and she hurried to get into the car. The young man saw the policemen too and ran round to the passenger side. 'Give us a lift, eh?' he said with a desperate attempt at cool.

She opened the door for him and he jumped in as she started away. She waved apologetically to the policemen as she passed them.

Her passenger's face had turned a dirty cream colour and was shining with sweat. 'Thanks,' he said. 'I'm . . .' He made an odd clucking noise in his throat and fell silent. Anna gave him a few moments to recover. Then she said, 'Hilary Simpson? But everyone calls her Roz.'

'That's the way it is in this game,' he said, unzipping his jacket. 'You get so there's *no-one* around who remembers your real name. Success means having a short memory. That's my trouble – I don't forget things.' He began to scratch his armpit, rooting under his jacket with long thin claws.

Anna looked quickly at him and saw for the first time the strangeness of his eyes. They were red-rimmed, steel-grey, and showed scarcely any pupils. The peppery smell of his sweat filled the car. He was still very pale and now he was beginning to talk too much. 'I've got her footprints all the way up my back,' he said. 'Me and a few mates had this band called In Hock – for obvious reasons – and we were playing pubs and clubs and we had this gig at Dockers in Limehouse. And there *she* was, just in from commuter country, all starry-eyed.'

He sighed. 'They're all the fucking same. They sit on the stage, and they bring you drinks and smokes. Oh, they'll do *anything* for you if you give them the chance. And I gave *her* the chance, and then I found out she'd do anything *to* me.'

Anna said, 'Look, where do you want me to drop you?' Having rescued him from the police, she couldn't wait to abandon him. She hated the bitter smell that came from his shirt, and his continual scratching was beginning to irritate her. What he was talking about might have been interesting, but she was repelled by the self-pity, and she had an instant distrust of anything a junkie had to say. It was like talking to a dreamer, not yet quite awake, to whom events that had not happened were as solid as those that had.

In the end she put him down at Goodge Street station and made her way back to Addison Road.

Chapter II

It could have been the middle of the night. The curtains were still drawn over shuttered windows and for some reason the room was lit only by candles.

This time Shona Una was wrapped in an olive-green towel, and looked like a pale forest orchid. Lena, Porky, and Van Vritski were there, but Avis and the wigmaker had been replaced by three unknown people Anna couldn't see properly because of the dim flickering light.

Nobody spoke when she came in, so she went across to Porky and gave him the plastic bag. 'Wha'sat?' he asked in a whisper.

'Your footswitch,' she said, whispering too. He looked puzzled and raised a finger to his lips.

'Zip the yapper,' Shona Una said angrily without taking her eyes off Lena. Lena shuffled a deck of cards. Shona cut them three times.

In a singsong voice Lena said, 'Your significator is the Page of Wands. The Page of Cups covers him. The Devil crosses him. Aha!' Shona leaned forward. Lena went on, 'This crowns him; this is beneath him; this is behind him; this is before him. Ah, the Ten of Cups.'

Shona said, 'That's good, isn't it?'

'Wait for it,' Lena warned. 'Everything depends on everything else. Himself – ' she turned over another card – 'the Hierophant. Interesting. His house; his hopes and fears; and lastly the culminator: Temperance.'

Shona lit a cigarette. Her hands trembled. Lena studied the cards, making minute adjustments to their position with fingernails that looked like crimson beaks. She looked up and saw Anna watching from beside Porky's chair. She said brusquely, 'Make us some coffee, Snoops.' Everyone waited in silence while Anna left the room.

In the kitchen she found a very young West Indian woman in tears by the sink. A plunger stood upright in six inches of filthy water. Cigarette ends and teabags floated on top. 'I try, an' I try,' she cried, 'but I cannot shift it.'

Anna took off her coat and pushed her sleeves above her elbows. She worked furiously with the plunger for a couple of minutes, but the mucky water simply splashed and washed over her arms. 'We'll have to get the trap off underneath,' she said, getting down on her knees and opening the cupboard under the sink.

'Mrs Blakemore going to be furious,' the girl said, tears spilling again. 'She told me to look after the place. But I can't.'

'This is hardly your doing,' Anna said. She wrestled with a joint connector. 'Is there a wrench somewhere? I can't shift this either.' The girl went away, and Anna cleared out the space under the sink. Even the washing-up bowl had been used for refuse. She found a dustbin bag and dumped everything into it. Some screwed-up paper smeared with grease fell on the floor. She picked it up and was about to throw it in the bag when she saw the word 'ugly' typed on it. This so neatly described Anna's state of mind that she flattened it out. It was so blurred and soiled with kitchen debris that she could only pick out a few words. '. . . ing ugly will ha . . .' she read. 'Honour your . . .' blank '. . . or . . .' And quite clear at the bottom was '. . . you will regret it.'

The girl came back carrying a tool box. Anna wrapped the filthy scrap of paper in a piece of kitchen towel and put it in her bag.

It took a few minutes to take the trap off and clear the blockage. 'Dear Lord, what they been doing?' the girl asked, gagging with disgust at the smelly waste. Anna turned her head away while it drained. They looked at each other, nauseated. 'A pint of bleach,' the girl said. 'That's what it needs.'

'Two pints,' Anna said. 'Two gallons.' They both giggled unhappily.

'Save some for the toilets,' the girl said. 'You ain't seen them yet.'

'Oh Christ! I forgot about the bleeding coffee.'

'I'll do that,' the girl said, standing up. 'Can you finish the plumbing? I'll throw up if I have to work down there any more.'

Anna fitted the bend back and screwed it tight. She washed her hands thoroughly and watched with satisfaction as the water flowed away. She poured bleach in after it. By then the coffee was made and Anna took it to the living-room.

There was tension in the room — she could feel it like grit between the teeth. As she came in one of the men got to his feet and stalked out. The front door slammed, and a sigh went round the room like a collective exhalation of breath. It was as if their sense of community existed only by excluding outsiders.

'I'm so fucking tired of scribblers,' Shona Una drawled. 'Always the same questions. You'd think there was a central question bank.' Everyone laughed. She secured the towel more firmly under her armpits and said irritably, 'Piss off, everybody. I got to get my head together.'

Lena said, 'Come on, Snoops. Let's get you kitted.' She led the withdrawal. By Porky's chair Anna noticed the plastic bag with the footswitch in it still unopened. And on the low table the Tarot cards lay forgotten beside the coffee tray. She suddenly had an acute sense of wasted time.

Chapter 12

She had to give Lena credit — she had never seen leather so fine or supple. The jacket was cut to give an angular look that suited her height.

'Plenty of room under the arms,' Lena said. She tweaked it here and there and settled the shoulders. 'Don't tell me I don't know my business.'

The skirt was shorter than Anna was used to but it fitted smoothly over the hips and still felt comfortable to move in. She was forced to admit that Lena had got everything right from the soft greeny shirt and the fine wool tights to the short low-heeled boots.

'The only thing wrong,' Lena mused, 'is you. Don't stand to attention, God damn it, sort of slouch a bit.' She stared critically. 'Think dirty. You look far too tight. Oh for Christ's sake – give a little – you make the thing look like a school uniform.' Anna laughed. 'That's better,' Lena told her. 'You can look almost human when you try.' Still, she seemed pleased and accepted Anna's thanks with an offhand shrug.

Encouraged by her comparative friendliness, Anna asked, 'Why is . . . er . . . she so scratchy at the moment?' She found that, for all of Shona Una's many names, she didn't know what to call her.

Lena was pecking through a bag of scarves. She looked up. 'Is she scratchy?'

'Isn't she?'

'How would you feel if you had to stand up in front of thousands of strangers and perform?' Lena asked sarcastically. It was unimaginable. Anna said, 'But she should be used to that sort of thing. Mr Horowitz says . . .'

'Oh, we all know what Danny Darling's worried about.'

'What?'

'Oh, you'll find out.' She drew a long silk scarf out of the bag and flicked the creases out as if it were a whip. 'Or maybe you won't.' She held the silk next to Anna's hair and said, 'Try that. Loosely, loosely! Everything's too tight with you. Hmm, not too awful. You need something to pin that boring old badge on and I'm not having you stick anything through that leather.' She thought of everything.

Anna asked, 'What did the cards say?'

'What cards?'

'The Tarot,' Anna said patiently.

'Oh, them. What do you want to know about them for? You don't look the type.'

'What type's that?' She was finding Lena's technique of turning every question back on itself hard to deal with.

'You want to be in control too much,' Lena said sharply. 'You wouldn't accept there are other influences. You wouldn't think a bunch of cards'd tell you anything.' She was right. Anna was startled but she said, 'I don't know about that.'

Lena smiled maliciously. 'Well, I do. We even thought the Page of Cups might be you – an effeminate young man, impelled to render service – a messenger. So why don't you bugger off and tell Marilyn to go out for some pizza. Some of us are going to want to eat before we leave.'

But Marilyn was hoovering in the hall. On her face was the hopeless expression of the small Dutch boy with his finger in the dyke. And in the kitchen a crowd of people were already making chaos of her work there. Van Vritski was at the table with a predatory gleam in his eye, so Anna slipped out and drove to Kensington High Street.

She was horribly conscious of the way people turned to look at her as she parked the big car, and of Beryl's open-mouthed stare when she got to the office. But, 'I hope you don't think that outfit's coming out of petty cash,' was all she had to say about it. There were catcalls from the builders, and Martin Brierly actually stood up behind his desk when she entered his room. For a couple of seconds they both stood facing each other, confused, and then Anna broke the spell by saying, 'I haven't much time, but I think Shona Una's received at least one threatening letter.'

'Is this it?' Mr Brierly asked. He pushed the soiled envelope of kitchen towel off his blotter with the tip of a pencil. 'Well, leave it here if you must. I'll get Mr Schiller to take a look.'

'Thanks. Would you tell him I'll call him at home this evening if I can.' She turned to go.

'It's all right for some,' Beryl called as Anna scampered down the stairs. 'But I wouldn't get too used to the high life, if I were you.'

'High life!' she muttered as she dashed to the Pizza Express.

Back at Addison Road she slipped one of the pizzas to Marilyn who hid it at the back of a broom cupboard – a subversive bond between women who felt misused was being formed. The rest she dumped on the kitchen table around which a right royal faff was going on about cars: who was taking one to Luton, who would be driving, and who would give whom a lift. There were more people around now than there had been for the Tarot reading, and Anna had no idea who they were or where they had come from.

She retired to the sitting-room for a few minutes of peace and found only the Siamese cat sitting like an ornament on the card table. She looked at her watch. They should all leave soon, and no-one appeared to be ready. The cat yawned and jumped off the table, scattering cards on to the floor. For a while it sat beside Anna, and allowed itself to be stroked.

On the floor by her feet a copy of *Smash Hits* was lying folded open to show the charts. *Bitterness* was at number four. The cat yawned again and Anna's feet began to feel twitchy.

Ten minutes later Marilyn came in looking flustered and carrying a wicker cat box. She said, 'Oh, thank goodness you're here. I can't find Barbarella.' The cat took a long contemptuous look at the cat box and disappeared under the sofa.

'Surely they aren't taking the cat?' Anna asked in disbelief.

They got down on hands and knees and peered under the sofa. Barbarella, wide-eyed and cool, stared back.

'Oh Jesus!' Anna said.

'Puss, puss, come on, sweetheart,' Marilyn coaxed. A note of desperation came into her voice. Barbarella flattened her ears and stayed put.

'Kitty, kitty, kitty,' Anna wheedled. 'Give us a break, you sweet little Siamese fur ball.'

'Cat won't budge – sofa must,' Marilyn said decisively, getting to her feet. 'I'll lift this end and swing it back. You catch Barbarella.'

Anna agreed without much hope. Marilyn heaved at the sofa and staggered back a couple of paces. Anna pounced. But Barbarella was already half way up the curtains.

'Only one thing for it,' Marilyn said. They went to the

window and Marilyn shook the curtains. Barbarella clung on. They exchanged a disconsolate look. Marilyn shook the curtains more violently. With a nasty tearing sound, Barbarella began to slide. Anna caught her at shoulder level.

Once she was caught, she hung limp in Anna's arms and purred. It was only when she was buckled into the cage that she began to protest in an eerie low howl.

'Poor darling,' Shona Una said, appearing in the doorway. 'What have they been doing to you?' Marilyn looked at the floor, her expression hidden. Anna choked and said, 'Well, we ought to be going.'

'So what's keeping you?' Shona Una asked. She was wearing a huge square-shouldered fur coat that looked as if it had begun life as a Hollywood prop. On her head was a platinum blonde wig, and her eyes were hidden by enormous sunglasses. She couldn't have looked more like an incognito pop star. By contrast, Lena wore a severe little cloth coat set off by a tiny cloche hat and button boots.

'Star, star's maid, and star's chauffeur,' Anna thought wretchedly as she ushered them into the back of the star's car. Clever little Lena. They were, after all, a designer set.

Chapter 13

'Well, get you!' Dave McPhee said, staring at Anna's legs. 'Hey, Kev! Seen Tiddler's new clobber?' They were standing in the corridor squeezed against the wall to let roadies with trollies push amp stacks past.

'Very nice,' Kevin said politely.

'Hope the fans don't rip it off you.' Dave grinned wolfishly. 'Now look, we got the two stage doors here, and as you can see, two men in sweatshirts. We got the two doors from the pit to backstage and we'll have two guys – Warehouse guys – in dinner jackets.' He led the way through to the hall. 'Now there's going to be a few people in the au-

dience – families, press, girlfriends, right? – along to see
the show. They've all got special passes, and they can come
through. How many, Kev?'

Kevin consulted a list. 'About twenty, Dave.'

'Right. So after the show there'll be a lot of faces backstage. Now most of our mob's in T-shirts, front of pit, taking
care of stage invasion, right? We'll have a couple more in
the wings if needed.'

On stage, Shona Una, Van Vritski and several others
were standing round the electric grand. Under the flat
house lights they looked small and insignificant.

Dave said, 'Pay attention, Tiddler.' He turned and
walked to the back of the hall. 'Here and here are the main
exit doors.' A couple of swing doors opened out into the
foyer. On one side was a bar, dark and with the grille down.
On the other some people were setting up a stand to sell
posters, records, T-shirts, and badges.

'Front of house,' Dave said, picking his way through
piles of merchandise. 'House staff take care of it but they
can call on us if need be. Now, up here. Don't hang about,
Tiddler. We haven't got all day.' He started up the stairs.
The lights were off and they made their way up in the dark.

The balcony was steeply raked. Most of the light came
from behind a glass panel where technicians worked on the
console. On either side of it were banks of spotlights.

'We should have a couple of chaps here at the back. But
there won't be any problem. It's all seating up here.' Dave
had to raise his voice to compete with the low rumble of
machinery. All the light trusses and an enormous structure
of interlocking girders were being lowered almost to the
floor of the hall.

On stage one of the men who had been at Addison
Road that morning was seated at the electric grand. He was
playing silently. Someone standing beside him signalled to
the console box. An almighty roar filled the hall. Everyone
jumped. The people on stage waved frantically and the
sound was cut off. The man at the piano went on moving his
hands over the keyboard as if nothing had happened.

'This way,' Dave said. 'There's a corridor down here,
leads from the balcony stairs round the side of the hall.
Right?' They went downstairs again, avoided the foyer, and

turned into the corridor. 'When the show's on,' he continued, 'this should be clear. Now all I want you to do is, when Superbitch is safely out front shrieking her little heart out, you come along here, up to the balcony, down the other side. It's like a perimeter, see. Just check everyone's where they should be. Anything out of order, report to me or Kev here, and we'll fix it. 'OK?'

'OK.'

'Just wander round. You should be able to manage that, eh? Apart from that, you keep an eye on the dressing-rooms. Make sure no unauthorized personnel take a fancy to anything that isn't theirs. Right?'

'I'll be floating around too,' Kevin said helpfully. 'But Dave's going to be backstage at all times. Come and meet some of the boys.'

They went backstage again. Anna was not surprised to discover that the J.W. agents had found the caterers and were collected like flies around the coffee urn. They were a nervous group with nothing better to do than to pass rude remarks about the band and the roadies and everyone else involved in the performance. They spoke to no-one outside their own circle, and no-one spoke to them.

To her chagrin, Anna was introduced as Tiddler from Small Fry Security. But after some ribald remarks about her appearance, the group closed in again, protecting itself with shop talk, and she was forgotten.

She slipped away to the dressing-rooms where she found Lena behind an ironing-board. She was pressing what seemed to be miles of parachute silk taken from the costume box in the middle of the floor.

After a while the man everyone called Ducks breezed in carrying a stack of wig boxes and he and Lena began a discussion about the three changes.

The rest of the band shared a larger dressing-room on the other side of a reception area. Anyone wanting to get to either dressing-room had to come through the reception room. It was furnished with sofas and low tables, and on a shelf that ran the length of the room the caterers had set up a small bar. There were plates of sandwiches there too, and bowls of sweets and crisps and several Thermos jugs of tea or coffee.

Anna poured herself some coffee, took a sandwich, and sat down. It was only half way through the afternoon and already she felt exhausted. It was tiring to have nothing to do when everyone else was so busy.

She had nearly dozed off when Van Vritski came in with another man. He was saying something about a clock oscillator going on the blink and the other man said, 'Well, leave 'em to it for a bit. No sweat.'

'Ker-riste, here's trouble!' Van said enthusiastically when he saw Anna. 'Wes, meet Snoopy. She's dangerous. Dane-jer-ouse. So watch your eyes, your wallet, and your nuts.'

'How can I watch my own eyes?' Wes asked, taking a plate of sandwiches and flopping down on a chair.

'Don't ask – just do it. She could've blinded me last night. Very rough. Ver-ree-ruff!'

Wes bit into his sandwich and said, 'Ugh, ham! Ain't there any without meat?' He stared accusingly at Anna. She said, 'There's egg and cress, or tuna salad.'

'What, no eyeball rolls?' Van jeered. 'You must be starving.'

'I am.' She got up. Van drew back a pace and Wes laughed. 'Reach us the egg and cress,' he said. 'Why do they keep giving us this white sodding bread?'

Anna passed him another plate. She knew he must be Wes Gardner, bass player. He had a studious look about him. Half-lens glasses perched on a short straight nose and a thoughtful furrow cut between his brows.

'Were you ever with a band called In Hock?' she asked, sitting down opposite him.

'Not me,' he said, examining the plate with utmost suspicion. 'Do you think that piddling cat's been at the eggs?' He looked round the room. 'I wish she wouldn't bring it. The bloody thing eats off people's plates.'

Van said, 'Well, you know where to get a new set of strings then, don't you? I'd use it myself if I still played skin drums.'

'It's unhealthy,' Wes complained. 'And the way she goes on about it you'd think it was her kid.'

'You mean she ignores it or mistreats it unless it suits her?' Van asked sarcastically. The intercom over the door crackled into life and he was requested to come back on stage.

When he had gone, Wes gave Anna a long level look and said, 'What's your real name? Why do they call you Snoopy?'

'Anna Lee. I suppose I inherited the name along with the job.'

'Oh yeah,' he said vaguely. 'I remember. That old cow who wanted all the little girls kicked out of the hotel. I don't go in for little girls myself. You never know where they've been. But they're drummer's perks to Van. He went up the wall.' He slapped out a drum roll on his knee and grinned. 'Where did you hear about In Hock?' he asked suddenly.

'Bloke I met in Rose Morris,' she told him. 'Said she used to sing for him.'

'Well, don't go rabbitting on about it. It's a sore point.'

'Why?'

'Well, it was in hock because it was a snow band. I never touch the stuff myself. It can burn holes in the lining of your nose. But anyway, they got busted, and you can get a fair stretch for dealing snow. Possession's bad enough. But a couple of the lads were dealing – which isn't the sort of thing you want to be associated with when you're in the public eye.'

'No.' She shook her head, watching him closely. But he went on calmly eating egg sandwiches. 'So what happened to *her*?'

'What do you expect – sweet young thing, fallen among thieves – a slapped wrist and tons of fatherly advice.'

'And you?'

He looked up sharply. 'I didn't say I was there.'

'No.' Anna waited. He finished eating and said quietly, 'Want a hand of rummy? I never play poker – it's bad for the nerves.' He went to his dressing-room and came back with a new deck of cards which he shuffled and cut with broad capable hands.

'Penny a point?' he asked politely.

Chapter 14

When Daniel Horowitz turned up, it was late in the afternoon and Anna was sitting in a dark corner of the wings watching the band on stage. He tapped her shoulder and, when there was a momentary hush, said, 'How's it going?'

'Looks like total chaos to me,' she told him. There had been some technical difficulties. There were problems, someone had explained blandly, getting a five piece band to sound like a twenty-four track recording. And the piece of electronic wizardry that controlled synchronization of the lights was having hiccups too. All in all, both stage and console box were filled with some very distraught people.

'No, no, darling,' Mr Horowitz said, 'I mean you and Roz. Are you hitting it off? Got anything to tell me?'

'It's too soon to say,' Anna said, not liking to tell him that her contact with Roz was so slight as to be nonexistent. He seemed disappointed but said, 'Well, never mind. Just stick at it, darling, I know you won't let the poor girl down.' He went off to look for the balding, Nordic-looking man who was the tour manager. Anna had seen him several times in the past few hours and he always had a queue waiting for his attention.

A few minutes later Shona Una came to the wings and began some suppling exercises. Watching her, Anna wondered if she had ever been a dancer. She moved beautifully. Her exercises brought her close to Anna and she said, 'What did Danny Darling want?'

'Nothing,' Anna said, surprised that she had picked him out in the dark. Now she dipped into a *plié* and said, 'Everyone wants something. He more than most – ten per cent for starters.' And as if to prove her point: 'Did he bring me something? Did he say he had anything for me?'

'Not to me.' Anna wondered why Danny should worry

about this woman. She did not seem at all vulnerable. In fact she appeared to be calling all the shots. Certainly her body was under complete control as she stood on one leg and stretched the other up on to a bar. The pale column of her neck was perfectly steady, and her light eyes looked quite indifferent. Even her previously irritable expression was hidden behind a calm dancer's mask and Anna felt as if she was talking to her through a pane of glass. Perhaps it was the effect of fame. It was funny how the famous seemed not quite human.

Shona bent double, holding her knees, and looking at Anna upside down, asked, 'You sure no-one's been looking for me?'

'Only everyone,' Anna said vaguely. Because of the lights and her position in the wings she could only see a corner of the balcony. But through the glare she thought she had caught a glimpse of a figure in a pale coat and peaked cap. She hurried down from the stage, along the corridor at the side of the hall and up the balcony stairs. When she got there she found a woman in pink overalls checking the seats. She said, 'Was there anyone else up here just now? A man?'

The woman looked round. 'Might've been,' she said. 'There's folk in every nook and cranny. Like an ants' nest, ennit?'

Anna went down again and walked slowly along the other side of the hall. The exit doors on that side had been opened and a van was drawn up alongside to let the roadies bring in boards and scaffolding. She stepped outside. There was no-one from security watching the door. She went back into the hall. The band had disappeared offstage and in their place a team of workers were using the boards and scaffolding to build up the stage to three levels.

Outside again, Anna walked the entire circumference of the hall and then entered, unchallenged, at one of the stage doors. She found Kevin sitting on a packing case eating a sausage roll. He said, 'Well, there's no need to have anyone on the doors till the fans start rolling in.'

'Only, about five this morning there was a geezer hanging round the house in Addison Road, and I thought I just saw him again in the balcony.'

'You sure?'

'Not absolutely,' she admitted. 'But if there's some nut following her about . . .'

'Point taken,' Kevin said, shoving the last of his sausage roll into his mouth. 'I'll take a couple of the lads and have a look-see.' He stood up. Behind him, at the other end of the passage, she saw Lena with Daniel Horowitz. They seemed to be arguing. Then a group of people appeared from the area under the stage, and they moved out of sight. Anna walked along the passage in their direction. Halfway there she met Ducks hurrying the other way. He said, 'Where in the name of God am I supposed to get a bottle of Evian?'

'Try the caterers,' Anna suggested.

'Her ladyship insists on Evian and she wants it yesterday,' he said, running a finger over his smoothly arched brow. 'Someone should tell her I'm a hairdresser, not an effing waiter.'

Anna moved off again but when she got to the point where Lena and Mr Horowitz had disappeared there was no sign of them. Instead she found the keyboard player sitting on the steps leading to the back of the stage. He held out a hand to detain her and said, 'Hi, you must be Snoopy. Listen, there's a window stuck in the dressing-room and it's goddamned cold in there. Can you get someone from maintenance to fix it?'

'Maintenance, eh?' Anna said, sitting down beside him. When she had circled the hall outside, none of the dressing-room windows had been open. 'There's a window open, and you want me to get someone to shut it for you?'

'Yeah, Van said you were the window expert.' He laughed suddenly. 'Hell, I guess if Van wants it shut he can shut it himself.'

'He's a big boy,' Anna said carefully.

'He sure is,' said the keyboard player, who was himself a slight figure. He was sombrely dressed and all his clothes seemed a size too large. 'What's he got against you, anyway? He was talking like you were a witch or something.'

'I dunno,' Anna said wearily. 'Nobody seems to like outsiders round here.'

'Don't look at me, babe.' He got a shapeless, half-

smoked joint out of his pocket and stuck it between his lips.
'Me and Craig stay out of politics where we possibly can.
We're both from New Jersey, see. We're only here for the
music.' He searched his pockets for matches, but Anna left
before he could light up. He looked the type who would
offer her a drag and she felt confused enough already.

Chapter 15

She found a phone in the cubbyhole behind the box
office and called Bernie's home number. 'Hello, love,' he
said. 'How's the whirlwind life on the road suiting you? All
sex and drugs and rock'n'roll, eh?'

'Well, there's drugs and rock'n'roll,' Anna told him.
'But I haven't seen much sex lately.'

'Don't despair,' he said consolingly. 'You could get
lucky.'

'Thanks a bundle,' she said huffily. 'What I rang about
was the bit of paper I left with his nibs.'

'Very nice!' Next time you send me a letter try *not* wiping the frying-pan with it first. Anyway, I cleaned it off a bit
but I don't suppose I made much more sense of it than you
did. Hang on while I get my notebook.'

Anna held the receiver to her ear and waited. Through
the box office grille she saw Lena come down the steps from
the hall, cross the lobby and walk out through the glass
front doors. On the other side of the lobby the merchandise
stand was finished and two girls in tour sweatshirts stood
experimenting with the till and giggling.

Anna looked through the glass doors to the street.
Lena was standing at the kerb looking up and down.

'You still there?' Bernie said. 'What I've got is something like, "It's not just the money," and then splodge,
splodge, splodge, "something very ugly will happen to you
or," splodge, "close to you." And then it's nothing but mess

till you get to "Honour your contract." At least I think it's contract. It could be compact or contrast but contract's most likely.'

A blue Datsun pulled over to the kerb and stopped. Lena bent down to talk to the driver. Bernie went on, 'At least that's as near as I can make it.'

Anna said, 'Sorry, I missed the last bit.'

'Cloth ears,' Bernie grumbled. 'Well, after "contract" it goes something like, "If you ignore this or think we're kidding, you will regret it." But as I say, I'm only guessing with some of it.'

'Sounds heavy.' Outside, the car pulled away. Lena stood looking after it.

Bernie said, 'There's nothing to show who it's addressed to, but I suppose we've got to assume it's for your singer. Have you spoken to her about it?'

'That's a laugh.' She saw Lena come in and walk across the lobby. Her face was expressionless and she didn't see Anna watching her. 'I can't talk to her because she's never alone, she doesn't want to know, and I don't want to cause a wobbler. Apparently, there was an upset before the last gig in Birmingham and she nearly didn't go on.'

'Tricky. What about the other runners and riders?'

'God, Bern, there's so many of them and I haven't even sorted out who's who.'

'Well, look, unless you find out for certain who the letter's to, how and when it was delivered, who saw it first and above all, what it really says – you can't say more than someone in that house received what looks like a threatening letter.'

'I know. But so far, I'm only hanging on by the skin of my teeth. They think I'm a bit of a joke. But if I start asking questions systematically, they'll have me out so fast my feet won't touch.'

'Then you'll just have to watch and wait; the old routine. What about J.W.?'

'Oh, I'm a *very* big joke to them. You know – Tiddler from Small Fry Security.'

'Well, look, don't get sorry for yourself. And remember the one about the boy scout who helped the old lady across the road.'

'What?'

'She didn't want to go.' Bernie laughed comfortably. 'So if your client doesn't want to share her problems, you aren't doing her any favours trying to force her to. Take it easy, love. Wait till you're asked.'

'But if someone's hitting on her?'

'That's her lookout. She's not a kid. If she wants your help, she'll ask for it. Till then . . .'

'I keep my eyes open and my hand on my ha'penny.'

Chapter 16

As she turned the corner into the passage behind the stage Anna bumped hard into Avis. They knelt over Avis's dropped briefcase and picked up the scattered paper. Avis was out of breath. 'I'm in trouble,' she said. 'The PRO from Dog's on her way here. She's bringing someone from the Colour Supp. They might want to do a spread on Shona. And there's someone from *Melody Maker* who wants an interview with the whole band. They'll be here in a minute and I can't find Van.'

'Cutting it a bit fine, aren't they?' Anna asked. It was nearly dark, and already there were a couple of hundred people in the hall, the committed Shona Una fans who wanted to be sure of a place at the front.

'I wouldn't ask, only I'm in a jam,' Avis said. 'I've got to meet the PRO, and if I don't watch out one of the others'll escape from the dressing-room.'

'It would be Van,' Anna muttered. She went down the passage, stopping every J.W. man she met to ask if anyone had seen him. At last one of the men on the stage door said, 'You don't mean the hairy git in riding breeches, do you? He went out in the car park not fifteen minutes since.'

'Riding breeches?' Anna asked incredulously.

'And braces.' The man sniffed. 'Looks a right twot, if

you ask me.' He stood back to allow two women and a man, all waving press passes, through the door.

A cold wind buffeted the side of the hall. The car park was filling up and while Anna stood there a coach pulled in. About sixty boys and girls got out and stood in groups chattering excitedly.

As she passed one of the groups she heard a girl exclaim in a thrilled whisper, 'Over there! It's one of them. Look!' They all turned like a herd of startled deer. Anna looked too and saw Van sauntering between parked cars. He was a strange sight on such a cold evening, in nothing but riding boots and breeches, his bare chest crisscrossed by the rainbow braces which he was wearing back to front.

'He'll catch his death,' the whisperer said in a motherly tone.

Anna hurried over to him. At the same time, she noticed a car leaving the car park. It was noticeable because, with the car park filling up so quickly, it was the only one leaving. It could have been a blue Datsun. It was too dark for her to be certain.

In spite of the cold Van gave off an animal heat. He flung an arm round Anna's shoulder saying, 'Snoopy snooping, eh? Want to catch me with a groupie, do you, or do you want some yourself?' There was an electric feeling of exhilaration about him. Anna pulled away, conscious of hundreds of curious eyes.

'Save your charm for *Melody Maker*,' she snapped. 'There's someone wants to see you.'

'Ker-rap!' he said angrily. 'Can't they leave us alone? We go on in an hour. You're security, Snoopy – protect me!'

'What! Miss a chance to get your ugly mug in the papers!' she shepherded him through the stage door.

'Everyone wants a little piece,' he protested. 'Did you see them out there? Chip, chip, chip.'

'Well, think what they give you back.' She pushed him down the passage. 'Where would you be without an audience?'

'You're a hard woman, Snoops.' He opened the dressing-room door. 'But I'll get you in the end.'

'Not while there's an ape in the zoo, you won't,' Anna said as the door closed.

The whole area behind the stage was crowded. Now that the audience had begun to pack the hall all the technicians, roadies, and organizers retreated backstage. The J.W. agents, some of them very self-conscious in their black sweatshirts, gathered beside the caterer's table.

Dave bustled into their midst and said, 'Right, troops! Let's be having you. It's time we deployed. Everyone know their stations? Tiddler?'

'Yes.'

'Where?'

'Down here till she's on stage. Then hoof it round and about.' She was furious with Dave for picking on her and only her in front of the others.

'And then? Come on, Tiddler, full routine.'

'Down here. Check dressing-room. See her offstage. Wait till she wants to go. Bring car round to stage door . . .'

'Doors locked, engine running – go on.'

'Wait for you lot to escort her out. Unlock doors. You get her in. I take off.'

'Proceed without stopping,' Dave said severely. 'You don't stop for nothing, right?'

'Yessir Boss. Fans on the roof, road blocks, ice-cream vans – I proceed without stopping. Right, Boss.' Someone snorted. Dave said, 'Don't come the smart arse with me, my girl. Okay you shower, on your bikes!'

Anna slouched back to her place by the stage door, pausing only once to kick the wall.

Chapter 17

The show started ten minutes late, but that wasn't Shona's fault. When the time came, she strode across the passage between dressing-rooms and stage as if she hadn't a nerve in her body.

Anna missed the first number but was in the balcony

for the second. Shona ran down from the top level of the stage to the front. Yards of silk billowed around her and caught the coloured light. A wig of white and yellow hair streamed out behind. She shook her head down and up, making a flash of silver and gold fan around her face. Van started on toms and was joined by Wes in a running riff. Then they crashed into a song called *Logodaedaly*.

The impact of the sound came not so much through the ears – it started with the feet from the huge roaring vibrations in the floor, and spread upwards until the whole body was immersed. It was loud enough to shake muscle from bone. And all the while strobing white light pierced the eye and flickered straight into the brain like the onset of epilepsy. The great structure of girders, now ablaze with thousands of flashing bulbs, descended gradually from the rafters and spun slowly above the audience like a ferris wheel.

Anna was impressed – not by the music – she liked music to be more raw and not so finely balanced, but the show itself was highly dramatic. Shona's act was a mixture of song and mime. She was not a woman – she was a figure from a fairy tale who caught the eye and held the imagination. Anna watched, entranced.

After a while she remembered her instructions and squeezed her way along the back of the balcony. Dave's orders had seemed fairly simple in an empty hall, but he hadn't reckoned with an audience packed into every spare inch.

She got backstage in time to see Shona, Lena, and Ducks race across the passage for the first change. The band stayed on, playing the long introduction to the next number. When Shona came back, a few minutes later, she was all in black shot with silver glitter. It was the costume Anna recalled from the *Bitterness* video. She was helped into a steel cage and someone started the machinery that lifted her on to the stage.

Even from so far back the audience could be heard shrieking its approval. 'Wha'd'you think?' Lena asked, on her way up to watch from the wings.

'Terrific,' Anna said. 'They're lapping it up.' Lena nodded and passed on.

In Shona's room Ducks was pinning the white and yellow wig to its block. The dressing-table was a jumble of towels and tissues smeared with make-up. The cat slept undisturbed on the ironing board.

She went on to the reception room where the caterers were clearing piles of paper plates, cups, and plastic mugs. She managed to eat a sandwich and drink half a glass of milk before Kevin poked his head round the door. 'We ought to make another tour round,' he said. 'You take the right side. We'll meet at the bar, front of house.'

When she got to the bar, she found him already buying drinks for the two girls from the merchandise stand. She said, 'I can't get through the back of the balcony.'

'Nor can I,' he told her cheerfully. 'Just open the door and take a shufti. You can do my side too – I'm going Mutt and Jeff with all this racket.' The girls giggled and he raised his glass to them. Anna trudged upstairs. Her feet dragged.

She looked in on the heaving mass of backs. People were out of their seats now. They jumped up and down and drummed on the floor with their heels. In her tiredness Anna could imagine the balcony giving way under the weight, bodies and masonry crashing into the packed hall below. She went back to the foyer.

Kevin was still drinking and didn't see her. Some of the Warehouse staff were huddled by the doors peering into the hall. Anna craned over their shoulders and past the jumping audience to see Shona haloed in eerie blue light. It was a relatively quiet number. Her voice, a piercing high whisper, accompanied only by synthesizer and bass, filled the hall like the sea at night.

Anna made another trip backstage. The dressing-rooms were deserted except for Barbarella who was still asleep, so she wandered into the corridor. She joined a group of roadies at the caterer's station and drank tea until Dave chivvied her back to work.

She was in the balcony again for part of the final number. Shona was now in a black and red costume that made her look half orphan, half whore. Her make-up was stark white – eyes and mouth like holes in a sheet. She stood alone in a circle of white light while the band played in the dark.

Anna shivered suddenly and turned away. As she passed down the long corridor to the back the audience erupted into applause. She started to run and arrived back-stage just as the band came off. They spilled across the corridor into the reception lounge, grabbing for beer cans and towels.

But it wasn't the end yet. They waited till the barrage of shouts reached its peak and then they went on again.

The passage was deserted. Everyone squeezed on to the edge of the stage to watch the finale. Anna shivered again and opened the dressing-room door.

The room was empty except for Barbarella stretched out, still asleep, this time on a wig box. The cold tingle at the back of Anna's neck subsided. Her own face, looking back from the mirror, wore a strained, worried expression. There were circles under her eyes.

As she turned to go her sleeve caught a glass and sent it rolling off the edge of the dressing-table. She stooped automatically to pick it up.

As she looked up, she saw something was wrong. The cat's eyes were open. The mouth was open too. It seemed to be laughing.

Anna stared. A tiny drop of blood hung like a scarlet tear from one sharp tooth. It gathered weight, stretched, and dropped to the floor.

She straightened abruptly, and reached out an unwilling hand to touch the creamy fur. Her hands were clammy.

She ran her fingers down the little cat's side. There was no sign of life but she found the hard circle of a nail head hidden deep in the fur. The point had been driven through Barbarella's chest pinning her to the lid of the box.

A storm of clapping and shouting broke through from the hall. There was movement in the corridor.

Anna picked up a dirty towel and flung it over Barbarella's body. She lifted her, but the lid of the box came up too. She levered it off.

Voices sounded in the reception room. She rolled the limp body in the towel and looked around wildly. The nail tore through the cloth and scratched her hand. She scarcely felt it. The only thought in her head was to hide the sad little body before Shona came back.

A frantic search revealed the wicker cat basket in a corner. She pushed Barbarella, nail, towel and all into it and kicked it under the dressing-table.

The door opened. Danny, Ducks, the tour manager, and Shona burst in. 'A triumph!' Danny was saying. 'Simply a triumph. Darling, you were magnificent.'

The tour manager, his face wreathed in smiles, cried, 'Better than ever!' They all seemed light-headed with pleasure and relief. No-one noticed Anna.

'Not bad, was it?' Shona said, as more people pushed into the room. Someone popped open the first bottle of champagne.

Chapter 18

Avis was jammed in the doorway flanked by two stylish middle-aged men from the record company. Anna was pushed back against the ironing-board. Someone thrust a plastic cup full of champagne into her hand. More people arrived.

She started to squeeze through the crush. Everyone congratulated everyone else. At one point, trapped between backs and bellies, she found herself beside Shona. She met the glazed, expectant eyes and said, 'Fantastic! Great show.' The eyes turned hungrily to the next face, and Anna slid nearer the door.

When she got there, Avis was at the other side of the reception room. It was hardly less crowded there. The band mingled with organizers, managers, sponsors, and their friends and families. Wes stood primly with his wife and, surprisingly, a teenage daughter. The two Americans looked dazed, still in their make-up, talking to an elderly couple who might have been someone's parents. Van, his chest shiny with sweat, drank from the neck of a bottle.

Danny came through with a fat man. Anna touched his elbow and said, 'Can I have a word, Mr Horowitz?'

'Just a minute, darling,' he said, distracted as his fat companion wandered away to find something to drink. 'Listen, sweetie, that man – ' he pointed with his chin – 'he's the managing director of the company promoting the tour. Someone told him about the kerfuffle in Birmingham, so he came to this gig to see for himself. Thank God everything went off smoothly.' He squeezed Anna's hand. 'Ring me in the morning, if you want to talk. I've got to keep this guy sweet.' He drifted away.

'Just think of all that gelt!' Anna turned and found Lena at her shoulder. Her eyes glittered beneath thickly painted lids. 'There's millions in this room. See her? The one in cream velvet.' Anna looked, and saw a tall, red-headed woman in deep conversation with Ducks. 'She's Madeleine Hatching of Rose Cosmetics. You'll see the name in the programmes. She's worth a couple of million. All the make-up's Rose. Look at Ducks kissing arse. He's got the right idea.'

Avis appeared with a champagne bottle in each hand. 'Bubbly, anyone?' she asked.

'Bubbly?' Lena sneered, disgusted. Avis looked at her coolly and said, 'The guy from Fake Four's turned up.'

'Shit! Where?' Lena stood on her toes and craned her neck. 'Oh no! Not with Van! He'll screw everything.' She dived into the throng.

Avis grinned. 'Fake Four's a chain of boutiques,' she told Anna. 'Little Lena's dying to get her stuff in there.'

'Another sponsor?'

'I wouldn't be surprised. I don't know much about that side of things. But I do know you have to pull every trick in the book to make a tour break even these days. It's a hell of a risk.'

'No wonder Mr Horowitz looks ready for intensive care.'

'You look a bit under the weather yourself,' Avis said. 'Heavy day?'

'Not half,' Anna admitted. 'Look, can you spare a minute?' Avis followed her out into the passage. This was swarming with people too. Roadies had begun to break up the set and move the equipment out. At the far end Dave McPhee and some of his men had scores of fans corralled by one of the stage doors. The queue stretched back into the hall.

Anna said, 'You were back here all through the concert, weren't you?'

'That's right,' replied Avis, puzzled. 'I had a seat, but I stayed here in case I was needed.'

'Well, did you go to the dressing-rooms at all?'

'No-o. Oh, I got a drink for the road manager about twenty minutes from the end.'

'Anyone else there?'

'I don't think so. I only went into the reception room, though. Lena, Ducks, and Shona had just come out after the second change.'

'And after that?'

'I wasn't watching. But I should think just about the whole band went in after they came off and before the encore. You know – to towel off or have a drink. Why?'

'Did you see the cat?'

'No.'

'Or any strangers go in there?'

'No. Come on – why?'

'Well, look,' Anna began cautiously. 'You've got to keep this under your hat for a while – promise?'

'Sure,' Avis said, bewildered. 'What's up?'

'Someone's killed Shona's cat.'

'No! What for? How?' Avis looked astonished.

'Someone nailed it to a wig box. Sh-sh.' Two couples emerged from the reception room and walked slowly past.

'Nailed Barbarella to a wig box?' Avis looked incredulous. 'What a horrible thing to do. Does she know?'

'Not yet. It didn't seem quite the right time to tell her.'

'I should say not!' Avis said with a shudder.

'I've hidden the body, but now I haven't the foggiest what to do. I shouldn't even have told you. You represent the record company, after all.'

'So what,' Avis said stoutly. 'I won't tell anyone. But I know what you mean. There's so much lolly hanging on this tour – a lot of rats to run for cover if it looks like anything's happening to the ship. Like if Shona showed herself to be too temperamental.'

'Like if she got hysterical. Or if it looks like someone's got it in for her. Has someone?'

'Why should they? Oh, I know a lot of people are jealous – they always are when someone comes through the ranks. I mean, a year ago she was one of a thousand – playing clubs and student gigs. And there's a lot of bitching in the band. Nobody feels secure.'

'How do you mean?'

'Well, apart from Van, who's always been a performer, the rest are basically session people, you know, scraped together for recordings. They aren't a band as such. And let's face it, once the tracks are laid down, a gig is just a technical problem. Neil could do it all from the keyboards. None of them are really needed out front, It's Shona's show and everyone knows it.'

'What about Wes?' Anna asked carefully. 'He's been with her a long time.'

'Off and on, so I'm told. But he's a case in point. He hasn't much bezazz and actually he's not that good. His only chance of some limelight is backing Shona.'

'Then it'd seem that most of the band have it in their interest to keep Shona happy – not scare the hell out of her by snuffing her cat.'

'My point exactly.' Avis shook her head. 'It's a stupid, cruel thing to do.'

They fell silent for a few moments. Anna's hand began to sting.

'Nails!' she exclaimed, reminded. 'A long nail.'

'All around you,' Avis said. 'What do you suppose the carpenters tacked the false floors down with?'

Once she looked, Anna saw piles of wood shavings, off-cuts, and debris everywhere. There were plenty of discarded nails long enough to pierce the side of a Siamese cat.

'Who's that guy waving at you?' Avis asked suddenly. 'Is that your boss?'

'Oh, flaming Norah,' Anna said. At the other end of the passage Dave McPhee signalled impatiently. 'I got to go. Listen, can you get yourself into Shona's dressing-room?

The cat's in its box, out of sight under the dressing-table, and I don't want anyone finding it yet. Can you sort of stand guard?'

'I'll try,' Avis said uncertainly. 'But I'm not much good if anyone throws their weight around. Will you tell your boss?'

'I don't think so, yet.' Anna started moving off towards him. 'He's the type'd have everyone up against the wall – do a full-scale search of the premises.'

'Then for Christ's sake keep your mouth shut,' Avis pleaded. 'Those guys from *Melody Maker* and the Colour Supp are still here.'

Anna ran down the passage to find Dave. 'What're you doing, having mothers' meetings in corners?' he barked. 'I want to know when we can let this mob through.'

The mob of fans showed signs of bad temper. They were pushing each other and quarrelling about places in the queue.

'Find someone!' Dave ordered. 'We can't hold this lot all night.'

Chapter 19

By the time she got back to the dressing-room a lot of guests had left. Nobody wanted to know about the fans except Van. 'Let's have 'em all in,' he suggested. He sat, arms outstretched on the back of the sofa, his head lolling. 'Let's look 'em over and suck on the sweet ones.'

'Shut it, Van,' Shona snapped. 'I'm not seeing anyone else tonight.' Her wig was off and she was wrapped in a pale yellow kimono.

'Couldn't you see just a few?' Danny asked unhappily. 'They've been waiting a long time, darling. You don't want to make enemies.'

'I've just worked my guts out for them for three hours.

Isn't that enough?' The mood of elation had soured: she looked drained.

'Well, why don't we get them to send their programmes and things through,' the front-of-house manager suggested. 'You could all sign them while you're changing.'

'Stuff their programmes,' Shona said wearily. A few of the guests exchanged glances.

'She's exhausted,' Danny said, even more unhappy

'Right. But we'll compromise,' the tour manager said, sizing up the situation and taking charge. 'We'll have the first fifteen in the queue. The rest can send their things in for autographs.'

Anna was sent back to Dave with the news. The fans took it badly. 'Just who does she think she is?' one boy said. 'We've been stood here ages.'

'I'd never've bought the bleeding disc if I'd've known,' another remarked. And Anna found herself looking at a host of resentful eyes. They were all prepared to hate the one they'd come to worship. She collected up record sleeves, programmes, and autograph books. But some of the fans went away without bothering. She could feel their disappointment like fingers plucking at her skirt. She understood their point of view, but all the same it seemed strange that the same fans who had clapped their hands raw for Shona now had no sympathy at all for her fatigue, when by any standard it had been a very tiring performance. It didn't seem reasonable.

And there was nothing reasonable about the way the chosen fifteen rushed along to the dressing-room in their panic to be allowed in. Anna, who was supposed to conduct them, was pushed aside in the charge. When they got inside, though, they stopped and stood abashed as if they'd forgotten what they'd come for.

Craig, Wes, Neil, and Van signed everything that was given them. Anna passed round the mementoes she had collected. Shona sayed in her own room, but the fans were allowed to stand by the open door while books and record sleeves were brought in to her. She was surrounded by Lena, Ducks, and Porky. Anna was glad to see Avis in there too.

Some remarks were passed, like: 'Wonderful show,

Miss Una,' and 'Can you write "for Tracy"?' and 'It's for my brother, Mark,' but Shona just signed whatever was put in front of her without looking up.

Afterwards, when Anna took them back, there were more comments. 'She's got lovely hands,' one girl said. 'Did you see her ring? Amethyst, wasn't it?'

'I never thought she was that old,' another one complained. 'She looks about eighteen on the video. Must be the make-up.'

'Anyone can look fantastic if they're made up right,' said someone else. Anna, who had never before witnessed the way an idol is cut down to size, was rather shocked.

'What a bunch of ijjuts,' Dave exclaimed as he shut the door behind the last one. 'No-one but a loony'd pay good money for that rubbish. Call that entertainment?'

'"It's only rock'n 'roll, but I like it,"' Anna quoted, half under her breath. 'You don't think much of the band, then?'

'Load of tossers. Isn't she ready to leave yet? Some of us got homes to go to.'

'Think of the overtime. I dunno,' Anna sighed, 'why does everyone slag everyone off so much? I've never come across such a slagging match.'

'You've never been security on one of these tours before, have you?' Dave looked down his nose at her. 'You'll learn. It's because there's a lot of vultures on only the one carcass – not enough to go round and everyone's hungry.'

There was some truth in that, she mused on her reluctant way back to the dressing-rooms. Only who were the vultures and what was the carcass? Fame and fortune was the simple answer. But what about Shona who had achieved it? She had stood in front of thousands of screaming, applauding fans and yet she still needed Anna's few distracted words. And now the fans themselves needed to be noticed. Look at me, look at me, no – look at *me*, seemed to be the cry in every throat. *I* could look like that if I had the right make-up . . . *I* could do that, if only someone'd notice me. Fame and fortune were only by-products in the universal need to be seen.

Chapter 20

Nearly everyone except the band had gone. Danny had left with the promoter and the record company honchos. So had the journalists.

Now only Wes's wife and daughter, a few friends of the Americans, Porky, and Avis waited in the reception room. Shona's door was open, and she waited, already in her fur coat, for Lena and Ducks to finish packing up. The men were shrugging into coats and stowing away odd bits and pieces. They were arguing about the order of the programme – whether *Logodaedaly* should change places with *Sweet Hot Night*, and if *Bitterness* should come earlier. They all showed signs of tiredness and irritability.

Anna drew Avis aside. 'I've been going crazy,' Avis whispered, 'thinking someone'd find the cat basket. But nobody did. And do you know? Nobody's even noticed the poor little brute's missing. What are you going to do?'

'Tell her.'

'Now?'

'Yes.'

'Would you mind awfully if I went home now?' Avis mumbled, blushing.

'Chicken!' Anna said ruefully. 'No, go on, and thanks for your help.' She went to Shona's room. Shona looked up and yawned. Anna said awkwardly, 'Look love. I've got something to tell you. It's about your cat.'

Shona yawned again. 'Yeah?' She turned her head. 'Where is she anyway? Anyone seen Barbarella?' Lena and Ducks stopped what they were doing and looked at her.

Anna said quietly, 'She's dead. I'm really sorry.' Shona looked stunned. 'What d'you mean, she's dead?' she asked, her voice rising. 'Where is she?' Lena and Ducks had their mouths open.

Anna said, 'She's in her basket, under the dressing-table.'

Shona shouted, 'If this is a sick joke, Snoopy, I'll kill you!'

'Hush, dearie, remember your voice,' Ducks muttered mechanically. Lena stooped and dragged the basket out.

'Don't open it,' Anna said.

'Go on, open it,' Van urged from the doorway. Behind him were Wes's teenage daughter and Porky, both craning their necks to see. Shona leaped up furiously and slammed the door on them. She turned to Anna. 'What have you done to her?' she cried.

'I found her dead just before you came off,' Anna said evenly. 'I wrapped her in a towel and put her in her basket.'

'But she was only three years old,' Ducks pointed out. 'She couldn't've just died.'

'What happened, Snoops?' asked Lena. 'Accident? You can tell us.'

'No accident,' Anna said. She was trying to watch them all at once. In a way she was sorry Shona had slammed the door. 'She was killed. Look – perhaps you can tell me where she was when you came in for your change.'

'I don't remember seeing her,' Ducks said. 'Do you, Lena?'

'Jesus!' Lena exclaimed. 'We're in and out of here, like Road Runner. You can't hang about playing with cats. It's a panic.'

Shona said, 'I don't remember seeing her since we first went on. She was asleep on the ironing-board.'

'That's where I saw her after the first change,' Anna told them.

'She never got in the way,' Shona said sadly.

'Well, I suppose we'd better find out who was in here between the first change and when you finally came off,' Anna said.

'You know, I blame you, Snoops,' Lena said. She got up from her crouch by the cat basket. 'You're security. You're paid to see things like this don't happen. But any bastard can walk in here and kill a cat. What if he'd planted a bomb or something?'

'Right!' Anna said. 'Which is why you need someone like me around. But you don't make things very easy, do you? You give me the cold shoulder and send me out on useless errands instead. You didn't want me here at all, did you?' A silence followed. Then the door opened and Avis put her head through. Anna gave her a relieved smile and said, 'I thought you'd gone home.'

'Changed my mind,' Avis said sheepishly. 'Listen, they want the costume box. Everyone's waiting to go home.'

'Let them take it,' Shona said. 'Everyone's tired – why don't you all fuck off home to bed? Why should anyone care? Barbarella was only a cat, after all. Why should anyone give a monkey's for my cat?' She marched into the reception area. Everyone stayed where they were.

'Some obscene bastard killed my cat!' she went on loudly. 'Well, good night! I hope you all have pleasant dreams.'

'Nobody's going anywhere,' Neil said. He exchanged a puzzled glance with Craig who said, 'We'll stick around as long as you want.'

Dave McPhee tapped on the door and looked in. 'Everyone ready?' he demanded bossily. He was answered by silence and hostile glances. 'What's going on?' he asked suspiciously. 'We can't stay here all night.'

'Sorry, Dave,' Anna began, 'there's been . . .'

'Keep it in the family,' Shona warned suddenly. She turned to Dave. 'Get outside and shut the door.' He went. Shona stood with her back to the door and said, 'Anyone says a word about Barbarella outside this room gets fired. Right? I mean it. You're all replaceable.'

'That's not very fair,' Wes said. 'We're all sorry about the cat, but . . .'

'Shee-it!' Van said angrily. 'No-one gives a toss and you know it. But she's right. This'd look just great in the *Mirror*.' There was a moment's quiet and then everyone began to talk at once.

Anna sidled up to Avis. 'Did you tell anyone how it happened?' she asked in a low voice.

'No,' Avis whispered back. 'And nobody seems to know either.'

'Well, don't say anything.'

'Okay. But they're all very curious.'

'Yes. But what was said?'

'Oh, nothing much.' Avis shrugged. 'Everyone wanted to know what happened, of course. But I didn't let on I knew. And then Van started making jokes about what a shame it was no-one played fiddle. He really is a cold-hearted son of a you-know-what. *He* could've done it, you know. He's mean enough and he doesn't like cats.'

'There's lots of people don't like cats. But . . .'

'What're you two whispering about?' Lena asked. 'Something you haven't told us, Snoops?'

'We were wondering what to do next,' Anna said vaguely.

'You could always hold an interrogation.' Lena smiled maliciously. '"Where were you on the night of the murder?" – that sort of thing. Listen, everyone – Snoopy wants to play detectives!'

'Shut up, Lena,' Anna said coldly, and Van, at the top of his voice, said, 'I don't give a wet fart what anyone else wants. I'm pissed off and I'm going home.'

'What do you want us to do?' Craig asked Shona. 'We'll stay here all night if you want us to. We'd like to help, but what can we do? None of us killed your cat.'

'We hear you saying so,' Lena said.

'Shut up, Lena.' This time it was Porky.

'Bitch!' said Wes.

'Just shut up, everyone!' Shona cried. She was very pale and looked as if she were about to faint. 'Go home! You make me sick, all of you. Snoopy – get my car.' There was an immediate rush for the door and Anna slipped into the dressing-room for the cat basket.

She found Dave waiting for her in the passage with a face like thunder. He fell into step beside her. 'What was all that about?' he asked. 'Who the hell does she think she is?'

'Don't ask,' said Anna. 'You wouldn't believe me anyway.'

'I suppose she wants her car now. Well, there's still a few of the faithful waiting. I hope they tear her apart.' But by the time they reached the car park he calmed down enough to repeat his instructions: 'Even if they climb on the bonnet, Tiddler, keep going.'

'Okay.' Anna was too tired to kid him any more.

'And I don't care what moody the stupid cow pulls — don't stop on the way home. Some of the ijjuts might try to follow you.'

Chapter 21

Some of them did try to follow. The BMW rolled majestically away accompanied by a carload of yelling boys who hung out of the windows and waved scarves. Behind them came two motor scooters, and further back, a VW Beetle.

Shona cowered between Porky and Lena.

'It's all right,' Anna told her, 'they can't see you. And we'll lose them on the motorway.'

'Lose them now,' Shona pleaded. 'I don't trust anyone.'

A little later Dave's XR3 cut in between the BMW and its pursuers. The radio-telephone crackled and his voice came over. 'You're in a built-up area, dummy. Want to spend the night in Luton nick?'

Anna said, 'I told you never to call me at work.' She eased up on the accelerator and Porky snorted with laughter.

On the motorway, the only lights in her mirror were Dave's, but they parted company at Brent Cross with Dave saying, 'Think you can manage on your own now? See you in the a.m. Don't be late.'

Addison Road was deserted when she stopped the car outside Shona's house. She turned in her seat and said, 'Want me to go in first?'

'Oh, for Christ's sake!' Porky muttered. But Shona said, 'Give her the keys,' and Lena handed them over without a word. They sat together in the back of the car while Anna padded up the steps and let herself in.

The flat was dark and silent. She went through the hall,

opened the doors one by one, and turned on all the lights. So far she had only seen the kitchen and living-room. Now she found a small study, four bedrooms, and two bathrooms.

Obviously, Marilyn had been at work all afternoon because the flat was in quite good order. There were suitcases, piles of clothes, and magazines strewn about, but the beds were made and the bathrooms clean, and there were no dirty cups or dishes. The place was by no means tidy, but at least it wasn't a slum.

She looked in cupboards, behind sofas, under beds. There were no bodies, no hidden fans, no surprise packages, so she went outside and called the others in. They went straight to the kitchen where Porky found himself a bowl and a packet of cornflakes.

'Are you expecting anyone else tonight?' Anna asked.

'What's it to you?' Porky looked up, his mouth full. Lena was uncharacteristically silent.

'Nothing,' Anna replied lightly. 'I was merely going to give the usual warnings about chaining the door, and all that moody. You've probably heard it all before.' She turned to Shona. 'Don't you think it's about time we had a talk?'

Shona hunched deeper into her fur coat. She murmured, 'It was only a cat.'

'It's a bit more than that.'

'Only a cat,' Shona repeated. 'Look, I'm out of it – right out – I've got to sleep.'

'I know. But you were warned, weren't you, that "something ugly would happen".'

Shona looked at her, the pale, colourless eyes pink-rimmed with fatigue. Lena spoke up. 'What crap! Can't you see she's out on her feet?'

Shona said, 'Come with me,' and Anna followed her into the hall. 'What's happened to Barbarella?' Shona asked when they were alone. 'You didn't leave her at the Warehouse, did you?'

'No. She's in the boot of the car.'

'Take care of her for me, will you? I can't face all that.' She leaned wearily against the wall, her face sunk into the collar of her coat.

'I was going to,' Anna said. 'But the point is that someone's trying to freak you out. Who? What do they want? What are we going to do about it?'

'Listen, Snoopy,' Shona began, and then changed her mind. 'No, you've done me a favour tonight. Several favours one way or another. What's your real name?'

'Anna.'

'Well then, Anna. I know what you're thinking, but it isn't like that. This is nothing to play amateur detectives about. I don't know what you've been told or what you've found but the truth is that I get fan mail, and I also get hate mail.' Her voice was flat and monotonous, almost as if she were talking in her sleep.

'Danny and Dog Records filter most of it out – everyone wants to protect me – but some of it gets through somehow. It can be pretty filthy. People threaten all sorts of things. But, Anna, people in my position expect that. We can't get freaked out by hate mail. It doesn't mean anything except I've got to have people like you around.'

'But someone killed your cat in a particularly nasty way,' Anna said.

'Don't tell me about it.' Shona bit her lip and stared down at the carpet. 'Maybe I should take security more seriously. Perhaps we could talk about it in the morning. But I've got to sleep now. I'll be useless tomorrow if I don't get to bed. Where are we tomorrow?'

'Bristol.'

'Okay, Bristol. And Anna?'

'Yes.'

'Thanks for everything.' The white lips turned up minutely in a sad smile.

Anna found herself out on the street feeling much better. Maybe the job wouldn't be so bad after all. All the same, she took note of the cars parked near the house and glanced sharply up and down the road before driving away. But everything looked normal and there were no lurking figures in raincoats.

In fact, the only suspicious figure she came across was in her own street, not a hundred feet from her house. It wore a navy coat and watch cap and hurried furtively along with a canvas bag clasped to its chest. As the lights from the

BMW flared over the pavement, the figure dropped to a crouch behind a parked car.

She braked and rolled down the window. 'Selwyn,' she called. 'What on earth are you doing out so late?'

'Sh-sh-sh,' came from behind a Morris Oxford. She got out, leaving the engine running, and went over. 'Selwyn! What're you *doing* dressed up like a burglar sitting in that puddle? Get up – you look ridiculous.'

'How did you know it was me?' He got stiffly to his feet. To her amazement she saw he was wearing a false moustache. The canvas bag clanked as he got up. She took it away from him and unzipped it. Inside was a short crowbar, three screwdrivers, a glass cutter, and a brick. Everything except the brick belonged to Anna.

'I couldn't sleep,' Selwyn explained lamely. 'I was just going for a walk.'

'Oh, well, sorry to've interrupted you,' Anna said. She took her tools out of the bag and gave it back to him with only the brick left inside. 'That'll be a bit easier to carry,' she went on. 'It's a long walk to Camden Lock. You'd never make it with all that weight.'

'What makes you think I'm going there? It's just a breath of fresh air I want.'

'Looking like a pantomime burglar, yes, I see. I just thought since Foolscap House is in Camden Lock, and *Wholes and Corners* is at Foolscap House . . . but no. Silly me.'

Selwyn hung his head. Anna said, 'Come on, love, don't be a blockhead.'

'But I'm a desperate man,' Selwyn said uncertainly.

'I know. But it's bloody cold, and a very long walk. And besides you forgot your gloves. You can't B and E without gloves – you'd be the laughing-stock of the underworld.'

Selwyn stared at his hands. They were pink and plump and utterly useless for manual work. He said sadly, 'You take everyone seriously but me, don't you?'

'That's not true,' she said. Although in a way it was. 'But love, I've never known anyone quite so hopeless as you at the things you aren't good at.'

'You could help me. You know how these things are done.'

'B and E? Thanks a bundle! I've told you, Selwyn, there's a far simpler, *legal* solution.' They stared at each other. Then he said, 'It may be legal, Leo. But it's immoral. Why should I have to buy my own work back? – just because I didn't open a bloody letter in time.'

Anna didn't know how to reply. Put like that, without his usual histrionics, it did seem unanswerable. Even with a joke moustache struck crookedly under his nose Selwyn had an air of simple dignity.

In the end she said, 'Well, come home, old thing. I'll make us both a mug of hot chocolate, and then you take a couple of Bea's sleeping pills. I'll think of something, I promise.'

Chapter 22

The alarm went off with a sharp waspish beep at eight the next morning. Anna rolled out of bed. She showered, made coffee, and then, against all her habits, cooked bacon, eggs, tomatoes and toast. If yesterday was anything to go by, it would be the only square meal of the day.

At half-past eight she rang the office and was told by Beryl, in peevish tones not unlike the alarm clock's, that no, Brierly Security had no dealings with any vet, and if Anna wanted to dispose of a dead cat she should make her own arrangements. And if this was Anna's idea of a joke, there were better subjects for humour. Anna pulled a face at the phone and turned to the friendlier Yellow Pages.

After leaving Barbarella at the local vet's surgery, she rushed home again and phoned the Horowitz Management number. The woman on the switchboard told her that Mr Horowitz was urgently engaged on another line. Anna left a message. Then she hurriedly packed an overnight bag. The whole tour would spend the night in Bristol and leave for Brighton the next morning.

She had just finished with her bag when the phone rang. Daniel Horowitz said, 'Anna darling? Thank God. Listen, there's an awkward . . . No, it might be a little crisis. Just drop everything and run round to her place now, will you? I'm sorry I can't talk, darling, I've got people here.'

'I was just leaving anyway,' Anna said. 'What . . . ?'

'You were? Good – great. I'm sure it's nothing, but ring me when you get there. All right?' He rang off. Anna grabbed her bag and ran.

Porky let her in. He looked unworried, the same unhealthy, S-shaped figure of emaciation as the day before, a slice of thickly buttered toast in one hand. He interrupted his chewing long enough to say, 'What you doing here?'

'Mr Horowitz told me to come round.' She stared at him. They were due to leave for Bristol within the hour. He must've known that.

Lena appeared from one of the bedrooms. She was all in black and looked like a tiny Mediterranean widow. Porky said, 'What's he want to call you for? We can manage.'

'So manage!' Lena said, exasperated. 'I can't get her up.'

'What's happened?' Anna asked.

'Nothing.' Lena turned back to the bedroom. 'Go and make some coffee if you want to be useful.'

'No,' Anna said. 'You make the coffee for a change.' She pushed past into the bedroom.

It was dark. Shona lay on her side under a pile of tangled blankets. A light snore rattled at the back of her nose. Anna pulled the curtains back. Lena protested, but Anna repeated, 'Make the coffee. Black and strong.' She went over to the bed. Shona's breathing sounded healthy enough, and her pulse, when Anna felt for it, was strong and regular. Anna slapped the hand she was holding, and shook her shoulder. Shona groaned. Her eyes opened to a slit and she mumbled, 'Ge' los', Snoo.'

'Yeah, get lost, Snoopy.' Lena hovered behind her like a black mosquito.

'What's she taken?'

'Just shove off, will you?'

'Do you want me to call a doctor?' Anna asked, 'No?

Then get that coffee and I'll think about it. You think about it too, eh?'

When Lena had gone Anna turned back to the bed. It was hard to see in the tangle of bedding, but it looked as if two people had slept there. The bed was, in fact, big enough for four. The ashtrays on both night tables had cigarette butts in them, and there were dirty glasses. She sniffed one of them. The sweet smell of Southern Comfort mixed with something strange wafted up. She put the glass down and started to search for bottles of pills. There was nothing by the bed, but in the bathroom she found a bottle of chloral hydrate. The label on the bottle showed it had been prescribed for Mrs E. Blakemore.

She ran cold water into the basin, soaked a towel and wrung it out. The towel was thick and fluffy, and heavy when wet. She took it in to Shona. She pulled her into a sitting position and began to wipe her face and the back of her neck. She struggled weakly, trying to die down again. Anna wouldn't let her. She supported her with one arm and continued to pat her face and neck with the cold towel.

A pillow fell to the ground and exposed a matchbox which had been hidden under it. Anna let Shona fall back, and picked up the matchbox. Inside were about a dozen white tablets. Each one had the letters *Mx* etched on the surface.

Shona began to snore again. Anna closed the matchbox and slipped it into her pocket. Sighing heavily, she stripped the sheets and blankets from the bed and shook them out, but nothing else was concealed there.

Shona wore a pale green silk shift, a skimpy thing wound up round her hips. Anna examined her legs and arms. The creamy skin was firm and smooth. She looked closely at her feet. But there were no punctures or track marks there either.

She pulled Shona upright again and applied the wet towel energetically. 'Wake up!' she shouted close to her ear. 'Come on! Up. It's time to go!'

'Le' me be,' Shona whined, like a child.

Lena came in with the coffee.

'Drink!' Anna yelled. She supported Shona and held her head while Lena fed her some coffee. Some of it spilt

and dribbled down her chin but some went the right way.
'More!' Anna shouted. 'Come on! Don't be so pathetic.'

'Bastards,' Shona said quite clearly. She struck out and
sent the coffee flying all over Lena.

'Stupid cow!' Lena exclaimed. 'Look what you've
done!'

'Don't care,' Shona moaned. 'I gorra sleep.' Lena
slapped her face. 'Oh no you don't!' she yelled. 'You're getting up and going to work, you silly bitch. I've had you up to
here!' She slapped Shona again.

'That's enough,' Anna said sharply. 'Let's get her into
the bath.'

'Oh, right,' Lena sneered, hauling Shona's arm. 'I
wouldn't want to mess with Superstar's pretty face, would I?
It wouldn't be marketable all bruised up, would it?' She
dragged Shona to the side of the bed. It might have been
sheer temper, but she proved surprisingly strong for such a
frail person.

Together they half hauled, half carried Shona to the
edge of the bath. Anna eased her over the rim and let her
down slowly. Lena got hold of the hand spray and turned on
the cold tap. She directed the stream of icy water full into
Shona's face.

The shock jolted Shona up. She spluttered and
squirmed, trying to avoid the spray, but Lena was implaca-
ble. 'She's coming out of it now,' she told Anna. 'Sorry I lost
my rag. But if you knew how long it took me to make this
dress – it's cut on the cross, see.'

Shona struggled up to a crouch and protected her face
with her arms. Cold water played all over her.

'It won't wash,' Lena went on. 'You've no idea what this
fabric cost.'

Anna turned off the tap and said, 'Let's see if she can
get out by herself. Otherwise we'll have to get Porky in to
help.'

'I won't have that cretin touch her,' Lena said. 'Come
on, Sho, get your arse out of there. Or do you want another
shower?'

Shivering and swearing, Shona got slowly up and
crawled over the side of the bath. Anna was ready with a dry
towel. She wrapped her up in it and started rubbing briskly.

'We need more coffee,' she said. 'And lots of orange juice if there is any.'

'I feel ghastly,' Shona protested.

'Your own fault,' Lena told her and skipped off to the kitchen.

After a while Shona stopped shivering. She stripped off the wet nightdress when Anna told her to, and accepted another dry towel. She looked awful. The left side of her face was blotched and puffy from Lena's slaps and her eyes seemed loose in her head.

While her back was turned Anna took the bottle of chloral hydrate from the bathroom shelf and poured the contents down the drain.

'Oh God, I think I'm going to throw up.'

'Good idea,' said Anna. Shona bent over the lavatory bowl, retching, while Anna filled a glass from the tap. When she had finished, Anna handed her the water. She drank slowly, experimentally. She kept it down.

'How many did you take?' Anna asked.

'Wha'?'

'Mandrax. How many?'

'Wha' does it matter?'

'I just want to know whether you're suicidal or stupid.' Anna suddenly found herself stiff with annoyance. She jammed her hands in her pockets. Lena came back with coffee and orange juice.

Shona managed to get herself to a chair where she sat slumped, her hands slack in her lap, eyelids heavy over murky eyes. Lena coaxed, and obediently she drank from cup and glass.

Eventually, when Lena went back to the kitchen for more coffee, Anna went out too. She said, 'I'll have to phone Mr Horowitz. She's not well enough to go to Bristol.'

Lena stared at her, horrified. Porky said, 'I phoned Van. He'll be here in a minute.' He looked pointedly at Lena. She said, 'Don't be stupid, Snoops. The show must go on and all that crap.'

'She's still got a skinful. She's had Southern Comfort, chloral hydrate, Mandrax, and God knows what else. She won't be fit by tonight.'

'She'll be okay,' Porky insisted. 'I've see her come out of much worse than this.'

'Big tour, thousands of people? How's she going to manage? She can't even see straight.'

'She'll be all right.'

'Read my lips!' Anna said angrily. 'She-is-not-well-enough.' The doorbell rang and Porky went to answer it. From the hall they heard Van say, 'Where's the patient?' and Porky mumble something in reply.

'Just wait a bit, Snoops,' Lena said softly. 'You're very good at managing in an emergency, I grant you that. But you don't understand a thing. Here's where you step out the way. Softly, softly, right? Now, I'm going to help the girl dress. And you wait here like a good little Snoopy. You will not pass go. You will not phone Danny Darling. Wait till I get back, or we'll have your guts for skipping-rope.'

Chapter 23

At eight that night Shona Una went out on stage at the Old Theatre, Bristol, clear-eyed, bounding with energy, and in total command of herself. It was a polished performance. Anna realized just how polished it was when she saw all the little things repeated that she had taken as spontaneous or accidental in Luton.

The Old Theatre was grand, with red plush seats, boxes picked out in gold and ivory, and Greek columns supporting the proscenium arch. But no-one appreciated the beauty. In fact everyone complained. To the technical people it presented problems of acoustics and lighting. The stage wasn't large enough for the band. The dressing-rooms were cramped and squalid. And Dave McPhee found the narrow corridors, the boxes, and the three balconies difficult to police.

Anna performed her function as part of security with

mechanical precision but she was tired and despondent. She dutifully toured the corridors and made sure no ambitious fans tried to creep backstage. She checked for bombs and unauthorized cameras, but her heart wasn't in it.

In the corridor to the left of the auditorium the booming sounds from the speakers lost their clarity. They were reduced to a muffled roar that shook the walls and felt like earth tremors in the floor. There was no sense in them. She met Kevin coming the other way. He said, ''Lo, Tiddler, keeping your head down?' It sounded as if he had found someone to drink with again. 'I'd play it safe if I were you,' he went on. 'Cap'n Dave's still doing his nut. He says you couldn't organize a singsong on a coach trip.' He laughed loudly and went his way.

Anna had been nearly two hours late for the rendezvous in Hammersmith. Dave had wanted a neat military-style convoy up the motorway. Instead there was a flurry of phone calls and excuses, and half the party left without him. She couldn't tell him the truth about what had happened – not with Lena and Van eavesdropping.

She hadn't told Mr Horowitz either, and anyway, the only question he had asked when she rang was, 'Is she functional?' Anna did not like that question. After Van's ministrations Shona was certainly functioning, but functioning rather too quickly. Her eyes glittered and stared, she moved jerkily, and her temper was bad. Anna harboured uneasy suspicions about what Van had done but nobody told her anything.

Ducks was in the dressing-room where he'd been throughout the performance. He looked morose and his exquisite satin shirt was rumpled. 'Everyone's in a foul mood,' he groused. He was teasing the black and red wig into artful disorder for the last part of the show.

'How can you tell?' Anna asked. 'They seem about average to me.'

'Well, I don't see why I should rot in here for hours. There's no more cats to kill.'

'That's right,' Anna said. 'Only people left now, so why bother?'

'What's got into you? You're getting as bad as everyone else.'

'That's true,' she said, startled. 'It must be catching. Sorry.'

'I don't know how I stand it.' He sighed and sprayed the wig with firm-hold lacquer. 'Don't think I have to either. I've had offers. There's one I'm considering very seriously right now.'

'Rose Cosmetics?' she asked idly.

'I could do very well for myself there,' he said, looking dreamy. 'I'm a top-class stylist, not some jumped-up tart's dogsbody. One more word out of Madame and I'm off. I won't even see the tour out. You can tell her that.'

'Not me, mate!'

He laughed. 'No. You're not exactly flavour of the month, are you? They don't like strangers prying into their sordid little secrets.'

'I'm not interested in their secrets,' she lied, 'just their safety.'

'You're the only one, then. There was one guy from some paper last week who offered me . . . well . . . a lot to tell him bedtime stories. You should tell her that too. If she wants loyalty she might be polite at least once a week.'

'I thought you were friends.' She poured two cups of weak coffee from a Thermos on the table and gave him one.

'So did I.' He sighed loudly and accepted the coffee. 'I did her hair for free when she was broke. "Wait till I crack the big one, Ducks. We'll be laughing," she used to say. Well, she cracked it, and I'm on the payroll, but do you see me laughing? You do not. Successful people don't have friends, they have sycophants. At least that's what she thinks.'

'Did you know her back in the In Hock days?'

'When I first met her she was Rosalind Greenwood. She and another kid shook their tambourines and their fannies in front of a band called de Blank. It wasn't bad. They made an LP that got to 23 in the UK. And then the lead singer died of . . . well, throat cancer, they *said* it was, and the whole thing folded. She went out on her own after that. You know what she said? The day after the funeral, it was. She said, "Ducks, I'm pissed off with these fellas. They've got dirty habits and gross egos. I've got more talent than all of them put together and I'm going up front." Which, after a long slog, she did.'

'What's wrong with that?'

'Nothing. She was right. You take whatever you can grab in this game. You don't grab, you don't get. Except now *she's* got the dirty habits and a gross ego to match, and I'm not putting up with it much longer.' He reached up and flicked the loudspeaker switch. The closing sequence of *Down Down Down* thundered into the room. He switched it off again and said, 'Battle stations!' Anna cleared out fast to give them space.

Chapter 24

There were not many people backstage after the show. It was too far from London. Mr Horowitz hadn't come, nor had Avis. The only representative from Dog Records was a PRO who had arranged the interviews with local press and TV beforehand and was now in charge of a couple of photographers.

The fans did better because the Old Theatre management had a well-practised system. A fair number got through to see the band, and more of them went home happy. But of course they weren't the same fans.

At least Anna thought they weren't until she pulled up outside the hotel where the band and crew were staying. As she got out to open the door for Shona she saw a VW Beetle crawl slowly by. When it had passed the hotel it speeded up and shot out of sight. She was reminded so forcibly of the VW which had followed them out of the Warehouse car park that she memorized the number.

Rain spattered down and she opened the umbrella provided by J.W. as standard issue with their celebrity cars. Shona and Lena scurried under its protection to the hotel lobby. Porky grumbled loudly and got his hair wet.

She stowed the car in the underground car park and found Dave and Kevin waiting by the lift. They both looked jaundiced, but that was the effect of the dim yellow lighting.

Anna told them about the VW. It gave her a curious sense of relief to tell somebody something that was on her mind. Dave laughed emptily and his laugh echoed off the concrete walls. 'Seeing little green men again, Tiddler?' Kevin asked.

'Little green men in VW Beetles,' Dave said scornfully. 'Well, he won't hurt anyone. You want to know why he won't hurt anyone, Tiddler? He won't hurt anyone because he is a masochist. Anyone goes to just one of these frigging concerts is plain stupid. Anyone goes to two is a masochist. Stands to reason.'

'QED,' Anna murmured. She wondered why all car parks, even under the best hotels, smelled of urine. The lift came and they got in.

'Tell you what, Tiddler,' Dave said with an exaggerated sigh as they ground up to the lobby. 'If you want to prove how sodding efficient you are – if you really want to impress us – you'll get your little troupe of freaks out of their pits on time tomorrow. The big boys are getting tired of carrying you. Got it?'

'Oh, right-o, Boss,' Anna said. 'Can I borrow your cattle-prod, then? Better still, why don't you get your mate, Julie Ibbotson, back on the job? I mean, she managed so jolly well and I'm sure you must miss her.'

The lift stopped and they walked into the lobby. Dave said, 'At least she knew better than to exercise her lip where it wasn't wanted.' They parted. Dave hunched his beefy shoulders and followed Kevin to the bar. Anna went to the desk to collect her key and study the sleeping arrangements.

Tour personnel took up a whole corridor on the third floor, and Shona occupied an executive suite. Anna found her still in her imperial-sized fur coat posing for photographers. She was draped over the end of the bed like a seal on an ice floe. Shutters clicked. The PRO said, 'Just a couple more, boys, and we'll go down for drinkies.' Lena curled her lip and began to unpack a pigskin nightcase.

Anna went down to her end of the corridor to check her mattress for lumps. There weren't any so she lay comfortably on her back for ten minutes and thought about how to clear her mind of the day's vexations. Thinking about it didn't help. She took the lift down to the restaurant instead.

The restaurant was open, but the kitchen had closed for the night. Behind a buffet table a man in a waiter's suit shaved transparent slivers off a turkey breast, a ham bone, and a beef sirloin, and arranged the slices on empty plates. Anna helped herself to half a dozen varieties of salad. They looked exotic but they all tasted the same.

She was joined by a group of technicians and roadies. It surprised her to learn that she had made a name for herself as the only female member of the security team. The name was Puss in Boots, but she didn't mind much as it was an amiable crowd, and she enjoyed being in the company of even-tempered people for a change.

As she got up to go she saw Wes sitting alone at a corner table. He waved her over. There was a circle of watercress and shreds of lettuce on the tablecloth round his empty plate. He said, 'Enjoying yourself? Guess where everyone else is? Craig and Neil have gone to the casino, and Van's out clubbing it. As if this life wasn't unhealthy enough already.'

'Where do they get the energy?' She was at that moment longing for a hot bath and bed. Wes grinned sardonically. 'Out of a plastic straw,' he said. 'As if you didn't know. They can stay up for weeks at a time. Never touch it myself . . .'

'I know. It burns holes in your nose. You told me. Listen, you seem to know about these things, how long can Shona go on taking the stuff she's taking? There are lots more gigs and a long way to go.'

Wes pushed his bottle of Perrier away. 'You mean like this morning? I heard about that. It's insane. She could put the lot of us on the dole doing that.'

'It's funny. Ducks was telling me about de Blank and how she decided not to depend on anyone – well – unreliable. Were you there then?'

'Not me,' he said. He picked up a leaf of watercress and popped it in his mouth. 'But I know who you mean. That's just what I'm saying. One guy does a nonsense and bingo! – twenty others out of work. You'd be amazed if I told you how many guys I used to know, burnt out, dropped out, dead. They think I'm a hypochondriac but I just look after myself.' He folded his arms across his chest as if to keep his precious health from escaping.

Anna said, 'The bloke I met in Rose Morris, the one from In Hock, he looked pretty ill.'

'That'd be Ferdo Howe. You should ask Porky about him. They used to be mates.' He nodded his head towards the buffet table. Anna turned to see Porky loading up a tray. He shambled over.

Wes said, 'Snoopy here saw old Ferdo yesterday.'

'So?' Porky scooped a gigantic forkload of potato and coleslaw into his mouth.

'She said he wasn't looking too brilliant.'

Porky filled his face again. 'He wouldn't,' he said. 'He's gone on the jab.'

'Job?' Anna asked, surreptitiously wiping coleslaw off the front of her jacket.

'Jab,' Porky said through the spray. One of the roadies came over and said, 'Want to go bopping? There's a disco next door.'

'Disco?' Porky asked. Anna got up quickly. If Porky was going to talk about discos, she wanted to be elsewhere.

'Coming?' asked the roadie.

'Thanks, but I've got to get some kip.'

Wes got up too. Porky was the kind of chap who would always find himself eating alone.

They walked into the lobby together. The roadie made for the bar in search of women to dance with.

'I don't suppose you want a nightcap?' Anna asked, knowing already what the answer would be.

'Not me. Never touch it,' Wes said, true to form. 'But I'm not stopping you. Poison yourself if you want to. Speaking of which, here's little Miss Malice.'

Lena got out of the lift and went over to the reception desk. Wes yawned. 'I wonder what those reporters'd say if they knew about her and their favourite sexpot,' he said from behind his hand. The light gleamed off his glasses, hiding the expression in his eyes. Spite or truth, Anna wondered. 'Would it matter?' she asked aloud.

'Who knows?' He shrugged. 'Not to the kids, I shouldn't think. The whole recording industry's built on the generation gap. It wouldn't make a bean if it relied on the sort of people your mother'd approve of. On the other hand, they say twenty-eight per cent of Dog Records are bought by oldies for the tinies. Me, I always forget a load of our fans are under twelve.'

'Sounds like you've been reading the market survey,' Lena said as she joined them. Wes grunted and looked disconcerted. 'I like to know where my wages come from,' he said and blushed.

'Oh, don't let's forget that.' Lena measured the emphasis and waited for his blush to deepen. Then she turned to Anna and said, 'You're wanted upstairs, Snoops.'

Wes yawned and said, 'Don't mind me. I got to phone my wife. She don't like it with me on the road.'

They went up to the third floor in silence. Lena tapped her tiny foot all the way. Outside the door of Shona's suite stood a trolley bearing piles of chicken salad sandwiches, half-eaten, and an untouched Black Forest gâteau.

Shona was in the bedroom. She sat on the end of the bed nervously rasping at her toenails with an emery board. The silk gown she had on was of an old gold colour that made her skin look like white eggshell. She looked up when Anna came in, and her eyes were so heavily circled it looked like smudged mascara. She said, 'I'm wired up. I got to sleep. But I'm wired up and I can't.'

'I'm sorry,' Anna said. She wondered how a recommendation for hot milk would go down. Shona stared at her. 'You got turd for brain?' she shouted suddenly. Anna jumped. Lena said, 'She wants her mandies, Thicko.'

'Mandrax!' Shona yelled. 'You nicked them. Who the hell do you think you are? My nanny?'

'You bleeding well need one,' Anna shouted back. 'You fall all over the place at ten in the morning, need lifting into the bath. Jesus, haven't you got any pride?' They were both bristling with hostility. Anna had completely forgotten about the matchbox. She had been carrying it in her pocket all day.

Shona recovered first. 'Yeah. I don't know how it happened,' she said quietly. 'I must've woken up in the morning, thought it was midnight and taken some more.'

'It can happen like that,' Lena put in.

'Only if you're totally zonked in the first place,' Anna said.

'You've seen her perform,' Lena said. 'How do you think she does it? Would you have the nerve? And afterwards, how do you think she feels?'

'I need something to come down,' Shona pleaded, 'a glass of wine, a couple of sleepers, just anything to take me off the edge. Just two, Snoopy. I promise I won't let it get out of hand again. I need them. Really. Just two, Snoopy. You can keep the rest.'

Anna dug the matchbox out of her pocket and opened it. 'Why don't you get your doctor to prescribe something a bit safer?' she asked as she picked out two tablets. Shona watched hungrily. 'I will, I really will,' she promised. She held out her hand and Anna dropped the two tablets in it.

'You know best, don't you?' Lena said as Anna left the room. 'Can't get by without giving some advice, can you?'

Anna didn't answer. She went straight to her room and turned on the taps for a hot bath.

Chapter 25

It was three in the morning. She lay on her side, eyes closed, and heard muffled sobbing. For a minute she thought it was part of a dream about a row of cats hung from butcher's hooks. When she was sure it wasn't she rolled over and switched on the bedside lamp. She threw her raincoat on over her pyjamas and opened the door.

A blonde girl in a short white slip stood in the middle of the corridor. At her feet was a little heap of clothes: an electric-pink skirt, tights, and shoes. As the door opened she dropped to a crouch and crossed her arms to hide her breasts. Tears rolled down her cheeks. Her nose ran.

Anna took off the raincoat and arranged it over the

shaking white shoulders. She asked, 'What happened?'

The blonde struggled into the raincoat and buttoned it up to the neck. She said, 'They threw me out. I never knew it'd be like that.'

'Who did?'

'Them.' The girl pointed to the door opposite Anna's, Room 373. She didn't look a day over fourteen. Anna sighed. As far as she could remember, Room 373 was Van's. The girl said, 'I can't go home like this. My dad'll murder me. They won't let me have my bra or my blouse. And my coat cost the earth. I don't understand. Tracy's my best friend.'

'Go and wait in my room,' Anna said. 'I'll see what I can do.'

The girl picked up the rest of her clothes. She wiped her nose on the sleeve of Anna's raincoat and trotted obediently into her room. Anna hoped she'd notice the Kleenex. She went across to Van's door and knocked. Faint noises – giggles, grunts and groans – came from the room and went on uninterrupted. The door remained shut. All down the corridor rows of doors stayed shut.

Anna knocked again. The third time she hurt her fist and the door opened. The girl who opened it giggled. The room was dark, lit only by the TV screen. A blue movie was being played on the hotel video.

Anna switched on the light. Van and Neil sprawled on the twin beds with two more girls. Compared with them the blonde in the corridor was overdressed. The girl behind the door scampered back to Van's side, giggling. The bangles on her wrist chinked in a jolly way. She kicked an empty bottle as she ran. It chinked too.

Van's face broke into a broad grin. He said, 'Well, look who wants to party. Yum-yum.'

'The kid wants her clothes back,' Anna said.

'So search us,' Van cried gleefully. He pushed one of the girls away and revealed himself – all red, purple, and tumid. Anna preferred him in riding breeches.

Clothes, bottles, underwear were strewn all over the place. She looked around for something suitable, and her eye lighted on a soda siphon. She picked it up and pointed it at Van's proudly exposed crotch. 'Just the kid's things,' she said flatly. An ice tray with unmelted cubes swimming in cold water caught her eye. She picked that up too. Van hastily dragged a blanket up to his waist.

Neil did better. He covered himself with a sheet and rolled over, face down. He nudged the girl beside him and said in a bored voice, 'Joke over. Make with the threads, babe.'

The girl eyed Anna warily, but got out of bed and rummaged among a pile of garments. She came up with a lacy white bra and a flouncy pink blouse. 'Coat and bag,' Anna prompted. The girl rummaged again.

Anna put the ice tray down carefully so that none of it spilled. She was dying for an excuse to use the soda siphon, but nobody said anything so she accepted the clothes and withdrew backwards like a professional gunman. She left the siphon outside the door and went back to her own room. There were still the sounds of giggles, grunts, and groans but they were only from the video.

The blonde stopped crying and snatched her bra. She hardly needed it. Anna stared sourly at the carpet while the girl finished dressing. Fully clothed she looked older, about six months older, but no wiser. She sat at the dressing-table and tried to do something about her make-up. 'How'm I going to get home?' she wailed. Her nose was pink and shiny. She dabbed some powder on, which made it mauve but not so shiny. 'They said they'd take us home after, and I haven't got any money.' Her eyes spilled, making wet tracks on the freshly powdered cheeks.

'Come on,' Anna said. 'I'll get you a taxi.'

'They said there was a party,' the blonde explained excitedly as she followed Anna down the corridor. As they passed Shona's suite the door opened a crack and Lena peered out. She said, 'Still playing the Girl Guide? I wondered what all the fuss was about.' Anna went on without answering.

The blonde said, 'Me and Tracy was at the Tropicana. We couldn't believe it when he walked in.'

'Who?' Anna asked. She pressed the lift button.

'Van Vritski.' The girl said the name with a little gasp. Even after what had happened, she still had stars in her eyes. The lift came and they got in. 'Tracy dared me ask him for his autograph. He bought us a drink.'

Anna didn't want to hear the rest. She said, 'Didn't anyone ever tell you not go to out on dates without the fare home in your pocket?'

'I'm not allowed out on dates.' The girl sniffed unhappily. 'My dad says I'm too young. He won't let me do anything.'

'Well, now you know why,' Anna said. She felt like a forty-year-old social worker.

The lift stopped at the lobby. Anna went to the desk and asked the night porter to call a taxi. She arranged it so that the fare would be charged to Room 373. The night man looked curiously at the little blonde girl but he asked no questions. Anna gave no explanations either. She waited in silence for the taxi, and when it came she went back to bed.

The next morning she packed her bag and went down to the dining-room for a big breakfast – scrambled eggs, mushrooms, toast, and two cups of coffee. There was no sign of Dave or Kevin yet, but several of the others were up and around. The Nordic-looking tour manager was beginning to go quietly berserk as he tried to dig people out of their rooms.

Anna finished breakfast and took her bag down to the garage. She checked that the car had enough fuel to get to Brighton and looked cursorily in the boot, engine, and wheel arches for bombs. She felt pretty silly but it was all part of standard procedure.

She was just polishing the windscreen when two men got out of the service lift and came over to her.

'Nice motor,' one of them said. 'Yours, is it?'

'I drive it,' Anna said. Her heart gave a nasty double thump. She had nothing in her hands but a chamois leather.

'Anna Lee?' the man asked. She nodded. 'Police,' he said. 'Would you mind if we take a look in your bag?'

She opened her mouth. There was scarcely enough spit in it to speak. 'Warrant?' she croaked.

'Don't need one, miss. We have reason to believe . . .'

'Warrant *cards*,' she interrupted, clearing her throat. Both men flipped open their wallets. Anna sighed.

'Now, if you don't mind, miss,' said DS Lewis. He took her overnight case out of the boot and went round to the front of the car. DC Cage politely relieved her of her shoulder-bag. They emptied both bags and laid the contents out tidily on the bonnet of the BMW.

'Would you turn out your pockets, please,' DS Lewis asked, and when Anna made no move to comply he went on, 'We can always arrange for a body search in the presence of a woman police officer.'

Anna felt in her pockets. Besides the matchbox there was only a paper tissue and a pencil stub. She brought out the pencil stub.

'Excuse me, miss,' DS Lewis said, still excruciatingly polite. He ran a hand over her pockets. 'This yours, miss?' He held up the matchbox.

'No,' she said. He pushed the tray out of the box. The pills were still in it, but they had been joined by a clear plastic sachet. Anyone could see it contained about a spoonful of white powder, and even in her confusion Anna could tell it wasn't icing sugar.

Chapter 26

'We'll have to have blood and urine samples,' said WPC Muncie.

'Just let me call my boss, and you can have as much as you like,' Anna said. She had been asking for the phone for nearly two hours. The police had been asking about the illegal substances in her possession for nearly two hours as well. It was a stalemate. She had repeated over and over again that the drugs were not hers but would say nothing else. The police pointed out repeatedly that since she hadn't been charged yet they could withhold the phone as long as they liked.

The interview room smelled of disinfectant and cigarette smoke. It was decorated patchily with road safety posters. The chairs were hard.

DS Lewis came back with two mugs of tea. He looked

at the WPC, but she shook her head. Lewis sighed. He gave Anna one of the mugs and said patiently, 'I keep telling you, everyone's soft on a first offender. We just want to know where you get the cocaine.'

'I'm not an offender,' Anna said, just as patiently. 'I don't know anything about the cocaine. I don't even know that it is cocaine. May I please call my boss?'

'It was in your pocket,' he pointed out reasonably. 'Would you like to tell me how it got there?'

'I've no idea.'

'You must have. Or are you suggesting it was planted?' They had been over this ground before too. Anna answered as she had before, 'I'm not suggesting anything. I simply don't know how it got there.'

'I can understand how you feel,' Lewis said, changing tack, 'you a private agent and all. It's worse for you getting caught like this. But you'll only make things harder on yourself if you don't open up.'

'May I please use the phone?' She had got into a rhythm, and it was a police rhythm. The secret was not to get excited, to be as persistent as they were without losing her temper, to keep humour or sarcasm well under control and above all to have impeccable manners. It was hard, especially at the beginning when all she could think of was the tour leaving Bristol without her, and the fact that no-one knew where she was. Well, someone must have had a pretty shrewd idea, but she didn't think that whoever it was would bother to tell Dave or Kevin. That was something she didn't want to think about yet. It would only make her angry. And anger was an emotion she couldn't afford at the moment.

When DS Lewis left the room again she rested her head on her arms and composed herself for the next assault. WPC Muncie offered her a cigarette. Anna hadn't smoked for years but she took one. If there was ever a time to resume it was now.

'He's only trying to help,' the WPC said as she held the match under the cigarette. 'He could've charged you straight off. But with the problem we have in this area, it isn't the users we're really interested in.'

'I'm not a user.' She dragged in a lungful of smoke and coughed, 'And if I knew where the stuff came from I'd tell you. But I don't know.' The smoke made her light-headed. She smiled at the WPC and went on, 'I know I'm in the private market now, but I don't suppose I earn much more than you do. And I don't know what the current street price is either, but I shouldn't think I could afford it any more than you could.'

They discussed pay for a few minutes, but broke off sharply when Lewis came back. 'Let's go,' he said, holding the door open. 'You've got your phone call.'

They let her use one of the telephones in the CID room. She dialled the office number with three pairs of eyes boring into her back. Beryl said, 'This'd better be good, Anna Lee. Where on earth are you? Have you any idea the fuss you've caused?'

Anna said very clearly, 'I'm making this call in the presence of three police officers. Would you please let me speak to Mr Brierly.'

There were a couple of clicks and a pause. She hoped Beryl was warning Mr Brierly before he came on the line. You never knew with Beryl. She might be taking the time to file her nails.

'Miss Lee?' his voice came over, sounding cautious. She immediately told him where she was and then went on to the hard part. 'I'm being questioned about possession of an illegal substance,' she said. 'They say it's cocaine, but I don't know. I can't tell them anything about it.'

'You were in possession of cocaine?' In spite of his caution he sounded incredulous.

'That's correct,' she said flatly. 'But I can't tell them anything about it because I don't know where it came from or how it came into my possession. I need legal advice.'

'I imagine you do.' He hesitated. She could almost hear his brain ticking as he thought how to frame the next question. Eventually he asked, 'Is anyone else involved?'

'No, I'm glad to say.' She heard him sigh with relief. 'Well,' he said slowly, 'we'd better start wheels turning. Is there anything I should know that might help?'

'Not with present circumstances.' She thought quickly, then went on, 'I was down here a couple of years ago. Do you remember the Quarmeford business? Well, I was in touch with an officer in Bristol then. I can't remember who, but the name'll be in the files.'

'I hope whoever it is has cause to remember you kindly,' Mr Brierly said, with a touch of acid. 'Not all of them do, you know.'

'This one should.'

'I hope you're right. You need all the help you can get. Now, you haven't been charged yet?'

'Not yet.'

'Thank heaven for small mercies. Well, sit tight.' He gave an unexpected cackle. It might have been laughter. 'And be careful what you say. Not everybody appreciates your sense of humour the way we do here.'

They had both said as much as they could. But even so Anna was reluctant to hang up. She felt that while she was talking to him nothing too awful could happen. No-one could lock her up. No-one could charge her. At very least someone knew where she was.

On the other hand, if he had an outstanding talent it was for pulling strings, and the sooner he stopped talking and started pulling the better. She said goodbye and rang off. She must have looked a bit miserable though, because WPC Muncie gave her another cigarette before taking her downstairs again.

The morning wore on. She submitted unprotesting to a doctor's examination. She gave samples of blood and urine. Her photograph and fingerprints were taken. She spoke to a solicitor, Mr Goodall, a local associate of the firm Mr Brierly used in London, but he didn't really know what was going on. He was merely there to see that if she were charged she would not be unrepresented.

But as time went by and no charge was forthcoming she began to feel more confident. At lunch-time they brought her sausage and mash, and she was able to eat it with a reasonably good appetite.

By tea-time she was out. Mr Goodall drove her to Temple Meads Station. 'You were very, very lucky,' he kept saying. And Anna had to agree. 'It's a good thing you came out of that medical clean as a whistle,' he went on. She hadn't told him any more about it than she had told the police, and he was not convinced of her innocence except in the legal sense of not yet being found guilty. 'And it was most fortunate that Inspector York came and spoke up for you. That might just have tipped the balance. Because, you know, technically you were in a very tricky position. I know you claim it wasn't yours, but you *were* in possession of a small amount of cocaine. And you could give no satisfactory explanation.'

'Satisfactory?' Anna asked, 'I couldn't explain it at all.'

'Precisely. You're a very lucky girl.'

'I know. I want to thank you for your help too.'

'Oh, I didn't do much,' he said truthfully. 'But that Mr Brierly of yours must have. You're very lucky to have an employer like that.'

On this occasion Anna had to agree with that too. But as she stood on the platform waiting for the London train she began to wonder what on earth she could do to appease her wonderful employer. He wanted to see her immediately she got back, and she knew that by the time she got there he would have got over the triumph of wangling her release. Even now, she thought uneasily, he could be wondering if it had been worth the effort.

Chapter 27

Beryl had stayed late at the office to see the fun. She looked at Anna with something approaching awe. Most of Martin Brierly's agents, at one time or another, had got into trouble. But no-one had gone so far as to be arrested for possession. Beryl was tickled pink.

'Oh dearie, dearie me – cocaine,' she said, trying her best to sound shocked, 'Well, fancy that. I'd never've thought it, even of you.'

Anna liked "even of you". It showed a touch of class. 'I mean,' Beryl continued, 'when J. W. Protection rang and said you'd gone missing – well, we just thought you'd done something silly again. "Never around when she's wanted," I could've said. But I didn't. Some of us know the meaning of team spirit. The Commander could do nothing but apologize for you. You know how he loves that, don't you? And now drugs! I hope you've thought up a cast-iron story.'

Anna lit a cigarette and blew the smoke in Beryl's face. 'So sorry,' she said. 'I'm a bit jumpy. I haven't had a fix for ages and you know how us junkies get.'

'I'm glad you can joke about it.' Beryl fanned the air with her shorthand pad. 'And kindly don't smoke in my office. You know I'm allergic. Since when did you start smoking, anyway?'

'A policewoman gave me the packet,' Anna said. 'She thought it'd help me get off the hard stuff. Does Mr B. know I'm here? I mean, I'd just love to stop here all night swapping compliments with you, but I thought he was in a hurry. And if he isn't, I am. I've got this urgent appointment at the detox unit.' She blew another plume of smoke across the desk. Beryl pressed the intercom button.

Mr Brierly sat behind his big new desk, hands folded on his clean green blotter. His face was empty of expression but at least he wasn't rolling his thumbs. 'Take a seat, Miss Lee,' he said coldly. 'And think very carefully before you speak. I want to know if the stock of goodwill I used up on your behalf was justified. I have never in my life had to skate on such thin ice.'

Anna had been expecting something of the sort. She knew that the only thing he would listen to would be a plain, orderly presentation of the facts. She had practised one on the train. Now, she got out her notebook, sat up straight and gave him an unemotional, rather dreary account of what had happened since she met Mr Horowitz. None of her speculations were included. If there was any theorizing to be done, she knew Mr Brierly would like to be the one to do it. He was always suspicious of any conclusions but his own and it made him happy to think that he alone could find some order in a random collection of events. Happy was how Anna wanted him to be.

'Mmm, I see,' he said when she had finished speaking. 'The first thing I have to say is that you should have kept in closer touch. It would seem you have got rather out of your depth.' Anna humbly agreed. 'And it would appear,' he went on, brightening, 'that J.W. Protection have been of little help. I did warn you, Miss Lee, if you remember.'

'Oh, you did, Mr Brierly,' she said with just a trace of admiration. '"Quantity, not quality," you said.'

'You should listen more often to the voice of experience,' he said. He looked as though he was beginning to enjoy himself. 'I understand the need for absolute discretion, but you really should have asked for guidance after the cat's death. That might well be seen as a follow-up to the threatening letter.' He made a steeple of his fingertips and looked at her over the top of his spectacles. 'But on the other hand, Miss Lee, from what you describe, it is difficult to decide, in people such as these, what is normal behaviour and what is abnormal strain. Normal behaviour for them may well include such charming features as living in a pigsty, drug-taking, hysteria, and having their cats killed. You do see what I'm getting at.'

'Oh yes. And normal behaviour for a fan could include sending nasty letters, hanging around outside stars' houses, following them in cars, and so on.'

'Precisely. What a revolting world these people have created for themselves.' He leaned back and thought about it. 'So while in the normal world these events could be taken as significant, even bizarre, here they may have no significance whatsoever. And similarly, the events leading to your arrest can be interpreted in two ways. Undoubtedly someone wanted you out of the way. But whether it was because they had something of significance to conceal or whether it was simply because you were spoiling their fun is open to question.' He fell silent. Outside the evening traffic on the High Street growled steadily. He got up and unlocked one of the cupboards under his bookshelf. It was where he kept a first-aid box and his bottle of Johnnie Walker.

'It's interesting that you felt the need to get in contact with – what's her name? – Miss Ibbotson. I wonder what really happened to her.' He spoke musingly and poured a splash of whisky into a glass. 'A drink, Miss Lee?' he asked, hastily putting the bottle away. Anna wondered what would happen if one day she were to say yes.

'It's high time I spoke again to Colonel Beamish. I resent the notion that he knowingly put an agent of mine into a compromising situation and failed to warn me.'

'To be fair,' Anna said thoughtfully, 'the job would normally just be a problem of crowd control. J.W. wouldn't see women as much use at that. Julie Ibbotson is the only woman on their strength. She was only included because the singer's a woman too. They probably treated her as a spare part, like they did me. I don't suppose they took her seriously at all – even though she's one of their own.'

'Then it's about time someone did.' He pressed the button on his desk and asked Beryl to come in. 'Treated you as a supernumerary, did they?'

'Tiddler of Small Fry Security,' Anna said as if to herself, but in a voice pitched just loud enough for him to hear.

'We'll see about that,' he said grimly. Beryl knocked and entered, her eyes alight with unkind curiosity.

'I know it's late, Miss Doyle, but would you be so kind as to get Colonel Beamish on the line for me. If you can't reach him now, then first thing in the morning will have to do. I want to speak to Mr Horowitz of Horowitz Management too.' Beryl wrote the names down and turned to go. Mr Brierly raised a hand to detain her. 'And Miss Doyle, Miss Lee here has had a most unpleasant few days, so I won't expect her in the office tomorrow.' And to Anna he said, 'Stay close to base. I don't want you rejoining that tour until we've had some clarification on the matters just mentioned.'

Anna thanked him and said good night. She found Beryl in the outer office stabbing phone buttons as if they were personal enemies. 'How do you get to be so jammy?' she asked without looking up. 'With your record you should be on your way to the Job Centre by now. You jolly well would be if I had anything to do with it.'

'You do your best,' Anna said consolingly. 'It's not your fault nobody listens.'

'Don't think I haven't got my eye on you.'

'That's good.' Anna buttoned up her raincoat. 'Then you'll know I'm owed expenses from last month, and I won't

have to ask you for them, will I?' She tied the belt. 'Every
step you take . . .' she hummed as she left the room. 'Every
move you make . . .' down the stairs '. . . I'll be watching
you . . .' and out onto the High Street.

It was wet and cold on the street and there were few people
out. Those that were hurried by with umbrellas down over
their eyes and collars up to their ears. She caught a bus to
Shepherds Bush and walked home from there.

With the gas fire lit, the leather suit hung in the wardrobe, and her feet warm in old slippers, she opened a can of
soup and left it to heat on the stove.

The show would be coming to a close in Brighton. She
pulled the phone close to the sofa and dialed Avis's number.
There was no answer. She tried Daniel Horowitz. He was
out too. Maybe they had both gone to Brighton. The flat
seemed separated from the rest of the world by a wall of
silence.

She put a Big Bill Broonzy record on the hi-fi and went
to the kitchen to stir the soup. Bea tapped on the door. 'I
thought I heard you come in,' she said. She peered into the
steaming saucepan. 'That's out of a tin, isn't it? You
should've come down – I've got lots of fish and potato pie
over. Selwyn's right off his food. I don't know what to do
with him – he's still all *Misérables* and sulks. It's getting on
my nerves.'

Anna poured soup into a bowl. 'There's tea in the pot,'
she said as she sat down to eat. 'And there's biscuits in the jar.
Help yourself.' Bea sat on the other side of the kitchen table
with a mug of tea and a chocolate digestive. 'I don't know,'
she sighed, 'I can't do a thing right. He just snaps my head
off all the time. I was thinking of Marriage Guidance or
going to stay at my sister's.'

'Bad as that?' Anna said sympathetically.

'And he's always been a jolly sort of drinker, if you know
what I mean. Well, you can put up with a lot from a jolly
sort of drinker can't you? But the last few days he's turned to
spirits and it's made him quite nasty.'

'Selwyn – nasty?'

'Really quite nasty.' Little frown lines appeared between Bea's brows. 'I mean, I know I'm not educated the

way he is, or sensitive or artistic, but I've always held things together for us. I may not be much inspiration for him, but at least I know how to earn a living.'

'Which is more than he does,' Anna put in.

'Don't think he doesn't know that,' Bea said quickly. 'It's part of the problem. He says he's a failure because he compromised. He says he'd've been a better poet if he'd starved. You'd think I'd ruined his career with a few hot dinners the way he's carrying on.'

'What a rubber brain.' Anna was becoming cross. It was far from unusual to be cross with Selwyn. He was always pretty free with his insults, but in the normal way of things they were never designed to hurt. 'Wage earners of the world unite,' she said after a moment's thought. 'We have nothing to blow but our brains. This is all because Foolscap's gone bust, and he doesn't want you to know he's lost his money and his books.'

'Bankrupt?' Bea asked, shocked.

'As a Scotsman's pocket on Sunday morning. And he didn't find out about it in time to put a claim in. So *Wholes and Corners* is now part of company assets.' She explained the problem.

'Well!' Bea said eventually. 'What a silly fool! When I first met him my mother said . . . Well, never mind what my mother said. I didn't listen then so there's no point remembering now. What're we going to do?'

'You could go downstairs and warm his ears for him,' Anna suggested.

'I wouldn't mind,' Bea admitted. 'But on second thoughts maybe his pride's been through the mangle already. I could telephone the receiver from the office, couldn't I, and find out what's what?'

Anna nodded. 'See what he'll accept, and then if it's reasonable we'll think about how to raise the cash.'

'I feel better already,' Bea said, relieved. 'I suppose I'll have to pretend I'm still in the dark, won't I?'

'That's up to you,' said Anna, who had never been married and didn't understand the importance of subterfuge in marriages such as the Prices'. 'I'll play it whatever way you say.'

'Secretly, then,' Bea said and got up to go. 'Selwyn's

damn pride is just as important as his damn books, I'd say.'

Anna didn't agree, but as she wasn't married to him she had to take Bea's word for it.

Chapter 28

It was another hard grey morning. A touch of late frost whitened the west-facing rooftops and made spring look farther off than ever. Anna consulted the J.W. schedule and found that Shona was back in London that morning. At eleven she was booked in to film her new video, and the band was playing Clarkestead Leisure Centre that night.

It did not seem a good idea to spend the morning at home. She was reluctant to meet Selwyn, having told all his secrets the night before, but she couldn't think where to go. The office was out, what with the builders and dust and Beryl, who was at her most dangerous when she was a goal down.

She knew she should wait for Brierly's permission, but there were a couple of notions she wanted to pursue while she had the time. She was still wondering which one had priority when the phone rang and Dave McPhee said, 'Colonel Beamish asked me to call.'

'Oh yeah?' Anna said suspiciously.

'We all want to express our sympathy about what happened yesterday morning.'

'Oh yeah?' she repeated, waiting for the punch line. It didn't come. Maybe Colonel Beamish was listening.

'Yeah. Tough luck, eh?' Dave sounded cautious too.

'Hardly a matter of luck,' she told him.

'No. Listen, we had a word with our Julie. She seems to think, in the light of what happened to you, there might've been an organized attempt to get rid of her too.'

'Pity you didn't tell me about it before. I could've been better prepared.'

'She never told us the details, just reported sick. It was something she was embarrassed about. She's not too quick, you know. Doesn't have your know-how with the soda siphon. Your guv'nor told us about that. He doesn't feel we gave you proper support.'

'Well, not to worry,' Anna said awkwardly. 'It's spilt milk now.'

'Nice of you to say so.' Colonel Beamish was definitely present. 'I don't know if you're coming back or not,' Dave continued, sounding quite unlike himself, 'but if there's anything we can do . . .'

'There is, as a matter of fact.' She was thoroughly relaxed now. If the sun was out, it was the only opportunity she'd get to make hay. 'Have you got an old copper in your mob? Someone who can get a quick result from Criminal Records? Only we thought a little background might come in handy and there's a name came up.'

'Who?'

'Ferdo Howe. Junkie. Old associate of Shona's. I think there should be a sheet on him. What I want is a current address. I'd do it myself, but there's a flap on in the office. Everyone's tied up, and I thought with your resources . . .'

'Can do,' Dave said quickly. 'Like I said, anything we can do. Stick around, we'll get back to you.'

Anna grinned and rang off. Whatever Mr Brierly had said to Colonel Beamish must have been very good indeed. She took the phone book over to the window.

The Dockers Club had an address in E. 14. She opened the A – Z and looked it up. The phone rang again.

Dave said, 'OK, Tiddler, so you've got us doing chores for you.' He gave her an address in King's Cross. 'I was told to be nice to you,' he went on. 'But don't take advantage. Just like a woman, hiding behind the Old Man's apron. So you got yourself nicked. Tough titty. If it'd been me, I'd've shopped the whole dirty bunch of 'em.'

'That's why small fry firms like us do so well,' Anna said loftily. 'We know the meaning of confidentiality.'

'Hah! Arse-licking, more like.' He made a rude noise at the back of his throat. 'Well, don't take too many liberties with me, my girl.'

'Wouldn't dream of it,' Anna said with reverence. 'And

thank you so much for the cooperation.' She rang off. Her coat and bag were hanging behind the door. She grabbed them and hurried down to the car.

Chapter 29

She drove to Addison and parked behind a delivery van while she waited for the BMW to show up. It didn't. A black Rolls-Royce came instead. The chauffeur wore a grey uniform with two rows of buttons. He held his cap under his arm while he rang the doorbell. He was obviously not in security.

Shona only kept him waiting for eleven minutes. She appeared at the door wearing ragged jeans and a sheepskin-lined jacket with the sleeves torn off. No-one could have suited a Rolls-Royce less. Craig and Porky followed, looking just as disreputable. The Chauffeur didn't bat an eyelid. He bowed them into the car as if they were royalty. The car purred away at the pace of a hearse.

Anna started her motor. She was about to move off when a black cab pulled up outside the house. The driver got out and walked up the steps to ring the bell. A girl came out so quickly she might have been waiting behind the door. She slid into the cab like a shadow. The cab did a U-turn and started up the road. Anna blinked. It took her a few seconds to realize that the girl was Lena. She had never seen her without make-up or wearing off-the-peg clothes. All she had to do to disguise herself was to dress like everyone else.

Anna made a U-turn too and set off after the cab. Luckily the traffic was quite orderly, and they didn't go far. Lena paid off the driver at Paddington Station.

There was nowhere legal to park so Anna pulled in behind a Post Office van on a double yellow line.

Lena was not in the ticket office. Hundreds of people

milled about in the main concourse. Anna threaded her way slowly through them. Clusters of travellers stood under the information board. Lena was not there either. The loud-speaker gave out information in such a way that everyone turned to his neighbour in bewilderment. The voice bounced around the steel and glass vaulting and came back like a duck quacking in panic.

Anna moved slowly and looked carefully. In the end she saw Lena on a bench outside the buffet. A grizzled old tramp sat on the bench too. No-one wanted to sit next to him so there was a long space between him and Lena. Be-side Lena on the other side was a woman in a shaggy pink coat. She held a shiny red handbag on her knee and her hair was piled up like whipped cream on top of her head. They leaned close together and talked.

The tramp slid down the bench towards them and spoke to the woman in the pink coat. She said something. It couldn't have been nice because he shuffled quickly back to his end of the bench. He had no socks on. There were about four inches of dirty ankle exposed between the end of his trousers and the old canvas shoes.

Lena opened her bag and took out a fat white enve-lope. The pink woman opened her bag to receive it. She patted Lena on the arm. Lena got up and left. She caught another cab at the rank by platform 7. Anna cursed. Her car was at the other side of the station. She went back to the bench. By the time she got there the pink woman had gone too. She stood for a moment, irresolute.

The tramp looked up and caught her eye. 'I see you watching,' he said and grinned. There were more gaps than teeth in his mouth. 'You want someone? I know everyone comes here regular.'

'The one in the pink coat?' Anna asked.

'I know her.' He cackled suddenly. 'Tell you what I like. If a person wants a chat, I like to have a nice friendly smoke with them.'

Anna still had the pack of cigarettes the policewoman had given her. She dug them out of her bag and handed them to the old man. He accepted them politely and put one in his mouth. She lit it for him and gave him the matches too. He said, 'Her name's Odette.'

'Just Odette? Where does she live?' And as the old man shook his head she said, 'That's not much help.'

'If I wasn't so hungry I'd give you her phone number,' he said cunningly. 'Can't remember a thing when I'm hungry.' Anna laughed. 'You wouldn't be conning me, would you?'

'Cost you a sandwich to find out.' The old man showed his gums again. 'You can afford that, nice young lady like you. Cheese and pickle's what I like.'

Anna went to the sandwich bar and bought him two. She brought them back and sat down beside him, not too close because he smelled of rotting vegetables.

'Odette's number?' she asked with her hand firmly clamped round the sandwiches.

'Over there.' He nodded towards the phone booths and chuckled. 'What she likes is uniforms.' Anna stared at him suspiciously but she went over to the row of telephones. Messages and labels were plastered all over the booths: 'Fräulein Lotte – stict disciplinarian,' 'Simone – French lessons,' 'Sherrie – model.' Among them was 'Odette—loves uniforms' and a phone number.

The old man waited patiently on his bench. She went back to him and gave him the sandwiches. She bought him a cup of tea too. He didn't ask for money which probably meant he didn't drink. Or it could have meant he was an eccentric millionaire. Anna could never tell with tramps.

She fed money into the phone and dialled Odette's number. The phone rang for a long time. She disconnected and phoned the office instead. Beryl said, 'I thought you were supposed to be at home. I tried to get hold of you half an hour ago. Why d'you never stay put? You're back on the Horowitz account. Someone from J.W.'s bringing the car to you at five.'

'That's okay,' Anna said. 'I'll be home by then. Are any of the lads in?'

'Why?'

'There's a woman I want to speak to and I don't think she'll talk to me. She'd expect a man to ring.'

'You want one of the boys to drop everything and telephone a woman who won't talk to you?' Beryl sounded as if Anna had asked the butler to stir her tea. 'And who is this paragon? I thought everyone was just dying to talk to you. I thought you were famous for your tact and diplomacy.'

'I think this one would stretch even *your* famous tact and diplomacy,' Anna said. She took a deep breath and tried not to lose her temper. 'It's Odette. She loves uniforms.'

'Pardon?'

'I don't think she's your type, Beryl. She's blonde, blue-eyed, about five and a half foot and very well built. She advertises herself at Paddington Station and, odd as it may seem, she'd probably think it a waste of time telling you or me where to find her.' There was a muffled snort from the other end of the line and then silence. Anna pressed more money into the coin box. After a while a voice said, 'This sounds like a job for Super-John.'

Anna put her finger to her free ear to cut out the racket from the station, and said, ''Lo, Johnny. You're right. A john's just what I need.' She told him about Odette. 'I just want to know where to find her. It's only a phone call, unless you haven't anything better to do, in which case a little background'd help.'

'How far back do you want me to go?' Johnny asked innocently. 'I mean, I'm supposed to be rousting some poor berk who can't pay for his car, but this sounds a lot more interesting.'

'Well, whatever you do, get a proper receipt for it or Beryl won't love you.'

'Never paid for it in my life,' Johnny said, indignant.

'You know, I've never met a bloke who didn't say that,' Anna said. 'I can't imagine how these poor women stay in business.' Just then her money ran out so she didn't hear his reply. She went back to the car and found a parking ticket fluttering under the windscreen-wiper.

It was the sort of day where grey dawn lasts till midday and then without drama turns slowly to dusk. Office lights stay on all day and the shops glow like nightclubs in the dark. The balloon-sellers outside Madame Tussaud's were doing a poor trade. Their white breath hung on the air like smoke as they stamped their feet disconsolately on the curb. Anna passed them on the way to King's Cross.

She found the address Dave had given her in a narrow

street that backed on to the track. It was the sort of place where only a neurotic would bother to clean the windows. They would need to be done twice a day. The houses might have been home to railway workers long ago, but now half the street had been condemned. The rest were squashed together for safety, grey net curtains hung defiantly like flags to signal occupation. Anna knocked at one of the doors. No-one opened it. She went back to the car and waited.

After a while she turned the key and let the engine idle with the heater turned on. Later she switched on the radio. The street was dead. It was as if the houses were not the only ones to be condemned. An hour passed and she found herself looking at her watch every five minutes and thinking about lunch. Half an hour longer, she told herself, not a minute more. Who knew if Ferdo Howe was coming home? Who knew if he even lived there any more? No-one'd live in that street if he had somewhere better to go.

Chapter 30

But he didn't have anywhere. She saw him walking up the street, his hands buried deep in his pockets, head bent, a scarf wound twice round his neck. She got out of the car to wait for him.

'Hello,' she said when he got to her. 'Remember me? I gave you a lift from Denmark Street the other day.' He stared at her with dull eyes.

'Yeah?' he said, fitting his key to the lock. 'Look, I'm sick. I got to lie down.' If he didn't lie down he'd probably fall down, she thought. His colour was bad and he needed a shave.

'Anything I can do?' She gave him a false bright smile. He looked at her speculatively. She had done him one favour so she might do him another. He opened the door and she followed him in. He went straight to a tiny living-room and switched on the electric fire.

'I'm freezing,' he said. 'Whatever I do I can't get warm.' With with the grime on the windows and the net curtains she could scarcely see him till the fire began to glow pink. She found the light switch.

'Turn that off,' he snapped. 'My eyes hurt.'

'You are in a bad way.' She switched the light off. 'Shall I make you some tea? That might warm you up.'

'Tea!' he jeered, but he pointed to the kitchen.

It was as small as a sentry-box. A forty-watt bulb brushed her hair and showed up the worn patches on the lino. But it was clean, a sort of desperate cleanliness only the very poor can achieve. Anna filled the kettle and lit the gas. She wondered if this was his parents' house. He looked as if, left to himself, he'd reduce any place to squalor.

When it was ready she brought the tea through to the living-room. Ferdo was where she had left him, still in his coat and scarf, huddled over the fire. He took the cup and stirred in three spoonfuls of sugar.

She sat down on a patched-up easy chair with sagging springs. 'You said you knew Shona when she was Hilary Simpson,' she began. 'Did you know Porky Wall and Wes Gardner too?'

'God,' he said, 'is Porky still around? I thought he died and went to Paris. I'm surprised you remember all this.'

'I don't,' she told him. '*You* do.'

'Do what?' he sighed. 'Shit, I feel lousy.'

'In Hock,' Anna reminded him.

'Could've been a good little band. But it never had a chance. We needed money. We needed a manager. We didn't need all the hassle.'

'You got busted,' she prompted again. He shivered and folded his arms. 'Did I tell you that? I never got on my feet after that. Six months!' He hunched his shoulders up to his ears. 'You won't remember Will Graef. Nobody does. He got six months too. He died in there. Best mate I ever had.'

'What happened to the others?'

'You want to see a picture?' He went down on his knees next to the fireplace. There was a sideboard and he opened the bottom cupboard. 'I know it's here. My mum keeps all my pictures in here. Christ – my head hurts.' He dragged a cardboard box out and sat cross-legged in front of the fire. Anna switched the light on again. He didn't notice. He was too busy sorting through old photographs.

'The way we were,' he said, holding up a photo with shaking hands. 'You didn't believe me, but it's true.' It was a four by five glossy. Anna got down on the floor beside him to look. There was a small stage surrounded by fairy lights. Ferdo stood at the front holding the microphone. He had a guitar slung round his neck. His face was fuller then and he had plenty of hair. Behind him and to the right was a dark-haired girl in a tight dress.

'That's Shona?' Anna asked. It could've been anyone.

'That's Hilary Simpson,' Ferdo said. 'Shona Una's a different chick. About a million quid different. That's Will.' He pointed to a skinny, baby-faced figure behind the electric piano. Wes hadn't changed much. He had looked like an aging student in those days too. He stood with his head bowed over his bass, haloed by the cymbals.

'And the drummer?'

'Ron Greene. He got out after two months. I never heard from him again. Ron, Wes, Hilly, Will, and me. Refugees from a mean ol' world. One of us died. Some of us wish we had. And two of us made it into the charts and lost their memories. That's par for the course in this game.'

'Wes remembers you,' Anna said. 'He said you were friends with Porky.'

'I haven't got any friends.' Ferdo leaned back against the sideboard. 'Turn the light off, will you.' Anna got up and did as he asked.

'How do you feel about them now, Wes and Shona?' She was curious. Wes seemed stable enough, but in spite of her success Shona at times looked as much of a casualty as Ferdo.

'Are you going to write about it or something?' he asked. 'Only I'm all wrung out. I ought to go to the clinic, but I can't raise the fare.'

'Are you registered?'

He nodded wearily. Half his face was stained pink by the fire. It shone oily with sweat but he still shivered occasionally.

'I'll give you a lift if you like. Where is it?'

'University College. But I'd rather have the bread. I don't know if they'll see me today.'

'They ought to. You look like hell.'

'You should give me some bread if you're writing about it,' he said craftily. 'The pic should be worth something to you.' She didn't want to give him any money. She said, 'I'm not writing about it.'

'What, then? You her new little chickie? Or maybe you want to get a line on her. Something tacky could set you up for a long time.'

'Are you kidding? The way I see the music business, something tacky'd set *her* up for a long time.'

'Some things wouldn't. There's some things'd send her straight back to the bottom.'

'Like what?'

'Oh no you don't.' He snatched up the picture, as if she had tried to steal it from him, and stuffed it into the breast pocket of his coat. 'Nasty secrets don't come free in this town.'

'Don't get ideas!' Anna said sharply. 'You try selling dirt, dirt's what you'll get paid. There's laws against extortion and blackmail. So don't try it unless you're hooked on porridge as well.'

'Jesus,' he whined, 'can't you see I'm sick?'

'Clearly,' she said and got to her feet. 'Come on. I'll take you to the clinic. If you go in I'll even give you a couple of quid to get back – but no more. I'm not buying any nails for your coffin.'

She drove him to UCH and took him round the side to the clinic. She left him with a nurse who wrote his name at the bottom of a very long list. When that was done Anna handed him two pound coins. The nurse looked at her pityingly and shook her head. There's no fool like the one who tries to help a junkie, the look said.

Chapter 31

A dietician would have had a coronary just looking at the egg and chips served up at the Narrow Road café. Anna was hungry so she didn't look too closely. Someone had left a paper at her table. It was folded open at an unfinished crossword. On the other side of the road to the left a dark young man stacked crates of empty bottles on the pavement outside Dockers Club. She wiped the steam off the window and watched him.

He looked up and saw her. She stuck some more chips in her mouth and turned to the crossword. She couldn't decide if 23 down, an anagram for 'law scowl (with animal connections)', was 'cows wall' or 'owl claws'. Neither looked right. When she looked up again the dark man was gone and the neon sign winked on and off over an empty pavement. Something had gone wrong with the sign. Sometimes it said DOC ERS CLUB and sometimes DO KERS LUB.

'Not many dockers around these days,' she said to the woman behind the counter.

'You been watching the sign, dearie?' the woman asked, patting her hairnet. 'Why don't they bleeding fix it? It's been driving me potty for months. I can see it from here, see, and it's bad enough when it works proper.'

Anna took her cup over to the counter and asked for more tea. 'Do they still have live music over there?' she said while the woman slopped milk into the cup. The tea urn spat out a vicious cloud of steam and a few drops of tea. 'Bleeding thing!' the woman cried and thumped it with a fist wrapped in a dishcloth. 'It ain't just the sign. Nothing bleeding works round here. I can't wait till they have us all down and we get our bleeding compensation. The council promised it five bleeding years ago.' The urn belched and

112

parted with a miserly dribble of tea. 'If you're thinking of going there alone – don't.' The woman wiped the bottom of the cup with her cloth. 'It's a drinking club, dearie. The music's only at night, and then it's for the rough trade. Not your sort at all, dearie. The only girls go in on their own's scrubbers. Know what I mean?'

'I wasn't thinking of going in,' Anna said. She had been, but now she changed her mind. She thought about Shona, standing well behind Ferdo Howe, singing her sha-la-las to the rough trade. If she hadn't met Ferdo, Anna would've thought that the only direction after Dockers was up. Ferdo proved her wrong. She finished her tea and left.

Outside, the smell of the Thames caught her un-prepared. It was like opening a very old book – a sudden waft of damp paper, old stories, and secrets. She got the car started and drove to the West End where the smell was of fried food and the sweat of fast people chasing an even faster buck. Soho had all the style and sublety of a fruit machine. It was crowded with people thinking up new and very old ways to make ripping off the suckers look like fun.

Horowitz Management was an unlikely place for hope-ful young people to exchange their dreams for profit. Daniel Horowitz was watching an amateur video of six teenagers playing a rock-reggae number. He looked tired and cau-tious. The cuffs on his blue-striped shirt were turned back, his tie was loose, and his jacket hung over the back of his chair.

'Not a chance in the world,' he said. He turned down the volume and left the singer mouthing silently like a fish in a tank. 'Derivative,' he said. 'Stale. Not my cup of tea at all. I don't know why I bother listening to some of the junk they send in.' Racks of tapes, cassettes, and directories were stacked behind his desk. By the window stood an exer-cise bike. Anna could picture him pedalling furiously, get-ting nowhere. He said, 'Listen, darling, I'm sorry you had all that whatsit in Bristol. But it proves I was right. There is something going on I should know about.'

'Just what is it you're afraid of?' Anna asked. He looked at her with sad pouchy eyes. 'I told you,' he said. 'I'm afraid Roz'll crack. And Dog and all the money'll get frightened. And she'll be back where she started.'

'And where was that?'

'When I first met her she was backing a very talented young guy called Borg de Blank. Only he had a frailty, if you see what I mean. We had to put him in a private nursing home. Cost a fortune, and the group broke up. All that work down the drain. Tragic. He took his own life, you know – cut his wrists.' He shook his head. 'What a waste. But look – ' he smiled suddenly. 'You've done very well, darling. I know you think they don't like you, but you're in there. They'll get used to you. And nothing's happened to Roz since you got there, has it?'

'I don't know about that,' Anna said. 'Her cat was bumped off in Luton. And before Bristol she took so many sleepers she couldn't wake up.'

His face fell again. He fiddled with his cigarette butts in his ashtray. 'Yes,' he said gloomily. 'But you sorted it all out, didn't you.'

'I woke her up. But it was Van and his little box of magic got her going again. It's no bleeding good for her.'

'I know. I know.' He pushed the ash into square patterns. 'Once we get this tour over we can sort her out.'

'Oh, great,' Anna said. 'So we pump her full of the hard stuff to make her perform and then we fill her up with sleepers so's she can rest. And meanwhile someone's putting the frighteners on her. And you're letting her spend all her money to buy him off. We're all buying time and she's paying.'

'Is that what's happening?' he said, suddenly attentive. 'She's paying someone. Is that why she's always crying to me for cash? You'd think I kept her short – starved her even. She's paying someone?'

'I think so. It may be for supplies or it may be to keep her suppliers quiet or it may be something else entirely. She's always on at you for money, you say?'

'A grand I gave her at Luton. Now she wants more. Tonight already. Listen, darling, where's she been to spend a grand in three days?'

'Nowhere I know of,' Anna said. 'You handle her money – how long's she been tapping you for amounts you can't explain?'

He lit a cigar and thought about it. 'It could be since a month before the tour. But you see, there's her new flat – Hampstead – very expensive. And all the new gear for publicity and the tour. I take care of most of the bills from here but there would've been extras and a few cash transactions. And always the friends. They borrow, darling, and how they borrow, if that's what it's called.'

'What about Lena and Porky?'

'Lena's officially on salary while the tour's on. Porky? Well, who can say. Maybe she gives him pocket money. I don't know. Porky I do not understand. She says she needs him, so why not?'

Anna scratched her head. Why anyone should want Porky around was one of the mysteries of the universe as far as she was concerned. She asked instead about Lena.

'A bright girl,' Danny told her. 'And level-headed. Myself, I don't like what she does, but the kids love it so it works. Roz says her image really came together when she met Lena. It could be true. So what if I don't like it?'

'When did they meet?'

'Six months, seven months – some festival last summer. She's ambitious, Lena. She would've seen Roz was on her way up. She needed a clothes horse, I expect. But it's worked for Roz too, so who am I to judge?' The tip of his cigar glowed hot. He blew the rich smoke at the window. 'When you get to the top, or near the top like Roz, you like to have people around you can keep between you and the rest of the world. Someone to walk into the restaurant first, someone to go out for the milk or post a letter, someone who won't get robbed by shopkeepers or mobbed by fans. It's a hard life. No-one believes it who hasn't tried.'

'I can understand that,' Anna said slowly. 'I just wonder at what point your protectors become parasites.'

'Aha!' Danny rubbed his hands together appreciatively. 'Let me tell you a story,' he said. 'It's about a boy, made it right up there – he was a household name ten years ago – very big. Well, he had a friend, big beefy chap he was, worked with weights, that sort of thing. So one night they go to a club, a very *in* club. You had to go there if you were anyone at all. They had a few drinks and a few dances.

Comes the time our star has to go to the gents. Well, he'd been attracting a lot of attention as usual. So some girl with a camera follows him into the gents.

'She climbs up on the partition and starts flashing off snaps of the star who's in the next stall taking a leak. In the gents, this is. Can you believe? Anyway, the boy yells at her to stop, but she won't. So he pushes her and she falls, cracks her head on the pan. Out cold. Our star panics. He gets out of there, quick as a fox, and tells his beefy friend to handle it. There are columnists in the club and a nice juicy scene would've made their night. So the friend handles it. But while he's carrying the girl out through the fire exit, she comes to and smashes him in the face with her camera. He drops her and she breaks her leg. He loses the sight of one eye and our star is still paying both of them.'

'Blimey,' Anna said.

'Yes, blimey. When you get famous enough little things like going to the gents can become impossible. And the guy who helps you out of a jam can become a life pensioner. It could never happen to an ordinary chap. No-one gives a damn where he takes a leak. And no one'd think they had the God-given right to take his picture doing it.'

'Yes, but that's an extreme example, isn't it?'

'It's a rather mild one, actually. Ask Mick Jagger. And the things people write – you should see some of the mail comes through here.'

'About that,' she put in. 'Who deals with it? How does it get to her?'

'Well, some comes here. A lot more goes to Dog. Some of it'd go straight to Roz if she had a proper address. We have someone here who does nothing but sort out fan mail. Most of it's just requests for photographs and so on. Every now and then Roz comes and does a whole batch, so we have a stock of signed photographs to send out. But while she's on the road anything important gets delivered to her personally.'

'Do you know what gets sent?'

'Not exactly. Why?'

'Well, could you personally check everything that leaves this office for her from now on? I've seen the remains of one letter that wasn't just a request for a signature. If it wasn't sent through the post it might've been slipped into a batch of mail from here or Dog. It'd be a help to know there was one clean source at least.'

'All right, I'll check.' His cigar had gone out and he tossed it into the ashtray and frowned. 'But you can't ask Dog to do the same. They aren't to know there's anything wrong.'

'You're the boss.' She looked at her watch. It was time to go. 'Are you coming to Clarkestead tonight?'

'I suppose I should.' He looked beleaguered. 'She's got to get her money somehow.'

Chapter 32

Anna put on the Puss in Boots suit and looked at herself in the mirror. The suit, she thought glumly, had stood the pressure of the last few days better than she had. The black leather shone with vitality while her own skin looked pale and she had dark circles under her eyes. She sat down and did a two and a half minute make-up job. What she needed was a re-spray but there wasn't time.

On the stairs she collided with Selwyn. 'No time for old friends, I presume,' he said acidly.

'Not enough,' Anna said. She pretended not to notice the acidity. 'I want to talk to you soon but it's a bit hush-hush. In the meantime could you think up a code word for the operation? It's all totally illegal and we need to be very careful indeed.'

'You're going to help!' He was instantly gleeful as a child. 'What do I do?'

'For a moment, just the code word. This is going to need meticulous planning. For God's sake don't tell Bea — she'd do her nut.'

'On my honour,' Selwyn whispered, following her to the front door. 'Leave it with me.'

When she got to Addison Road she found the Rolls parked outside the house. The chauffeur sat capless in the front seat reading the *Evening Standard*. Anna tapped on the glass and asked him what he was doing there.

'Waiting for my passengers, if it's any of your business.' He was middle-aged, grey, and bored. She flashed her security badge and he said, 'Oh, right. It's her ladyship's parents. I was supposed to be off by six. Now I don't suppose I'll see my kip before midnight.'

Shona herself let Anna in. She looked reasonably fresh and wore a cricket sweater over a very straight-cut pair of slacks. But she was not calm. 'Do me a favour, Snoopy – sorry, Anna,' she said quickly. 'My mum and dad're in the living-room. You wouldn't sort of chat them up, would you? Make them some tea. I daren't let them into the kitchen. They think Porky's subnormal.'

It hadn't occurred to Anna that Shona might be worried about what her parents would think of her. It made her seem a lot younger somehow and a lot more human. She said, 'I've got to get ready and I don't like to leave them on their own.'

'Where's Lena?'

'Getting ready too. They aren't all that fond of Lena either. I don't know what they wanted to come for. They haven't got the foggiest about music.' Shona shifted her weight from one foot to the other, embarrassed and nervous.

'Well, I suppose they won't bite,' Anna said reluctantly. Shona's nervousness was infecting her.

'Thanks a lot.' Shona sighed with relief. She opened the living-room door and led Anna in. The parents sat side by side on the sofa. Shona said, 'Mum and Dad, this is er . . . Anna . . . er, Anna. She's in charge of security. She'll look after you till I'm ready.'

The scent of furniture polish came up from the woodwork in sickening waves. Someone, probably Marilyn, had given it emergency treatment. The place sparkled like a show-room. The old man got to his feet and held his hand out. 'Security, eh?' he rumbled. 'Well, well. We always use Securicor at my bank. I expect you know them.' He wasn't really old, probably he was only in his fifties. He was just one of those men who look as if they've never been young. His wife too had a timeless quality as if every change of style in the last thirty years had passed her by.

'Simpson's the name,' he said awkwardly. 'I don't suppose you knew that. Hilary's been through a few changes since she left home.'

Anna made polite conversation for a while, asking them about their journey and whether they were looking forward to the concert. It was hard going. Mrs Simpson had a paid of gloves which she kept fiddling with, while Mr Simpson watched her with great suspicion as if he expected to find evidence of plague, perversion, or feminism. After a while, as she didn't either break out in buboes or polemics, they began to relax and Mrs Simpson started a conversation about vitamins. Anna left them and went to make tea.

Porky had done his best. He was wearing a suit. He was also eating a banana sandwich and there was quite a lot of mashed banana on his shirt. Anna gave him a wide berth. She made the tea and arranged the tray in a way her own mother would approve. Mrs Simpson reminded her forcibly of her mother. She even smelled the same, Pears soap and anti-dandruff shampoo. Anna's mother had never suffered from dandruff in her life, but she used the shampoo as a precaution. 'You never know, dear,' she had once said. 'You can even catch nasty conditions from library books.' She made similar remarks about money and always wore gloves when travelling by public transport.

When she got back to the living-room Anna asked Mrs Simpson if she collected china. She did, and Anna's sense of familiarity deepened. Both the Simpsons chatted quite happily about their success in junkshops until Shona arrived, and an air of constraint became apparent again.

Shona was wearing her Hollywood fur coat but it was Lena who attracted the attention. She was at her most outrageous in something that looked like a fiery wet suit. Her make-up was an astounding combination of black and primary colours. Altogether she looked more like an abstract painting than a human being. It was as if she had designed herself solely to provoke the parental generation. Mr and Mrs Simpson were nonplussed. The one to be most provoked, though, was Shona, who glared at her through slitted eyes. Lena was obviously not playing the game.

They quarrelled about it in the back of the BMW on the way to Clarkestead. Lena said, 'You can't still be worried about what your parents think. It's too juvenile.'

'I don't care what they think,' Shona snarled. 'But I don't see them often and I want them to enjoy themselves.'

'They'll be having a ball, then,' Lena snarled back. 'Because if there's one thing they enjoy it's disapproving of me. I'm not pretending to be a stodge just to please them. Look at Porky's suit. It's pathetic.'

'Leave my suit out of it,' Porky grumbled.

'I wish I could,' Lena said sweetly. 'But I can smell it from here.'

'Zip it, both of you,' Shona said. The rest of the journey was completed in icy silence. It was true about the suit, though. Every time Porky moved the odour of carbon tetrachloride and stale food drifted through the car.

The Simpsons had been taken to an expensive restaurant for an early dinner so they were not present when the smoke generator went wrong and covered the stage with acrid fumes. The area was cleared and everyone went up to the dressing-rooms.

The Leisure Centre was designed to be what the architect called 'flexible space'; it was not custom-built for a concert. The dressing-rooms were an arrangement of thin temporary partitions put up next to some cloakrooms. They were adequate but draughty and uncomfortable, and no-one wanted to stay there. Everyone milled about on the mezzanine floor. Except for the men who were struggling with the smoke generator, they all seemed to be at a loose end.

As a venue, Clarkestead was the least significant on the tour. The technical crew was reduced because fewer effects were needed. The audience would be the smallest yet so Dave had brought only three men with him, and Anna so far had managed to avoid all of them. With only two main entrances the security job was easy, so Dave, when she bumped into him, was in a relaxed mood.

'Back in harness, Tiddler?' he said. 'Better watch out the freaky bastards don't slip you a mickey. I've told all my people to frisk each other down at regular intervals. We don't want any more plants, eh?'

Martin Brierly said almost the same thing when she phoned him from the manager's office. 'Be very, very careful, Miss Lee. We don't want any more incidents. I'm sorry we had to put you back in so quickly but J.W. could suggest no suitable alternative.'

When she got through to Johnny he gave her an address off Praed Street and said bluntly, 'It's a crummy neighbourhood. If you want to go there, take an escort.' Everyone was being very free with warnings all of a sudden.

Upstairs, Shona, Ducks, Craig, and Van were playing poker at one end of a trestle table. Ducks was winning. Wes lay full-length on a bench, a personal stereo plugged into his ears. Lena sat at the other end of the table stitching a minute tear in the black and red costume. Porky slumped on another bench reading a Spiderman comic.

'Just like one big happy family,' the tour manager said under his breath. He stood behind Anna in the doorway for a moment before walking away to look into the hall from the glass-walled observation deck. He was immediately mobbed by everyone who wanted something. Over his shoulder he called, 'Tell them the stage's clear. They can go down again.' Anna passed on the message.

Chapter 33

She was watching from the observation deck when Avis arrived. Down below the band were coming to the end of the sound check. They stood around on the stage while Craig played a few bars. The sound men made adjustments and Craig played the same few bars again. He nodded. Everyone looked up at the gallery and waited. Shona, seeing Anna and Avis, smiled up at them and dropped a deep theatrical curtsy.

'She's so nice when she's nice,' Avis said. 'She could get anything she wanted if she used her charm.'

'Some people despise charm.' Anna saw Van make a sign to the sound men with the middle finger of his right hand.

'I don't,' Avis said with emphasis. 'It's what makes being on the bottom rung of the ladder bearable. It's what makes you want to do special things for some people and nothing at all for others. I'm very susceptible to charm.'

'Me too, I suppose,' Anna said ruefully. 'In some circumstances I'm even a sucker for people who are only half way polite.'

'Me too,' Avis said, and laughed. 'When I first met Shona, when she was just going round with an electric piano player and a drum box, I would've counted her as one of my friends. This was when Dog were first thinking of putting her under contract. I don't mean I knew her well or anything like that. It was just I always felt she was pleased to see me. Maybe she wasn't. Maybe this tour has brought out the real Shona. But even if it was false I liked her better then. Charm takes the sting out of honesty.'

'Was it Neil then?' Anna asked.

'Who, the piano-player? No. I can't remember his name. He was from Oz and I think he went back there. He must be kicking himself now.' Below them, the band started to shuffle off stage.

'Did you go to the first gig?'

'Birmingham? Mmm – you could say that was the beginning of the end of my illusions of friendship with Shona.'

'Mr Horowitz said she threw a wobbler. Did you see what happened?'

'Did I ever!' Avis said with a shudder. 'You'd've thought it was my fault. I still can't think about it without sweating. I went up specially to wish her luck and lend moral support and I had to take a couple of hours off work to do it. You know, hours you have to make up some other time.

'A couple of other people were going from Dog too, but at the last minute one of them pulled out so he gave me a load of stuff to give her up there – a re-recording schedule, some programmes to sign, publicity, and so on. Well, when

I got there, you've seen it, it was chaos, so I left the stuff in her dressing-room and told Porky to see she got it.

'Half an hour later, bombshell! "Who brought this crap?" Me. "What makes you think I'm interested? Take it away. I don't want anyone fucking me up at this stage. You too, bugger off, I don't want to see you again." It was terrible. There was a roomful of people and they all heard. She wasn't exactly whispering.'

'What did you do?' Anna asked.

'Well, I was shattered. It was so unexpected. I suppose I was pretty feeble. I just said I was sorry, I hadn't realized she didn't want to be bothered with business. At first she got even angrier and then she burst into tears and locked herself in her dressing-room. Of course my name was mud that night. Everyone looked at me as if I'd put a hex on the gig.

'She apologized later, said the pressure was getting to her and all that. But it's never been the same since. I always feel I'm here on sufferance. The trouble is, the people at work still think we're mates so if there are any errands it's always me who gets sent. And I'm always afraid she'll blow up on me again.'

'What a pity,' Anna said. Avis seemed to be the sort whose instinct was to think well of people and who would be disproportionately hurt if anyone she liked treated her unfairly. 'What exactly did you have to give her?'

'I don't know really,' Avis told her. 'Just a big brown envelope. As far as the guy at Dog told me it was just routine stuff. Nothing urgent. If it'd been something important, they'd never've sent me with it.'

'I suppose business has to go on even if she is on tour.'

'Well, right. And any record company would expect it to go on. I can't go back to Dog and say, "Don't bother Shona with anything. She's too sensitive to choose publicity stills when she's touring," or something pathetic like that. She isn't big enough for them to wear it. Whatever she's said to me personally, I don't want to mess things up for her at Dog. So I come bearing papers – again.' Avis tapped her briefcase.

'Is that what you've got?' Anna asked. 'Publicity stills?'

'Some of them are lovely,' Avis told her. 'Want to see?' She opened the case and took out a stiff-backed envelope with several eight by ten glossies in it. 'This one'd make a great poster.' She held it up for Anna to see. Shona smiled out at her, a fond, ferocious smile.

'She's very photogenic,' Anna said. She went through the photos one by one and looked in the envelope to make sure there was nothing else. 'I don't think there's anything here to upset her.'

They went to the dressing-rooms together. Anna had the impression they were using each other as shields as they went through the door. It wasn't really necessary. Someone said, 'Hello, it's the Owl and the Pussycat,' but Shona was warm towards Avis and sat down with her to look at the stills. Avis glowed. They had rigged up a portable TV and everyone was watching an early evening pop programme expecting to see one of their own videos.

Daniel Horowitz turned up at seven-thirty. Shona was beginning to fuss about whether the box office had remembered complimentary tickets for her parents. Avis volunteered to find out and earned a grateful smile from Shona and a sneer from Lena. Dave poked his head round the door and summoned Anna to keep an eye on the incoming crowd.

There was no seating in the hall except for a few rows built up at the back. The rest was wooden flooring with lines painted on it – three basketball courts, a five-a-side football pitch, and four badminton courts – all in different colours, superimposed one on top of the other. The area nearest the stage was already packed.

Anna crawled under the rows at the back to make sure no-one had left any explosives there since she last looked. Then she ran upstairs to look at the gallery, and then down to the foyer to check that no-one smuggled in a shotgun or meat cleaver. In the main it was a well dressed crowd of suburban kids and their most offensive weapons were Instamatic cameras and a few bad cases of acne.

As soon as she could she exchanged places with one of the J.W. men and went backstage. She found Daniel talking to the tour manager at the bottom of the stairs that led up to the dressing-rooms. When he was free she drew him aside and asked if he had brought Shona any money. He had. 'A thousand in tens and twenties in an ordinary manilla envelope. She put it in the bottom of her make-up case. I wish she wouldn't. It's stupid keeping large amounts of cash in a place like this. There are hundreds of people around. It's just putting temptation their way.'

'I'll try to keep an eye on it,' Anna said. 'Did you ask her what she wanted the cash for?'

'She said, "Don't lecture me, Danny. It's my bread. I'm over twenty-one. I don't have to account to you for every penny I spend," something like that.' He ran a nervous hand through his hair. The watery blue eyes looked sad and anxious. 'There's the implied threat, of course. There are managers who'd give her what she wanted and ask no quesitons.'

'Could she up and leave your agency?' Anna asked curiously. 'Don't you have a contract?'

'Fah!' Danny said. 'Contracts have to be renewed, darling. If she doesn't like what I do for her there's always someone in the wings promising her the earth. If she doesn't trust me I can't nail her to my office floor and demand loyalty. I can't force her to let me do a job for her.'

'No more can I,' Anna said thoughtfully. 'We're both in a cleft stick.'

'Well, do your best,' he said. 'We'll just have to be very careful not to rub her up the wrong way. We could both find ourselves out on our ears. Then there'll be no-one looking out for her.'

'Will you be around when the show's over?' she asked.

'I'm only staying for a couple of numbers, then I'm off home. I haven't seen my wife for a week. I could be out on my ear at home too for all I know.' He smiled to show he was joking, but the smile was like an apple with a worm in it. He went upstairs and Anna waited a couple of minutes before following.

Dave was outside the dressing-rooms. He said, 'Been round the back, Tiddler? Any problems?'

'So far so good,' she told him. He nodded and she went to join the cluster of roadies on the observation deck. The hall seemed packed but more and more kids were pushing in from the foyer. They didn't seem to mind and stood patiently jammed together like sheep in a pen. Disco music was being pumped out of the speaker system to keep everyone anaesthetized.

She continued the tour of inspection along the back of the gallery and down into the foyer where she met Avis shepherding Shona's parents towards the gallery steps. They looked as uncomfortable as a pair of soldiers at a disarmament rally.

'I don't know if this was such a good idea,' Mr Simpson murmured as a hundredweight of healthy teenage muscle pushed past him and ran up the stairs yelling, 'We are the champ-yons.'

'We had to show willing,' Mrs Simpson said apologetically. 'You wouldn't want Hilary to think we weren't interested.' Behind her, Avis winked at Anna and said, 'You must be awfully proud of her, Mrs Simpson.' Anna said, 'Creep!' under her breath and Avis quickly transformed a giggle into a cough.

'It's a time when family and old friends *should* gather round,' Mrs Simpson said doubtfully. She turned to her husband, 'Did you see that young man of Hilly's outside? Freddy something.'

'Howell, wasn't it?' Mr Simpson said. 'I didn't see him. We should've stopped and said hello.'

'I didn't recognize him at first – he's aged so dreadfully since we last saw him – and by then we'd passed him.'

Avis said, 'Where are you off to, Anna? They'll be turning the house lights down in a minute.'

Chapter 34

Outside, a forlorn queue of fans waited to see if any tickets had been returned. They huddled close to the Leisure Centre walls for protection from the icy wind. 'Any comps left?' one of them asked Anna when he noticed her badge. She shook her head and moved on towards the car park. A few latecomers sprinted past her, scarves flying, their voices loud on the night air. It was too cold to walk slowly. She jammed her hands in her pockets and went briskly between the lines of parked cars.

At the back of the Centre the tour vans loomed out of the dark. From one of them cables as thick as an arm snaked along the ground and disappeared through a partly open doorway. They had brought a generator to augment the power supply. She followed the cables into the dimly lit passage. It was a service passage, all concrete and grey paint. The fire door that led into the back of the Centre was closed and would not open inwards. She leaned on it to make sure. The only other alternative was the short flight of stairs that led down to the boiler room and that was where the cables went.

She went down. It was dark at the bottom. She felt along the wall for a light switch. The wall was cold and greasy to touch. A soft sigh broke the silence. There was a small furtive movement close to her feet and something brushed gently against her ankle. She jumped back and as she did so a hand grasped at her foot. She kicked out. A low weak voice said, 'Never mind.'

She stood still and heard the sigh again.

'Ferdo?' she said. At that movement a muffled roar of applause came from above.

'Ferdo?'

'Present,' the weak voice said. He sounded horribly tired.

'Where the hell are you?' She still couldn't find the light switch. But she found Ferdo by tripping over his leg. From above them came the opening bars of *Logodaedaly*.

'Did you fall?' she asked and crouched down beside him. 'Can you get up?'

'Gotta sleep, man,' the whisper came.

'Not down here, you daft bugger.' She found his arm and pulled him towards her. He came up to a sitting position and flopped against her, nearly knocking her over. 'Are you hurt?'

'No pain, man.' He sighed again.

She slipped his arm across her neck and hauled him to

his feet. His whole body weight dragged on her shoulder. She struggled to the bottom of the steps. His legs buckled and he fell. She crashed down on top of him.

'He's not heavy,' he whispered. 'She's my brother.'

She could see him faintly now. The bony nose pointed upwards. His eyes were closed. She shook him. 'Ferdo!' she exclaimed. 'What've you done?'

'Sold my history, man . . .' The ghostly voice was close to her ear. His lips barely moved. '. . . for a song.' His breath tickled her neck. She felt his forehead. Fish on a slab might have been colder, but not much.

She straightened and then raced up the boiler room stairs, out through the service doors, into the car park.

Out of breath, she sprinted to the corner of the building, turned it, and found herself dazzled by twin beams of white light. If she hadn't jumped she would have been flattened. As it was, the wing mirror caught her shoulder and sent her spinning into the wall. She fell. A car swerved, revved, and sped away.

Her shoulder was numb, the heel of her hand grazed. She picked herself up and limped to the entrance. The foyer seemed deserted but the sound of raised voices came from the manager's office. She pushed the door open and said, 'Someone phone for an ambulance, please.'

Two faces turned to look at her. A grey-haired woman said, 'What's happened? You'd better sit down, but I don't think you need an ambulance.'

Anna said, 'There's a bloke in a bad way in your boiler room. He needs help fast.'

The fat man picked up the phone and dialled. Anna said, 'Where's the light switch for the boiler room?'

'My goodness,' the woman said. 'I've never been down there.' The fat man on the phone began to speak. Anna turned to go.

'But I can lend you a torch if that's any help,' the woman said. She began a painfully slow search of a desk drawer.

The fat man said, 'What's wrong with him?'

'I don't know,' Anna said. 'Looks like an overdose.'

'Damn!' said the man. He repeated the information into the phone.

'I knew it was here somewhere,' the woman said, and straightened up. She held out the torch. Anna took it and ran.

Ferdo lay where she had left him, sprawled along the bottom three steps. 'A blanket,' she said out loud as she went down. 'Why didn't I think?' She propped the torch on the bottom step. Ferdo's man-in-the-moon profile was turned to his right. There was silence. She thought he had stopped breathing. Then he sighed. Sigh . . . pause . . . sigh. She didn't know whether to get him upright or lay him flat. Flat was easiest.

She rolled him as gently as she could to the bottom of the steps. At least he looked more dignified lying straight. She pressed both hands against his ribcage to encourage his lungs and called his name. His eyelids fluttered once. She pressed again and again, her ears tuned for the sound of the ambulance. All she could hear was the thud of bass and drums from upstairs. She squeezed his ribs and thought about mouth to mouth.

As she paused for breath his coat fell open and a wad of fivers dropped from the inner pocket. She stared at them. Then felt quickly in the pocket. More fivers. No photo. She stuffed the money back. Ferdo gave another light sigh. His right hand crawled like a shelled crab up to his chest.

The fingers when they encountered hers trembled, then held on feebly. At last, from the car park, came the sound of the ambulance.

They were very efficient. They rolled Ferdo on the stretcher. They wrapped him in a warm red blanket. They clamped an oxygen mask on his face. They even found the light switch.

And they were gone in less than five minutes. 'I hope we won't need them again tonight,' the fat man said. He was Mr Pauly, manager of the Leisure Centre. 'Let's get out of the cold. If there'd been more time you should have had that shoulder seen to.' They watched the winking blue light of the ambulance as it turned out on to the main road.

'I think we can find a drink for you in the office,' Mr Pauly went on. 'What an upsetting sequence of events for you. But I'm glad it was a member of security who found the poor chap. Anyone else might've panicked and told the wrong people. This is *not* the kind of publicity the Centre needs, or the tour either, I imagine.'

Chapter 35

'Jesus Christ!' Dave said. 'Didn't you read your horoscope this morning? Or are you always this accident-prone?' He was sitting on the edge of Mr Pauly's desk while the grey-haired woman dabbed disinfectant on the oozing purple welt on Anna's shoulder.

'Just lucky,' she said, wincing.

'Who else'd get knocked over by a hit-and-run merchant on her way to call an ambulance?' He swung his legs and gazed at her morosely. 'And don't guzzle that brandy. You've got to be fit to drive in an hour. You *will* be able to drive, won't you?'

'She shouldn't drive,' the grey-haired woman said. 'This shoulder's going to be awfully stiff. It'll be a mass of bruises in the morning.'

The brandy burned the back of Anna's throat. She grinned at Dave and said, 'It's okay.'

'And your beautiful jacket,' the grey-haired woman mourned. 'The sleeve's only hanging on by a thread.'

'Maybe Lena'll put a stitch in it for me.'

'Is that the little freak who looks as if she's got nothing on but a lick of paint?' Dave asked. 'I'm surprised she didn't see you get hit. She went out just after the band went on, and she wasn't back till just before Mr Pauly came up and called me.'

'I saw her come through the lobby,' the grey-haired woman said. 'I couldn't believe she was going out dressed like that. It's amazing what young people wear these days.'

'Or don't wear.' Dave got up. 'Well, back to the grind,' he said. 'I suppose you should take it easy till it's time to go, Tiddler. Not that you ever do much else.' He went away with his hands in his pockets and the sort of look on his face people wear when they haven't said, 'I told you so.'

Anna took another gulp of brandy. It didn't help the shoulder but it blurred the picture of Ferdo's man-in-the-moon profile.

The grey-haired woman screwed the cap back on the disinfectant bottle. 'It's clean,' she said, 'but you ought to see a doctor.' She screwed the cap back on the brandy bottle too and put it firmly in a locker. Anna sighed and said, 'Thanks for your help. I'd better be getting upstairs now.'

She went up slowly, feeling heavy and clumsy. On the observation deck roadies and tour personnel had gathered to watch through the glass. 'It's going down a treat,' one of them shouted above the noise of the band. Anna looked over his shoulder and saw in the darkened body of the hall the audience heaving like waves. Shona stood, feet apart, almost suspended in a column of white light – her arms outstretched like a sorceress. It looked as if she was commanding the audience to perform for her rather than the other way around.

Anna moved on. She saw Avis silhouetted against the glass, and as her eyes got used to the shadows she picked out the others. She touched Lena on the arm and beckoned.

'That's designer gear!' Lena said, shocked, when she saw the damage. 'Shit, Snoops, you got to take care of it.'

'I told you I led an active life,' Anna said. 'Can you patch it up a bit?'

'This needs a bloody skin graft.' Lena examined the ripped seams. 'I'm not a cosmetic surgeon. I'm not your personal invisible mender either. I gave you a few hundred quid's worth of grade A skin. If you can't keep it together why should I bother?'

'Because you don't want to be seen driving around with a scarecrow,' Anna said hopefully.

'Give it here.' Lena snatched the jacket and made off for the dressing-room.

'And besides it was probably your mate who knocked me down.'

'How's that?' Lena stopped. Under all the paint it was

impossible to read her expression or even see if there was an expression.

'Weren't you out in front talking to a chap in a car?' Anna asked. 'Someone said she saw you just before I got hit.'

'She's dreaming,' Lena said. 'If I went out it was to look for that cretin, Porky. Have you seen him, by the way? He was supposed to fetch a can of hairspray out of Duck's car and nobody's seen him since. Ducks is having a tantrum.'

She opened the door to the dressing-room. In Shona's private area everything was set out for the final change. The black and red costume hung ready on a screen. The matching wig was on its block in front of the mirror. Ducks sat in Shona's chair contemplating his own reflections. Before him was a litter of brushes, combs and cosmetics. Lena pushed past him to get a needle and thread. 'Still a little moody, are we?' she said, rummaging in the depths of a linen sack.

'Still a little bitchy, are we?' he retorted. 'I get stuck back here in this piss-awful hole, minding the shop. They aren't even properly equipped here. I don't know when the next change is coming up . . .'

'Ten minutes. They're on *Towards Lunar Bay.*'

'. . . and bloody Porky can't be bothered to run a simple errand . . .'

'Belt up, Ducks,' Lena said indifferently. 'I'm here now, so run your own errands. At least get your bum out of that chair. I've got work to do.'

'Of course, I forgot!' Ducks leaped to his feet. He grabbed a towel and dusted the seat of the chair. 'Miss Pecci's the only one with any work to do. Everyone give way to Miss Pecci! She's got work to do.'

Lena sat down and calmly threaded her needle. Ducks glared at her through slitted eyes. He said, 'You're poison, Marlene Pecci. Pure arsenic. I don't know why Sho doesn't wise up and throw you out on your pointy little ear.'

'You bore me,' Lena said softly. 'God, how boring you are. You're weak, whiny, and pathetic. You'll never get anywhere on your own. You'll always cling to someone's apron strings.' It sounded like a curse or a prophecy delivered with cold indifference. Even Anna was chilled.

Ducks went pale. He held the towel in both hands like

a garrotte, his knuckles shiny white. Then he dropped it and left the room.

Anna said, 'Not too hot on industrial relations, are you?'

Lena stabbed her needle into the leather. 'Why bother?' she said without looking up. 'He doesn't pull his weight. He thinks he's got a meal ticket for life, and he does nothing but complain.'

'People work better when they're secure and feel appreciated.'

'Think so?' Lena asked without much interest. 'Some people are born freeloaders.'

'Well, think what'd happen if Ducks walked out,' Anna said.

'We won't be that lucky.' Lena's tiny fingers flickered over the leather. 'But if we are, I know ten stylists better than him. I could do his job myself.'

'But he's an old friend,' Anna protested.

'This is business.' Lena looked up briefly and gave Anna a hard glance. 'Friendship's not enough. Shona's on the move. Old friends get to be old drags. Like that!' She snapped her fingers. 'They all want a piece. Sho'll be astounded how many "old friends" she's got if she really makes it.'

'I just saw one in the boiler room,' Anna said grimly. 'He was in a bad way. I had to call an ambulance.'

'Who?'

'Ferdo Howe.'

'Never heard of him.' Lena tested the seam she had just sewn and then turned her attention to the torn flap.

'In Hock.'

'Oh, them. Well, Sho had to start somewhere. Look, I'm going to have to patch this from the inside. I can't sew it. In fact it'll have to be glued on to the patch.' She got up and rummaged in her sack again till she found a stiff piece of fabric that satisfied her. She snipped it into shape. Her hands were quick and clever. It was a pleasure to watch her work.

'There,' she said eventually. 'You can't wear it till it dries so you'd better let me have the shirt.' Anna stripped it off and gave it to her.

'Ugly,' Lena said, looking at Anna's shoulder. 'I hate wounds. It's disgusting to think what goes on under the skin. Skin's so pretty before it gets old and wrinkly or torn.'

'Best stick to silk, then,' Anna told her. 'You can always throw it away and get some more if it lets you down.'

'You're right,' Lena said seriously. She chose another smaller needle and silk to match Anna's shirt. Anna watched her while she sewed. The garment she wore clung to her, as Dave had said, like paint, and yet it was difficult to see her. The strong clear patches of colour acted like camouflage and drew the eye away from the shape underneath. It was hard to take anyone who looked like Lena seriously. She looked like a painted doll, and painted dolls weren't sharp or hurtful or ambitious. Nor were they expected to be clever or competent.

Lena snapped off her thread and handed the shirt back to Anna. The mend was barely visible. Anna could see the beautiful, tiny stitches if she looked closely, but not otherwise. 'That's great,' she said. 'Thanks.'

Lena shrugged. 'Soak it in cold water when you get home – to lift the blood out,' she said. 'And try not to be so clumsy. You bound around like a big dog. No wonder you get in such a mess. Good clobber's wasted on you.'

'Woof!' Anna said and stuffed the shirt tail into the waist of her skirt.

'Not like that!' Lena said, exasperated. She jumped up to help. 'You've got no respect, have you?' She tweaked the shirt into shape. Anna was glad of her help. She could scarcely move her left arm.

'Girl Guides!' Lena sneered. 'That's where your good deeds get you, Snoops. You won't be much use to us with one arm.' She looked at her watch. 'Right. I'm off. Got to get the girl up for her lightning change.' She slipped like a rainbow shadow from the room. Anna had no doubt that her sense of time was as precise as everything else about her, and that she would arrive behind the stage exactly when Shona came off.

She looked at her watch too. She would be lucky if she had three minutes. Shona's make-up case was on the floor under Lena's work sack. It was a square box made of fake alligator. Most of the contents were on the dressing-table.

Anna opened it and took the top tray out. The manilla envelope was there all right but it was light and flat. She looked inside. If Mr Horowitz had brought a thousand pounds, someone had already made very short work of most of them. Only two twenties and a ten remained. She fitted the tray back, closed the lid, and pushed it back under Lena's work sack. The sack contained nothing but the tools of her trade and a paperback copy of *Dead Babies*.

Shona's handbag hung on a hook on one of the screens. She snapped it open. Inside was a jumble of tissues and ordinary non-theatrical cosmetics, an address book, a change purse, a packet of peppermints, no £950, and no threatening letters.

A commotion in the outer reception area told Anna she had run out of time.

Chapter 36

Shona, Ducks, and Lena came by in a rush. The Velcro at the back of Shona's costume had been ripped apart so that all she had to do was let it fall to the floor. Ducks had her wig in his hands. She looked like a skinned rabbit. Anna backed way and left them to it.

She looked down from the observation deck. Without Shona, the band was like a yacht without a sail. They worked hard on the long bluesy introduction to the next number but it lacked colour or impact. Craig was up front under the spot. The short times Shona took off-stage were his only chances to lead, but he didn't have the presence to fill the space she left. Wes and Neil looked diligent but not exciting enough. Van had enough self-assurance for all of them but his kit was set off to one side. It would have been better, too, if he had had a classic drum kit. The shiny little pads he hit seemed unworthy of his attack. Still, he was a bundle of energy, and sweat streamed off his bare chest. But the stage seemed empty and the sound was thin. The audience waited hungrily.

Shona burst through the back curtains like dawn. She danced through the others and whirled up to the microphone. The hall came alive again, and Anna turned away from the window to look for Porky.

The obvious place to look was the snack bar. He wasn't there. She found Avis sharing a table and a plate of chips with a couple of roadies. None of them remembered seeing Porky.

She met Dave on the stairs but he couldn't help either. His only concern was that she should be on hand at the end of the show.

Porky was not in the bar, nor in the passage behind the stage. The only other place she could think of was the car park. She went back up to the snack bar and borrowed Avis's coat. As she walked through the foyer Mr Pauly called from his office. She went over to the door. He was sitting at his desk. The brandy bottle was out of the locker again and rested on a pile of papers. 'How are you feeling?' he inquired politely. He did not meet her eyes and went on hurriedly, 'I've just phoned the Royal Victoria Hospital. I thought you might like to know how that poor fellow was. But I'm afraid they couldn't save him. He died about twenty minutes after they got him there. It's a shame, after everything you did for him. I'm sorry.'

Anna leaned against the doorframe and stared at the floor.

'Have a drink,' Mr Pauly offered. 'It's not your fault. You did your best.'

'No, thanks,' she said absently. 'I've got to drive.' Her shoulder began to ache like a rotten tooth. She went slowly through the glass doors, around the building, and into the car park.

The cold air stung her cheeks and made her eyes water. She walked aimlessly up and down the ranks of empty cars, and passed Ducks's Peugeot twice before she realized that it was the only one with misty windows. She opened the door and looked in. Porky was lying on the back seat. Only a distillery would have smelled stronger. He was curled up on his side, the bottle cuddled against his cheek. His horrible suit was twisted as if someone had wrung it out with him still in it. The trousers had worked their way up his legs exposing several inches of calf like hairy celery sticks.

Anna leaned over the front seat and shook him. He groaned and the bottle fell on to the floor. She shook him again. He struggled upright and said, 'It wasn't me.'

'What wasn't?'

'Oh Gaw,' I think I'm going to puke.' He leaned forward. Anna shot out of the front seat. She pulled open the back door and hauled Porky out on to the tarmac. He staggered over to a neighbouring Ford and was spectacularly sick on the bonnet.

'Oh bloodyell,' he moaned. 'Oh Gaw'!'

'Oh, terrific,' Anna said. She turned her back and thought about the favour Ducks owed her if he ever heard about it.

After a while Porky said, 'Farkin' juice always gets me.' He took a few deep breaths and began to shiver. He wobbled back to the Peugeot on rubber legs.

'Feeling better?' she asked brightly. He sank down on the back seat, his feet on the tarmac, head hanging between his knees.

'What on earth made you do a stupid thing like that?' Anna asked.

'I was depressed,' he muttered at the ground. 'Some things bring a fella down. Nobody thinks I got feelings.'

'You saw Ferdo,' Anna said. She was really thinking about herself.

'Oh yeah?' He looked up and blinked slowly. His eyes looked like runny eggs.

'Yeah.'

'What's a clapped-out junkie to me?' He lay back on the seat and covered his face with a bent arm. 'Survival,' he said. 'That's what counts.'

'He used to be a mate.'

'So what? Junkies don't want mates – just the soft touch.'

'Did he see you?'

'No way. I ain't got bread to flush down the bog.'

'He had plenty of bread,' Anna said.

'Yeah? Looked skint to me. Looked on his last legs. I didn't want to know. I ain't no do-gooder like you.'

'Survival,' she said. 'That's what counts.'

'Right on. What'd he want if it wasn't no handout?'

'Maybe he was just looking up old friends.'

'Ha-bloody-ha,' Porky jeered into his elbow. 'Ferdo never did nothing without there was something in it for him. Could be he was pushing.'

'Why?'

'He come with that connection of Van's. Didn't see Van, though. He must be all topped up.' He struggled up on to his elbow and looked at her mistily. 'Nah,' he said. 'Couldn't be. They ain't fool enough to give Ferdo gear to peddle.'

'He had a skinful,' Anna said bleakly.

'Thought so,' Porky said. 'I seen the meat wagon. Did he make it?'

'No. Who's Van's connection?'

'What connection?' He suddenly looked a lot less misty. 'They don't call you Snoopy for nothing.'

'You ain't seen nothing yet,' she told him. 'Wait till the fuzz start asking.'

'You wouldn't,' he said confidently. 'You wouldn't blow it for her ladyship. I know you. She's a good little earner. You wouldn't blow that.'

'You should know,' said Anna sweetly. 'You're the expert. But don't bank on it. If I blow this one I've still got a job. What've you got? It could've been you out in the cold instead of Ferdo. That's what brought you down.'

'I don't smack.'

'No, but you eat,' Anna said. 'That's quite a habit you've got. Think you could support it on your own? You're right, of course. I don't want the police sticking their noses in. But they may come sniffing anyway. It's drugs. Naturally they'll want to know. And then what? The papers? "Old friend lets OD case die."'

'You wouldn't,' Porky repeated. His skin had a greenish tinge.

'I wouldn't be able to help it. You knew Ferdo. You're a witness.'

'Only if you tell the fuzz I am.'

'You're catching on.' She grinned at him. At least it felt like a grin. Maybe she was just showing her teeth. 'Who's Van's connection?'

'But I don't know a thing.' Porky put a hand on the doorframe and pulled himself up. He sat swaying for a few seconds. 'Shee-it, I feel rotten,' he said. 'Listen, I stay out of all that caper. I drink my coke out of a bottle, and I don't do Ferdo's thing neither. I don't want to know, see. Those're rough blokes to muck with.'

'But you know them by sight.'

'I may've seen them. You'd have a hard time not seeing them in this game.'

'So tell me,' Anna insisted, 'and keep it in the family.'

'You're no family of mine!' he said quietly. 'I'll tell you one thing, though – they call him Mr Hard, and he comes from the East End. Van thinks he's a gas. But I come from east of Tower Hamlets meself and I know Mr Hard ain't no rocker's playmate. You won't think so neither if you ever meet him.'

'Ferdo came here in Mr Hard's motor?' Anna asked. 'What does he drive?'

'A plain old Datsun,' Porky said. 'You wouldn't look at it twice.'

'Number?'

Porky shook his head. 'Nor his phone number. Nor his wife's maiden name. I told you, I stay out of that caper.'

'How about Shona?'

'She don't need to see no-one she don't want to see. She's got all the runners she wants. She's clean. Your really rich punters don't go shopping for themselves, do they?' Porky got to his feet and hung limply over the car door. He said, 'You want to know Shona's caper – ask her. Don't ask me. I'm wasted.'

Chapter 37

They walked through the car park to the front of the building. Porky tucked his head into the collar of his coat. He was still having trouble with his legs. Anna said, 'Do you remember a VW Beetle that followed us out of Luton? And again, maybe in Bristol? Is that anything to do with Mr Hard?'

'Don't you ever stop?' Porky complained. 'No. I never seen a VW, particular.'

'Or a tall geezer hanging around Addison Road at night?'

'Nah.' Porky pushed through the glass doors into the foyer. A blast of sound nearly blew them back outside. 'I feel horrible,' he said. 'Maybe I ought to eat something. My head's thumping like a jack-hammer.'

So was Van, from what Anna could hear. She said, 'Ducks's gunning for you. Better steer clear.' He gave her a bleary, cynical look and shambled off in the direction of the snack bar.

Mr Pauly was not in his office. Anna sat down at his desk and used the phone. Martin Brierly's housekeeper told her that he wasn't expected in till eleven. Anna left her name and called Bernie. He said, 'What's the news, kid?'

'I can't get hold of the Old Man,' she told him. 'The tour's moving on to Norwich tomorrow. But I've had a bit of a dust-up with a motor. I think there's something wrong with my arm. I'm not going to be too clever tomorrow.'

'What happened?' Bernie asked calmly.

She told him. She told him about Ferdo Howe, the money, and Mr Hard too.

'Ho-hum,' he said. 'Interesting. Can you get back all right?'

'The BMW's automatic.'

'Don't take any chances,' he warned. 'You like to think you're a bit stoical sometimes. Well, stoics cause accidents – so if there's any doubt, get someone else to drive. Have you told Dave McPhee about the junkie? No? Well do it now. Spread the load a little. You won't be in Norwich tomorrow so someone ought to keep an eye out. You don't have to bare your soul. But that lad died. He could've taken what did it himself or it could've been given him. If it was given him, Mr Hard or whoever wants watching.'

'The thing about Dave,' Anna began carefully, 'well, he's a bull. He thinks all musicians are freaks. I don't know what he'd do about drugs.'

'Same as you, love,' Bernie said. 'Your band may well be everything he despises, but they're also J.W. clients. He can't turn them in.'

'Okay, but it's difficult to see him as an ally when he acts like the enemy.'

Bernie chuckled. 'Don't be so sensitive, love. You know how blokes like that are. Just because he treats you like an outsider of the female persuasion there's no need to get on your high horse about it. It's happened before and it'll happen again . . .'

'All right already!' Anna interrupted. 'I'll talk to him. But I wish you were here to do it instead.'

After she had put the phone down Anna went upstairs. The band had just begun the reprise *Bitterness* and the hall was in an uproar. Tour personnel were starting to deploy themselves for a fast exit.

She found Dave outside the reception area. He stood with his arms folded, chin tucked into his thick neck like a guardsman. Anna went to stand beside him and for a moment they watched the roadies gather by the backstairs. She said, 'That bloke I called the ambulance for . . .'

'Yeah,' Dave said. 'He checked out. Heroin overdose. Mr Pauly told me.'

'His name was Ferdo Howe.'

Dave yawned. He didn't bother to cover his mouth and Anna could see his fillings. 'Ferdo Howe,' she repeated.

'So?'

'That's the name you gave me the address for this morning.'

'So?' He turned slowly to look at her. 'Don't tell me, Tiddler. You went to visit him and he was so affected by the experience he jacked himself full of smack rather than see you again.'

'When I saw him,' she said doggedly, 'he was stony. I took him to the clinic. Only about seven hours later, not only is he popped to kingdom come, he's got a wad of readies on him as thick as a brickie's sandwich. On top of that he was seen *here* with a known supplier called Mr Hard . . .'

'Look, Tiddler,' Dave butted in, 'what do we care where a junkie gets his fix? You've got a butterfly brain. Typical woman. We're in security, not narcotics.'

Anna bit her lip. 'Yes, boss,' she said, 'but Ferdo was an old friend of Shona, Wes, and Porky. Mr Hard is known at least to Van Vritski. He drives a blue Datsun. I've see it. So he's hanging round the gigs close to London.'

'Okay, Tiddler, okay,' he said tiredly. 'You get your spotter's badge. Along with wiping snot off the freaks' noses and protecting them from ten thousand loonies we will also keep an eye out for one blue Datsun, unregistered, driven by someone who may or may not be called Mr Hard. Thanks for your expert help, Tiddler. And judging by the way you're holding that arm of yours I suppose we can expect a sick note in the morning. You *are* going to see your GP, aren't you? Or do you plan to get nicked again? I mean, girls like you don't want to work every bloody day like the rest of us ordinary mortals.'

'What do you want me to do with the BMW?' she asked. Her fingernails dug painfully into the palm of her hand.

'Do you really want me to tell you?' He turned away and then swung back. 'No. If I had anyone spare I'd ask you to give me the keys now. As it is, you'd better leave it at Addison Road. Now, if it isn't too awfully jolly much for you, why don't you get your pretty little arse over to the bottom of the front stairs and see what arrangements Mr Pauly's made for the loonies.'

The sour taste of unsaid expletives was in her mouth as she marched off to find Mr Pauly. On the way she gave Avis back her coat. Avis said, 'I suppose I'd better watch out for the old folks. Make sure they don't get trampled to death in the stampede. Are you all right? You look a bit pale.'

'I'm fine,' Anna said, 'Thanks.' When she moved off the sour taste had gone.

In the foyer the doors had been thrown open and kids were beginning to pour out into the night. Some of them shouted or chanted, their excited voices quickly lost on the wind. The girls on the merchandise stand did quick business selling LPs, T-shirts, and posters. On some of the faces was the glazed empty expression of a dreamer who didn't want to wake into real life. The ones who wanted to prolong the dream gathered at the bottom of the stairs asking where to go for autographs.

Anna and Mr Pauly had their work cut out to keep the stairs clear for the people coming down. 'It'll be a long wait,' Mr Pauly warned the crowd kindly. 'The band has to change and sort themselves out.' To Anna he whispered, 'They'll thin out a bit if they know they have to wait. We can't take this mob up.'

He was right. After twenty minutes only the really keen ones were left. She counted heads and led them upstairs. Six more from the gallery were waiting.

The makeshift reception room was already quite full. Everyone had a glass of something and everyone was affected by the euphoria of another successful show. Only the Simpsons sat apart on hard chairs looking, if anything, embarrassed. Avis offered them more wine but they had hardly touched what was already in their glasses.

Anna stood at the door and let the fans in by threes and fours. Van pulled the prettiest fan down on to his knee and she sat there giggling helplessly while he gave autographs to whoever asked. The others formed a little group near him. They were all in an expansive mood.

As usual, Shona kept to herself in her private area, protected by Lena and the tour manager. But even she had a pleasant smile for the visitors.

Ducks came over with a glass in his hand. He looked relaxed now. He sipped wine and said, 'Funny, isn't it. These unimportant little venues are sometimes the best. Takes the pressure off a bit.'

'You cheered up quick,' Anna said. He opened his fist and allowed her a brief look at a brown cigarette with the girth of a Christmas cracker. Then he glided away to join two sound technicians by the cloakroom door. She leaned against the wall, and the room and its occupants seemed to recede for a moment, grow smaller. The noise of conversation blurred into a continuous hum. She closed her eyes.

'Porky told me about Ferdo. Tough shit, huh?' It was Wes. Anna looked round for Porky and saw him on a bench, picking flaked skin off his cracked lips. She said, 'Yes. Tough. Had you kept up with him?'

'Nah,' he said. 'You can see when a guy's on the skids. It doesn't pay to watch them fall. Tough shit, though.' He moved on.

Mr Pauly channelled some fans out through the door and Anna let another quartet in. She closed her eyes again. Someone said, '. . . and a CZ5000 synth, isn't it?' A gnome-sized fan with mad scientist's eyes was trying to interest Neil in a technical discussion. 'You got me there,' Neil said, bored. 'I just move my fingers.' The gnome wandered over to Craig. Neil winked at Craig and drew a thumb across his throat. Craig brushed past the gnome and disappeared into the cloakroom. Disappointed, the gnome made for Shona. 'I really admire your breath control, Miss Una,' he said. 'Have you studied the Djvorsk method?'

'Well, er, thanks,' Shona said. She signed his programme and looked bewildered. It was then Anna noticed the tall man who stood by himself near Shona's open door. He had a raincoat over one arm. A signed programme stuck out of one of his pockets but he also had a glass of wine in his hand. He could have been a guest except no-one was talking to him and the signed programme gave him away.

Anna was sure he had not been among the group she had brought up. She moved across the room so that she could see his face. He was trying hard to look rangy and casual, but he was too tense and too young – twenty at most. His clothes made him look older. They seemed to belong to someone of a different generation. A mother's boy out on his own.

He watched Shona with famished intensity. Anna moved into his line of vision and let him see her looking at

him. At first he raised his chin a couple of inches. Then he
began to look like a dog who has just made a mess behind
the sofa, and after a while he backed unhappily out of the
room.

She walked to the door to see where he went and just
caught sight of him sprinting like a maniac across the observation deck to the stairs.

Dave loomed out of the shadows and said, 'Nearly
through? Anyone making a move home?'

'Did you see that chap running?' Anna asked. 'Did you
let him in?'

'Not me,' he said. 'Can't you hurry things along in
there?'

Chapter 38

'Who was the weirdo?' Shona asked, *sotto voce*. 'The
one you cooled.' She swept the litter of cosmetics into her
make-up case. The last of the visitors had left and everyone
was packing up, putting on coats.

'You noticed him?' Anna was surprised. She examined
the patch on her leather jacket. Another of Lena's small mir-
acles.

'I noticed him in Brighton too,' Shona said. 'I don't like
him. Tell your boss, will you.'

'I already did.' Anna did not mention what Dave said in
reply. She said, 'I also told him I think that's the one hanging around your house.'

Shona looked up, her face impassive. Anna said, 'You
will be careful, won't you?' They stared at each other for a
couple of seconds. Lena bustled in with two roadies. 'Move
yourself, Snoops,' she said. Anna went back to the reception area and the roadies hefted the costume box.

Avis came over and whispered, 'The oldies are getting

restive. Is Shona nearly ready?' On the other side of the room Mr Simpson was pulling on his gloves and Mrs Simpson was snapping the clasp of her handbag.

'Okay. I'll tell Shona,' Anna said, turning back to the dressing-room. Porky appeared at her shoulder and said, 'I'm catching a ride with one of the lads. Don't wait for me.'

'Good thinking,' said Anna. He smelled like a barman's towel and Lena would never let him forget it. She pushed her nose round the dressing-room door saying, 'Shona, your folks . . .'

'Coming,' Shona said. She blew her nose and dropped the tissue, missing the bin by a yard. Her fur bedspread was draped over her shoulders and it swung rhythmically as she stepped out into the reception area. 'Why don't we all go somewhere to eat?' she announced. Everyone turned to look at her in astonishment.

'Great. Bandy's!' Van said.

'Not Bandy's,' Wes objected. 'Heavy meat.'

'Your father and I have already had our supper,' Mrs Simpson said timidly.

'Where's Bandy's?' Craig said, looking dubious. Anna's heart sank. Mrs Simpson stared shyly at Shona as if she were a stranger. Mr Simpson stared at his shoes. 'I really think we ought to be getting along, dear,' he said to his wife. He did not look at Shona.

'What about Tam's Garden?' Wes suggested.

'What's that?' Craig asked. Neil shrugged and said, 'Vegan, I guess.'

'Yes, we really *should* be getting along,' Mrs Simpson said apologetically. 'But we've had a lovely evening, haven't we dear?'

'Lovely,' Shona said, her face wooden. 'Snoopy, would you mind seeing where my parents' driver's got to?'

Anna tramped the length of the Leisure Centre once again. She found the driver, Dave, and Mr Pauly in the foyer. Mr Pauly had a bunch of keys in his hand which he jiggled wearily. Dave was saying, 'I wouldn't mind but the little bastards've got no sodding manners.'

'Pardon our French,' the driver said when he saw Anna approach. Mr Pauly unlocked the door and let him out to fetch the Rolls.

'You too,' David said to Anna. 'I'll roust Superbitch. We're not stopping here all night to suit her.'

Anna walked through the empty car park. The Rolls and the BMW were side by side. The driver was disgustedly cleaning lipstick hearts off the windows. Someone, probably the same person, had written 'We love you Shona Una' in letters a foot high on the BMW windscreen.

'It's a devil to get off,' the driver said. 'Here, I always keep some window-cleaner with me.' He passed her an aerosol can. Anna set to work on the windscreen. Her left arm was very painful and almost useless.

'Why do they do it?' the driver asked. His nose was running with the cold and his knuckles bunched arthritically. 'It's only us poor mugs as ever see what they write. Us poor mugs as have to clean it off. I wouldn't want your job, not for a night out with Miss World, I wouldn't.'

'I don't think much of it myself,' Anna told him through chattering teeth.

He finished his windows and drove to the front of the building. Anna scrubbed and polished and gradually the greasy smear disappeared.

The freezing temperature had one advantage: there was no-one hanging about waiting for the band to come out. Anna drove round the perimeter of the car park to make sure. No VW Beetle. She waited outside the front entrance with the motor running and the heater turned full on. The Rolls had already left.

It was another quarter of an hour before Shona and Lena came out.

'Where to?' Anna asked.

'Home, wherever that is,' Shona said moodily.

'Indecision,' Lena said. 'It's so absolutely tedious.'

Anna put the car in drive and pulled smoothly away.

'Next time you pick a band,' Lena said, 'either get all carnivores or all grazers. This mixture's too boring.'

Shona laughed angrily. 'Wanted: one herbivorous drummer.'

'What about the wrinklies?' Lena asked slyly. 'Had a good time, did they?'

Shona didn't answer and Lena went on, 'What you expect, Sho?'

'Nothing.'

'Right, nothing,' Lena said. 'Stick to your own kind, Sho. No-one else understands. What you say, Snoops?'

Anna didn't answer either. She was trying grimly not to move her hands too abruptly on the wheel. They went on for a few miles in silence. Then Shona said, 'Stop the car, Snoopy!'

Anna slowed and said, 'You know I'm not supposed to.'

'Screw that,' Shona said. 'Stop!'

Anna looked in the mirror. Shona was leaning forward, a determined frown on her face. Anna checked the road behind her. It was all clear. There was nothing ahead either.

'Fucking stop when I tell you,' Shona exclaimed.

Anna pulled into the kerb and stopped. 'Don't get out,' she said. But Shona already had her door open. 'Move over,' she said, opening the driver's door. 'Go on, shove up. I'm driving.'

'Better do as she says,' Lena drawled. 'She's so macho when she's disappointed.'

Anna climbed over the central aisle and sat in the passenger seat. Shona got into her place.

'Think I'm useless, don't you?' she said as she steered the car back on to the road. 'Think you can drive better with one hand than I can with two? What happened to you anyway?'

'Haven't you heard?' Lena said spitefully. 'Brown Owl here got wounded in service to the community over and above the call of duty. She got bonked by a speeding ambulance.'

'Did you?'

'No.' Anna swivelled in her seat and gave Lena a hard, direct look.

'Uh-oh, have I said something?' Lena asked. 'Sho has a right to know, doesn't she? He was a friend of hers.'

'Who was a friend of mine?'

'Are you insured?' Anna asked.

'She doesn't need to be,' Lena said. 'She's rich. Cash on the nail for everything, isn't it, Sho?'

'I meant you, Lena,' Anna said harshly. 'With a mouth like yours, you ought to be.'

'Who was a friend of mine?' Shona's hands were firm on the wheel. She seemed to be a good, steady driver. Anna faced front again. 'Ferdo Howe,' she said reluctantly. 'He OD'd.'

'Died happy, didn't he, Snoops? Very, very happy.'

Anna turned again and asked, 'What're you trying to do, Lena? Spread a little sunshine? Put a sock in it, will you.'

'"You are the sunshine of my life, Snoo-pee,"' Lena sang in a high, clear voice.

Shona took her foot off the accelerator. 'You two want to walk?' she cried angrily. 'All right then. Snoopy, in words of one syllable, stop-babe-y-ing me. Lena, belt up! What happened?'

Anna said, 'I found Ferdo in the boiler room under the Centre. He was pretty sick. An ambulance took him to hospital but he died. I don't know why he came. He didn't mention you.'

'He probably wanted a handout,' Lena said. 'Don't worry about it, Sho.'

'He had plenty of cash on him.'

'Then why?' Shona asked painfully.

'He was brought by Mr Hard,' Anna said. 'Maybe someone ought to ask him.'

Shona stiffened visibly but her hands remained quite steady. There was a short silence, then Lena said soberly, 'You never told me that, Snoopy.'

'I didn't know you were acquainted.'

'I'm not, personally.'

Shona said, 'You do get around, don't you?' In profile the pale head looked like a carved cameo. Anna looked at her. She said, 'What do you know about Mr Hard?' Shona didn't answer. Lena sat forward and very gently began to massage the nape of her neck. 'Take it easy, babe,' she said. 'Just take it easy.'

'This could get nasty,' Anna told Shona. 'If you know Mr Hard as well as Ferdo . . .'

'Did the police come?' Lena asked quickly.

'No, but I had to give my name to the ambulance crew. Now Ferdo's dead, someone may start asking questions.'

'Don't tell anyone anything,' Shona said. They had

been idling along at about twenty miles an hour. Now she put her foot down and the car shot forward throwing Lena back against the rear seat. 'I don't know any of these people, right?'

They were coming into London. Shona weaved recklessly in and out of the traffic.

'Slow down!' Anna yelled. 'You'll kill someone.'

Shona swung out past a post office van into the path of a Mini coming the other way. The Mini mounted the pavement. Anna hung on to the door handle. 'If you get hit,' she shouted, 'I won't be able to do a damn thing to help you.'

Shona tucked the BMW neatly behind another truck and slowed down. 'I'm not asking for help,' she said tightly. 'I'm asking for silence.'

'Same bloody thing.' Anna let go of the door handle.

'Scared?' Lena asked sweetly.

'I'll pay you,' Shona said.

'You're already paying me. Don't be so wet.'

Lena laughed. 'What d'you make a month, Snoops? Don't you want a little extra the taxman never hears about?'

Anna turned to look at Lena. 'If you don't put a sock in it, I'll put a boot in it for you.'

Lena said, 'Bad move, Sho. You shouldn't offer to pay them. They like to think they're being of service. Money spoils it for them. Makes 'em think they're just like everyone else.'

Anna clamped her mouth shut. If she hadn't, she was afraid she might begin to gnaw the dashboard. Shona looked straight ahead and drove. After a while Lena began to stroke her neck again.

Chapter 39

Sometime in the night two notes had been slipped under the door. The first one said, 'Dear Anna, The receiver will accept £500. Shall I haggle further? Love, B.' The second said simply, 'Raffles' in red ink. Anna grinned and smoothed both notes out on the kitchen table. The percolator bubbled and she turned it off. A stain of weak sunshine spread over the floor.

The doorbell rang. She went downstairs and let Bernie and Johnny in. Bernie blew on his hands for warmth. They were both wearing sheepskin coats.

'Bit taters out there,' Johnny said. 'Got the kettle on?'

Selwyn opened his door a crack and waggled his eyebrows dramatically. Anna went over to him. 'Raffles,' she whispered, nodding to the two men going upstairs. 'Listen, Selwyn, keep your head down till I tell you. You don't know anything, you don't say anything. Know what I mean?'

'Why?' he asked, crestfallen.

'Whose name's on the dust jacket, fathead?' she said, grinning demonically. 'Who will they question first if the whatsit hits the fan?'

'Right you are,' Selwyn said, and vanished behind his door.

Anna ran up to the kitchen and poured the coffee. The men had taken their coats off and were sitting by the fire. She distributed mugs one-handed.

'Anything broken?' Bernie asked. His eyes were on the sling she was wearing. 'Did you get it X-rayed?'

Anna nodded. 'Last night,' she said. 'Just a bit of torn muscle, but I'm not supposed to use it for a while.'

'So sit,' Johnny suggested, 'and listen to what the Old Fart's done now.'

'What?'

'He's only pinched your Horowitz account from under J.W.'s noses!'

'You're kidding,' Anna said, horrified. 'We can't manage that sort of cover.'

Bernie sipped his coffee placidly and said, 'He's exaggerating. J.W. are still doing the tour. But we've got the dainty work.'

'The Old Boy thinks there might be a quid or two in this celebrity escort caper,' Johnny told her. 'Apparently Colonel Beamish is hopping mad, because Mr B convinced Horowitz that J.W. just didn't have the subtlety for a case like this, ho-ho-ho. So you're back under the Brierly umbrella and we've all been hauled off the debt-tracer stuff for the duration.'

'Over-reacting a touch, isn't he?'

'Oh yes,' Bernie agreed. 'But you know what it is, don't you?'

'What?'

'He thinks he's going up-market, doesn't he? Expanding the premises, taking on new staff. He was thrilled to bits when J.W. wanted you.'

Johnny nodded. 'I bet he had it in mind to pinch the client all along. He's a devious old bastard.'

'Well,' Anna said. 'That's one way of expanding. I wouldn't put it past him.'

'Be that as it may,' Bernie said with his kindly, cynical smile, 'he's put all his eggs in one basket now. We've got Tim and Phil outside the house on Addison Road. The whole damn office is on standby.'

He drained his mug and set it carefully on the tray. 'Let's get a few things sorted. Someone's got the screws on Shona Una and you reckon it's got something to do with this Mr Hard, with Marlene Pecci as the likely messenger. And the last delivery was yesterday.'

'Yes,' Anna said. 'But Van Vritski and Porky Wall might be delivering too.'

'So we'll see who comes and goes.'

'Phil's had his car phone installed,' Johnny put in with a touch of envy. 'Mind if I give him a ring? See if it's working?'

'It's working,' Bernie said. 'He didn't get it from you.'

The corner of his mouth twitched. 'Next. We have an inquiry in the pipeline about that club, Dockers, and the cocaine bust. A little background could be handy.'

'Good,' said Anna. 'If Ferdo had something on Shona too it must have been from around the time In Hock were playing Dockers. I wish I knew where he went after the clinic and where the money came from. Did he get enough smack from Mr Hard to blow himself up? Or did someone give him too much to shut him up?'

'It's a pity you didn't see the man yourself,' Bernie said. 'Or his motor.'

'Or the motor that knocked me down. That could've been where Shona's money went to, via Lena. The timing was just about right.'

'Don't say that,' Johnny said. 'You aren't that big a klutz. Or maybe you are. You've been sitting right next to Shona Una for days and you can't get a thing out of her.'

'You try it,' Anna said, annoyed. 'Be my guest. It's like being on a bleeding seesaw, what with her nerves, her drugs, and her sodding street cred. To say nothing of all the prats she's got living in. Whatever's going on she wants to handle it herself and she's making a fine old mess of it.'

'So all right,' Bernie said soothingly. 'Any more coffee in the pot? Johnny, you pour, will you?'

Johnny picked up the percolator and gave each of them half a cup more. 'All the same,' he grumbled, 'she's let two dim girls give her the shaft.'

'So they aren't that dim.' Bernie put milk and sugar in his coffee and leaned back. 'Tell us about the household, love. We ought to have more details.'

Bernie and Johnny had copies of the J.W. tour file, and while Anna talked they both made notes. The weak sunshine faded to cold grey again and the gas fire bubbled rosily. It was a good day to be indoors.

'You know what?' Anna said when she had finished giving the men the facts they needed. 'There's one thing I keep thinking about. When I told Shona and Lena that Ferdo had been seen with Mr Hard they both seemed very surprised – as far as you can tell with them. Why should anyone be surprised about a hop-head being seen with a dealer?'

Johnny stretched his legs out in front of him and snapped his ballpoint pen. 'Maybe because he was *their* dealer. They didn't think Howe knew him.'

'They're a stony-faced pair,' Anna said, shaking her head. 'They wouldn't react to anything so trivial. Shona showed some emotion when her cat died, but she soon had that under control. Her favourite reaction's no reaction.'

'Is it?' Bernie asked. 'I thought you said she was a mess the next day.'

'That was her sleepy-time cocktail,' she said. 'Oh, I see what you mean.' The phone rang and she got up to answer it.

Phil Maitland said, 'That you, young Anna? Bernie there? Tell him a black cab just pulled up at the door, no passenger on board.'

'Well, let's see who comes out.'

Phil said, 'Let me speak to Bernie.'

She held the phone out to Bernie and he heaved himself out of his armchair to take it. He listened for a minute, then said, 'Yes. I know it's expensive. We'll both log the call, all right? Then Beryl won't be able to query it.' He raised his eyebrows at Anna. 'Yes. Okay. Now talk to Anna. She knows all the starters in this race.' He handed the receiver back to her.

Phil said, 'The meter's ticking away and I don't mean just the cab's.'

'Money no object,' she said airily. 'You're dealing with rock stars now, pal.'

'He's worried about his phone bill,' Bernie said with a laugh. he strolled into the kitchen and filled the kettle.

'Hang on,' Phil said. 'Door opening. Female, I think, Knee-high to a piss-pot. Gordon Bennett! You should see what she's got on!'

'That's Marlene Pecci,' Anna told him. 'Get after her, Rover.'

'Is that what Bernie says?'

'That's what I say.' She hung up. Bernie came out of the kitchen, looked at his watch, and made a note in his notebook.

Johnny got up. 'I'd better get over there and give Tim some backup. I wish we all had car phones. By the time I find a call-box working I might as well come back here and report in person.' He pulled on his sheepskin coat and went to the door. 'J.W. well-equipped, eh?' he asked as he went out. 'Must be all right working for them.'

The door closed. Anna went to the kitchen and watched Bernie make the tea. He said, 'Phil says a black woman opened the door to the cab driver. I wish we knew how many are in there.'

Anna went back to the Phone and dialled the Addison Road number. She cradled the phone against her cheek and held a finger over the button ready to disconnect if the wrong person answered, but after a couple of rings she heard Marilyn's musical voice say hello and repeat the number. Anna said, 'Hi Marilyn, it's Anna, the plumber's mate. How're you?'

'Hello there.' Marilyn sounded friendly but a little flustered. 'What can I do for you?'

'Is Lena there?' Bernie came out of the kitchen and stood in the doorway listening.

Marilyn said, 'You just missed her, and Miss Una's still asleep.'

'Anyone else I can talk to?' Anna asked.

'Just the thin one but he's in bed too. Shall I wake him?'

'Don't bother,' Anna said. 'He's got a hangover and he's no use to man or beast anyway.'

'Uh-huh,' Marilyn agreed. 'Someone was sick in the kitchen last night. I think it was him.'

'Poor you,' Anna said sympathetically. 'Listen, I won't be over today and I'm a bit worried about Miss Una. Do you think you could ring me later on? Let me know if she's all right?'

'I don't know 'bout that.' Marilyn sounded doubtful. 'Mrs Blakemore don't like me to use the phone.'

'Don't worry,' Anna said. 'Miss Una's manager will pay all the bills. But don't do anything if it bothers you.'

'Well, maybe I'll call when everyone's gone,' Marilyn suggested. 'You got a number?'

Anna gave it to her, thanked her, and rang off. 'Just Shona and Porky Wall,' she told Bernie. 'Marilyn cleans for the woman who owns the flat. She's okay.'

He poured thick black tea into two mugs. They sat down in chairs opposite each other and sipped in silence. Outside the wind shook the windowpanes. Bernie crossed his ankles and folded his arms. His eyes were half-closed and sleepy and he had the look of a bronze Buddha. There was something entirely trustworthy, Anna thought, about a man with a big nose and big feet. Downstairs she heard the clack of Selwyn's typewriter start up.

The phone rang. When she answered it a man's voice said, 'Mr Schiller, please.' She stretched the cord over to Bernie's chair. It seemed a pity to disturb such a picture of peace. He placed his notebook and pencil on the arm of the chair and took the phone. ''Morning Ted,' he murmured drowsily. 'Nice of you to call back.'

He listened for a while, making small, accurate marks on his pad. 'Yes,' he said at length, 'yes, got that. When?' After a few minutes he said, 'Well, that's grand, Ted, just what I wanted. I owe you a big drink. Yes. Syl was asking after you just the other day. You must come over for a meal. Yes? . . . soon.' He winked at Anna and hung up.

'Syl won't be too pleased,' he said. 'The old goat always tries on a cuddle in the kitchen when my back's turned.' He flipped back a couple of pages in his book and read through what he'd written. Anna waited expectantly.

'Yes. Ted,' he said eventually. 'Did a long stint at Market Square nick. Knows Dockers Club well, as does every copper in that neck of the woods. Over the years it's been done for, well, you name it, infringement of licensing laws, gaming, drugs, prostitution. Customs and Excise has had a go too. Once even – ' he grimaced – 'they were closed down for cock-fighting. Oh, and the building's listed to come down along with the rest of the street. It should've been condemned years ago but Ted reckons the owner's got a mate on the council.'

'I was warned it was for the rough trade,' Anna said. 'Who's behind it?'

'Property dealer called Witherspoon.' Bernie read from his notes.

'Oh yeah?'

Bernie smiled sleepily. 'Of course,' he said, 'he has to be straight because of the license. But behind him are two lovely fellows, the Brothers Grimm, you might say. Ever heard of Jack and Patsy Handle?'

'The Handle Vandals,' Anna said. 'The stars of a hundred, headlines after the Solomon Street hoist.'

'Them,' Bernie said. 'They're still inside, of course, and meanwhile their interest is being looked after by a cousin, Charley Handle and various managers. Well, that's Dockers Club. Get the picture?'

'You won't be sending me in on my own, then?' she said with a grin.

'Not on your nelly,' Bernie said wryly. 'Although funnily enough, a sprinkling of quite nice people go there on occasion. The place is so rough that it has something of a reputation among idiots like entertainers and sports people who pop in for a little real life.'

'Brushing up on *their* street cred,' Anna suggested. 'It's amazing how many people find villains exciting.'

'Well, never mind them,' Bernie went on. 'It's four and a half years ago we're interested in.' He looked down at his notes again. 'Acting on information received, a team from Market Square plus a couple from Drugs Squad paid a visit to Dockers. It was late afternoon. The club was closed. But they found some members of the resident rock band supposedly rehearsing. In their possession was a quantity of cocaine which they were packaging for sale on the street.

'Caught actually handling the drugs were Ferdinand Howe, Ronald Green, and William Graef. Hilary Simpson walked in while the raid was in progress and was hauled in with the rest of them. That's Shona Una, I presume?' Bernie looked up.

'Yes,' Anna said. 'What about Wes Gardner?'

'His name never came up,' Bernie told her. 'But wait for the good bit. Information received, remember? The informant was Hilary Simpson.'

'I don't believe it!' Anna said, getting quickly to her feet. She crossed to the window and looked out. Down below a cyclist pedalled doggedly by. The tips of his ears showed purple with cold. She felt deceived.

'It's on record,' Bernie said. 'She phoned in and gave her name.'

The phone rang and Anna jumped. She picked up the

receiver and a strange woman said, 'Is that Miss Lee? I've got Miss Doyle for Mr Schiller.'

Anna sighed and passed the receiver to Bernie. He said, 'Yes? Hello, Beryl. Coming up in the world, aren't you? Yes? Okay. Thank you,' and put the phone down. 'Got some poor girl acting as her personal secretary now,' he said. 'Anyway she's heard from Criminal Records. There's no such animal as Mr Hard on their files.'

Chapter 40

Anna stared at the rug. It had a soothing design of ochre, green, and a quiet autumn red on a cream background. Bernie's big shoes rested squarely at one end. They almost covered the faint mark where Selwyn had spilled his beer nearly a year ago. She said, 'That's really hard to believe. She shopped her own band and walked in on the bust. Why? To make it look good?'

'Apparently she denied ever making the phone call,' Bernie said. 'But look at the facts. Howe and Graef got two years apiece; Green, ten months. Hilary Simpson wasn't even charged, although some of the stuff was found in her makeup case.

'All the same,' Anna said softly, and then couldn't think of what to say next. In her mind she saw Shona, her sleek furry head in profile, the short straight nose, strong dancer's throat, long full eyelids; and superimposed on top of that the brilliant figure in black and red, everyone's fantasy of a bad girl, shimmying across a stage. All images, all image. Ah well. And she heard Shona's voice say, 'So what?' She couldn't remember if she had actually heard Shona say that, but it seemed as if she'd heard nothing else from her or any of the others; as if none of them gave a damn about anything which didn't affect their personal appetites or ambitions.

'Autism,' she said out loud. Bernie looked up. 'What?' he asked.

'Nothing.'

'You said "autism",' he said. 'You made it sound like a discovery.'

'I'm a bit slow,' she replied. 'I just figured out what was wrong with everyone I've met in the past few days.'

'Hope it's not contagious,' he said, smiling.

Half an hour later Phil turned up. His hat had pressed a ridge into his yellow-grey hair and there was a sprinkling of sleet on his shoulders. He hung his coat up behind the door and came over to warm his back at the fire.

'La Pecci went to an Italian café in Spring Row,' he told them. He put his hands in his pockets and rattled the coins in them. 'She's back at Addison Road now. Johnny got all excited when I told him and he's gone off there now. He said you had the address.' He looked at Anna.

She opened her own notebook and saw that Spring Row was where Odette did business. She showed the page to Bernie and said gloomily, 'That's the last we'll see of him today.'

'Johnny likes a bit of class,' Bernie said doubtfully. 'If they advertise at stations they can't be all that classy.'

'Who did Lena meet?' Anna asked.

'She left the cab waiting outside,' Phil said. 'So I thought it best to stay with that. She was only in the café five minutes and she went straight home after. Who's Odette?'

'Business girl,' Anna said shortly.

'Oh, I see.' He turned to Bernie. 'Johnny said to tell you he was following up some research of his own and he'd be in touch. Ha-ha.'

'You shouldn't leave Tim too long on his own,' Bernie said.

'I was just getting us some Kentucky Fried,' Phil told him. 'It's close so I dropped by for a warm-up.'

Bernie looked at his watch and said, 'I'll come too. I've got to check back at the office.' He put on his sheepskin coat. 'Stick by the phone,' he told Anna. 'And if we should be so lucky that Johnny calls in, remind him he's supposed to go to Norwich this evening. I'll bring us some lunch back. You rest that arm.'

The two men buttoned up their coats and left quietly.

Anna put her feet up on the sofa and gazed at the ceiling. Was that what Ferdo thought would ruin Shona, she wondered, that she had virtually sent three of her friends to prison? Was it enough? It was unpleasant. It would make her victims hate her bitterly. But would it turn her public against her if they knew? She simply didn't know how important the bad girl image was to Shona's fans.

When she examined her own reaction to the news she was surprised at her immediate distaste and sense of betrayal. She had seen enough of drugs to be glad whenever she heard about a raid which stopped some of the stuff reaching the streets. Logically then, she should be glad about what Shona had done. But she wasn't. Street law says you don't shop your mates.

And anyway, why had Shona done it? All the members of a band relied on one another. It was like the problem of the dead cat. Anna had already decided that, although it looked like an inside job, no-one connected with Shona had it in their interest to frighten her. In the same way she could see no reason why it would be to Shona's advantage to destroy the first band that had given her work. It was like sinking the stepping-stone she was standing on.

While she was thinking this, she heard furtive movements behind the door and after a while it opened a crack and revealed Selwyn's tousled head.

'On your own now?' he breathed. 'Can I come in?' He tiptoed across the carpet and sat down on the arm of a chair. 'Bea's just back from Saturday shopping. She's having a lie-down and I don't want her to know I'm up here. What's the plan?'

'A straight hoist,' she whispered.

'When?'

'I don't know yet. It'll need detailed reconnaissance.' She thought for a minute. 'If you want to help, give me a description of the premises, inside and out, and a list of the personnel. I'll have it copied and circulated.'

'Right you are,' he said. 'Perhaps I could cycle over to Camden Lock and refresh my memory.'

'Not on your life,' she said sternly. 'Don't go anywhere near. You aren't associated, remember? Your memory's good enough, isn't it? You're always sounding off about it.'

'Certainly.' He looked uncertain. 'But there's a difference between having a good head for mood or colour and remembering whether you turn right or left when you go through a lobby.'

'Close your eyes,' Anna said bossily, 'and follow your own footsteps. You'll be surprised what's in your mind.'

'You're telling me,' he agreed. 'Okay, then. I've got to get on. I told Bea I was going to the pub.'

'Did she believe you?' Anna asked. Selwyn looked at her suspiciously. Just then, luckily, the doorbell rang and she put her finger to her lips and hurried down to answer it. Bernie was on the doorstep with a brown paper sack clasped to his chest. Selwyn squeezed past him and whispered, 'Raffles!' as he went by.

'Raffles to you too,' Bernie murmured politely, watching him trip down the step on to the pavement. 'Battier than ever,' he said as Anna closed the door. Upstairs he unpacked thinly sliced salt beef, black olives, tomatoes, and pita bread. Anna filled the kettle and made him laugh by telling him her plans for rescuing Selwyn's books and pride.

'Should be all right,' he said. 'Hope you get your money back, though.'

'Bea's going halves,' she told him, sitting down. 'And she's taking charge of selling the books, so we shouldn't lose too much.'

Bernie filled a pita envelope with salt beef and tomato slices and squeezed some lemon juice into it.

While they were eating Phil called through to describe two arrivals at Addison Road. One was a delivery van from The Hungry Hunter and the other was Craig.

After lunch Bernie went off to find Johnny and organize the trip to Norwich. The wind dropped and the sleet turned to steady rain. Anna took a couple of aspirin and lay down again on the sofa.

At two-thirty Bernie phoned to say that Dave McPhee had turned up and they were getting ready to leave. If Johnny called, she was to tell him he was fired. Anna laughed and settled down again with a book.

It was after eight o'clock when Johnny phoned. He said, 'Pin your ears back, Anna Lee. The tart with no heart, aka Odette, was born Janine Pecci. Like it? Here's another. Her old man is Mickey Stone, aka heart of Stone, aka Mr Hard. Suck on that! I'm outside Odette's flat in Spring Row, and the lady has a visitor. His Datsun's parked on a double yellow. Ask Bernie, should I take the Datsun?'

'He's in Norwich,' Anna said flatly.

'Farkin' Ada!' Johnny said. 'Bolloxed that, didn't I?'

'Call Phil,' Anna suggested. 'He's with Bernie.'

'*Double* yellow,' Johnny said. 'No time for that. I'll take the Datsun.'

Anna's heart gave a quick thud. She said, 'Wait for me. I'll be there in ten minutes.'

'If he goes, I'm off too,' Johnny warned. He rang off.

Chapter 4I

Rain rustled in the gutters and gurgled down drains. Only two of the shops on Spring Row were lit up. One was an Indian general store which was open. The other was an Islamic bookshop which wasn't. The pavement streamed and light bounced off its mirrored surface in a yellow glare. A couple hurried by, sharing an umbrella.

It was a narrow street which those in the know used as a short cut between two main roads. The blue Datsun stood with two wheels on the pavement, its running lights glowing. Anna paid off the taxi. She found Johnny's Cortina tucked into a service entrance, lights off, motor purring softly. Johnny leaned over and flicked the catch on the passenger door. She got in.

She could smell the damp on his sheepskin coat. His face was just a pale blur. He said, 'Silly twat'll have a flat battery if he leaves it much longer.' He looked intently forward. The Datsun's running lights shone weakly, smudged by rain.

'Where's the flat?' Anna asked.

'Two doors down from the bookshop,' he told her, without taking his eyes from the Datsun. 'Third floor.' He stirred impatiently. There was a sheen of nervous sweat on his forehead. 'Come on, come on, let's be having you,' he muttered under his breath. Rain gathered on the windscreen and he snapped the wipers on for a couple of strokes to clear his vision.

Light flooded the pavement as a door opened. 'Hey up,' Johnny said. 'Chummy.'

The door closed. Two figures, one in a leopardskin coat, ran to the car. The man got in and the woman went round to the other side. He ran his motor and switched on the headlights before letting her in. The car moved off. It turned left at the end of the road. As it turned, Johnny flicked on his lights and pulled out after it. He turned left too and settled into the traffic several cars behind.

Anna picked out the swept-back antenna and kept her eyes on that. She gripped the door handle and felt sweat on her hand. After a few blocks the Datsun turned left again into a one-way street, and then left again into a mews.

'Cul-de-sac,' Anna said. Johnny overshot the mews and slipped into a parking space a couple of hundred yards from the corner. He cut his lights and left the engine running.

'Go and look,' he ordered. 'Hurry.'

Anna got out and ran to the corner. Her bandaged left arm banged awkwardly against her chest. She looked carefully down the mews. The Datsun's interior light was on and two women were climbing into the back. She went quickly back to Johnny. 'They'll be with us in two ticks,' she said as she got in. She buckled the seat-belt and waited. 'He's picked up two more women.'

Johnny's chin tilted up as he watched the mirror. A few minutes later the Datsun cruised by.

The first ten minutes were the most difficult. The Datsun made several apparently random turns. But then it became clear they were filtering through the one-way system to join Marylebone road, heading east. As soon as he knew it was not a local trip and they were staying on the main road for a while, Johnny settled down and relaxed a little.

'So,' he said happily, 'Chummy's got three of them in the same area. The dirty bugger!'

Rain drummed on the roof. Saturday-night traffic clogged and loosened and then clogged again. The Datsun in front kept going stubbornly eastwards: Euston Road, Pentonville Road, then south-east at the Angel.

At Spitalfields Anna said, 'He's going to Limehouse. He's got to be going to Limehouse.'

'Don't guess,' Johnny said.

A little later the Datsun turned left on to Commercial Road. Johnny speeded up to the corner. He missed the lights. Anna strained her neck to see what was happening. Johnny banged the wheel. The lights changed. He let the clutch out and sped down Commercial Road. No Datsun.

Anna kept looking to her right, down intersections that permitted a right-hand turn. Johnny looked everywhere. No Datsun. The Commercial Road became East India Dock Road. Still no Datsun.

'Too bloody far,' Anna muttered. Her fingers were slippery on the door handle.

'Shut up,' said Johnny. But a moment later he swung the car in a U-turn, and raced back west.

'Lost him, lost him,' Johnny repeated under his breath. 'Sod it! Lost him!' He banged the wheel again. Then he said, 'Limehouse, you reckon?'

'Narrow Road.'

'I'm not a bleeding taxi-driver!' he said furiously. 'Where is it?'

'Left,' Anna said. 'Hanger left.'

They drove through wet dark streets. Anna directed him as best she could. She missed the turning once, and they entered Narrow Road from the east end.

The building was lit up with coloured bulbs and the neon sign blinked DO KERS LUB into the rain. A small crowd of people had gathered under the sleazy awning. Umbrellas were being shaken. Cars jammed both sides of the road. Johnny drove slowly past.

'No bleeding Chummy,' he said, swivelling his head right and left.

Anna caught sight of a leopardskin coat. 'That's it!' she exclaimed. She craned over her shoulder and saw two more. She didn't mention them. Johnny turned at the next block.

'Shit!' he shouted. He stamped on the brake. 'Look at that.'

A broken sign hung crazily from a wire-netted gate. It said HANDLE CAR HIRE. USED VEHICLES – EASY TERMS. In the car park stood half a dozen blue Datsuns. The bonnet of one of them was steaming gently. Anna started to laugh.

Chapter 42

Johnny made a three-point turn and stopped the car on the corner. He switched off. 'Sod, sod, sod,' he said and knocked his forehead on the steering-column.

'No, really,' Anna protested, 'you did brilliant.' She was still laughing.

'Forget it,' he said morosely. 'And shut up laughing.' They sat in silence for a couple of minutes. Then Johnny said cheerfully, 'Well, it wasn't *that* bad.' After a few more minutes he said, 'Well, come on, then. Let's go in.'

'Hold on,' Anna said. 'That's Jack and Patsy Handle's little pied-à-terre. Heard of them?'

'Yeah?' He suddenly looked respectful. 'Let's go and see.'

'Hang about,' she said. 'It's a really rough dump. We can't just waltz in.'

'Why not?'

'Well, Bernie says it's too damned dangerous,' Anna told him. 'The Handles had an organization.'

'The Handles're banged up,' Johnny retorted. 'Bernie's a good chap but he's too fussy. Wait not, want not, I say.'

'And besides,' she went on, 'look at me. I'm not dressed for Saturday-night clubbing.'

'Oh, Gordon Bennett,' he said impatiently. 'Wait here if you're worried about your bloody frock.' He opened his door and got out. He took off his coat and threw it in the back. Under it he wore a respectable three-piece suit.

'This is a really bad idea,' Anna said. She pulled the sling over her head and jammed it in the glove compartment. She combed and fluffed up her hair. Johnny went round to the boot for an umbrella. He came to her side and opened her door. She hesitated and then got out.

'All right, all right,' he said, before she had a chance to speak. 'If anything goes wrong it's my fault. Satisfied?'

'This is stupid.'

He took her arm and marched her to the corner, saying, 'Well, you don't have to bloody come. You can stop in the motor if you want.' They walked to the club. A poster, tacked to a board said, ENTERTAINMENT! THE BED-DOE FOUR! DISCO! DANCING! GITA – EXOTIC ARTISTE!

'Jesus,' Anna whispered. 'An effing stripper.'

'Great,' he said and pushed the door open. They went in.

Anna stood in the lobby and waited while Johnny negotiated temporary membership. Two bouncers in dinner jackets checked cards and admitted snappily suited men and some women. There weren't many women, and those few tended to wear low-cut or backless dresses with nipped-in waists and wide shiny belts. There were a lot of very high heels and lamé bodice. It was her fate, she thought, to be so often found wanting in matters of dress.

'Come on,' Johnny said. One of the bouncers looked casually at his membership card and not so casually at his suit.

'You ain't been here before,' he said softly, 'so I'll tell you. We don't want no trouble, so if you're carrying anything, know what I mean, leave it with me or my mate here.'

'What *does* he mean, darling?' Anna asked, hanging back. 'Are you sure you want to go in?'

'In this way,' the bouncer said. 'Out that way. Makes no odds to me.'

'You'll love it, sweetie,' Johnny said. 'At least it'll be a change from the Barbican.' He took her arm again.

They followed a party of three men down some carpeted steps and into a large dark room. A tiny dance floor was surrounded by tables. To the left was the small stage she had seen in Ferdo's picture. To the right an enormous bar stretched the full width of the room. The tables closest to the stage and dance floor were all taken. But the real crowd was by the bar. Hostesses sat on stools or squeezed, with trays of drinks, between the men. Their skin glowed rosy in the dim red light.

Anna nudged Johnny and they went to sit at a table in a shadowy corner. A hostess in tight black slacks and a strapless top came and took their orders, beer for Johnny, vodka and tonic for Anna. She turned her attention to the Beddoe Four who were whaling the hell out of *Satisfaction*. The bass player was supposed to be controlling the coloured lights with a foot switch, but he kept missing the beat so the effect was haphazard. The music was careless too, but the Four crashed through the number and sweated profusely into their studded leather.

Not that it mattered. People shouted to each other across the space between tables, bought each other drinks, goosed the hostesses. There were better things to do than listen to a stoned, underrehearsed band.

Johnny moved his arm against her and said, 'Over there.' A group of men were coming through a pair of swing doors at the far side of the room. From their clothes they might have been taken for businessmen, but the evidence of a childhood in the street was on their faces – a missing tooth, a broken nose, a scarred eyebrow.

'One of them must be Charlie Handle,' Johnny said. But neither of them knew which. The men leaned against the bar and one of the barmen opened a bottle of champagne.

'The one on the left is Mickey Stone,' Johnny said. 'I mean, I think he is. He wore a leather coat at Spring Row.'

'Where's Odette?' Anna asked.

'Can't see her.'

The group of men broke up and began to circulate, greeting people, being greeted. The Beddoe Four began a massacre of *Brown Sugar*, and the bare-shouldered hostess arrived with their drinks. Johnny took his beer, but Anna's glass contained something cloudy with impaled cherries and pineapple chunks, and a pink and white striped straw in it.

'What's that?' Johnny asked.

'What did you order?' the hostess countered, bored.

'Vodka and tonic,' Anna said. 'Never mind.'

'You want to change your order?' The hostess asked with a tired sigh.

'Never mind,' Anna said again and took the glass. The hostess swayed wearily away.

'Dump is right,' Johnny said disgustedly. The swing doors at the other side of the room opened again and six or seven brightly dressed women came through.

'Odette!' Johnny said. She wore a scarlet dress, and her golden curls danced round her ears. The mass of smart dark suits at the bar opened for them, and one by one the colourful women were swallowed into the crowd.

'Well, well,' Johnny said with enthusiasm. 'They could do business till their eyes popped – given the proper facilities.'

'There probably are,' Anna said sourly.

'Almost certainly.' He smoothed his crinkly hair and ran a finger over his moustache. 'I think I'll change that bloody drink for you.' He got up.

'Be lucky,' she said even more sourly. He picked up her cocktail and made for the bar. Anna found a couple of aspirin in her bag and took them with what was left of his beer. She leaned back against the wall and waited for them to work. The Beddoe Four filled the club with a horrible approximation of *Behind the Lines*.

Fortunately that was the end of the set. A man in a midnight-blue dinner jacket got up on the stage and announced the DJ of the night. The baby spots switched on to the turntable and an elderly rocker introduced the first record. A few couples got up to dance.

The Beddoe Four unplugged their instruments and stumbled offstage. They joined their friends at a table near the door. The singer reached for a pint glass and, throwing his head back, poured the contents down his throat. His girlfriend timidly pushed another in his direction.

Anna looked over towards the bar. Johnny had disappeared. She got up and walked over to the band's table. 'Nice set,' she said when she got there. They stared at her, glasses arrested in midair. They were deservedly unused to compliments.

'Can I buy you all a drink?' she went on vivaciously.

'Pull up a chair,' the singer said. He tipped his own chair back and beckoned to a waitress. Anna sat down.

'Beer all round,' the singer said expansively when the waitress came. Anna handed over the money.

'How long've you been here?' she asked.

'Just the week,' the singer said. He ran a hand over his shaved head and eyed her speculatively. 'We close tonight.'

'That's a shame,' Anna said. 'I'd liked to've heard more. Got anything else lined up?'

'Pub in Hackney,' he told her. 'Starting Wednesday night. You want the address?'

Anna nodded. The singer's girlfriend produced an envelope and a ballpoint, and he wrote 'Prince of Wales, Fletching Lane,' in laborious capital letters.

'Thanks,' Anna said, accepting the envelope. 'Who does the booking here?'

'You want to talk to Mr Graef?' the singer asked hopefully.

'Who?' She thought she had misheard.

'Mr Graef,' he repeated. The waitress came back with a trayful of beer. Anna got up. The singer said, 'Put in a word for us, will you? We don't mind where we play.'

Johnny was not back at the table, and she couldn't see him at the bar. She waylaid one of the hostesses and asked where she might find Mr Graef.

'Dunno,' the hostess said. She examined her nailpolish and looked depressed. 'Should be around somewhere. He introduces all the acts.'

Anna moved off, looking for the man in the midnight-blue dinner jacket. He was standing near the stage talking to some customers. He leaned down, his big hands on another man's shoulders. He was stout, with a loose-lipped, genial face, and sandy-grey hair brushed straight back from his forehead. Anna waited in the shadows for him to finish talking. She kept her eyes open for Johnny while she waited, but there was no sign of him. She felt a little short of breath and vaguely uneasy.

Mr Graef moved away from the table. Anna swallowed and stepped forward. She said, 'Mr Graef? I was told to see you about bookings.'

'Not now,' he said, frowning. And then, 'Oh well, why not? It's a slow night.'

They were interrupted by the DJ letting loose a stream of patter in a bad American accent. The record he introduced was *Bitterness*. Anna started and said quickly, 'Sorry. I didn't hear what you said.'

'I said, have you got an act?' he shouted close to her ear. He didn't look so genial now. 'Come up to my office. I can't hear myself think.' He walked bad-temperedly towards the swing doors. Anna followed. She felt thoroughly unsettled and looked vainly around for Johnny.

Mr Graef pushed through the doors on to a concrete passage, and up a flight of stairs. The doors swung shut and cut off the insistent strains of *Bitterness*. Anna was relieved. It was the sort of coincidence that made her neck prickle. She wished she had waited for Johnny. She wished she had thought more carefully about accosting Mr Graef.

Ahead of her, his solid back moved steadily upwards. At the top of the stairs was another passage. This one had a crimson carpet and green flocked wallpaper. Several doors led off it. As they passed, one of the doors opened and Odette came out followed by a man. The man was Johnny.

Odette said, ''Evening, Mr Graef.'

Johnny's mouth dropped open. Anna gazed blankly at him and caught up with Mr Graef. He grunted something to Odette and continued up the corridor. At the end of it he opened a door.

Chapter 43

It was a medium-sized office that smelled of mushrooms. River damp had seeped through the windows and bubbled the paint. The ceiling was murky with cigarette smoke. A new, impressive desk with an IBM typewriter perched on it like an ornament made the place seem even more dilapidated.

Mr Graef sat behind his desk and crossed his legs. His meaty thighs strained at the fabric of his trousers. He leaned forward with his elbows on the blotter and said, 'Right, then, what's this act you're touting?'

'A trio,' Anna said. 'Female vocalist. But maybe this is the wrong venue. They're not at all like the band you've got downstairs.'

'No harm in that,' he said, winking broadly. 'They need more experience.'

'Yes.' Anna nodded respectfully. 'That's a bit like the situation we're in.'

'So what experience have you had?' He looked her over, eyes narrowed, like a good judge of horseflesh. He did not seem to be impressed.

Anna laughed nervously. 'Oh, I'm not a performer,' she said. 'No, they're friends of mine. They call themselves Smooth Talk and they're very versatile. Especially the vocalist.'

'What's she like?'

'Well, she's tall and dark. She projects very sophisticated.' Anna began to warm to her creation. 'Voice like warm honey. What she likes best is the romantic ballad, but she can really belt them out too.'

'She's not black, is she?' he interrupted. 'We don't have no blacks acts here. The punters wouldn't wear it.'

'Oh, er – no,' Anna said, hurriedly changing horses in

midstream. 'Look, maybe I'm wasting your time. I'm just trying all the live music venues in the area.'

'You represent them, eh?'

'On an informal basis,' Anna said. 'As you can see, I'm not very good at it. I'm hoping that as they gain experience someone a bit better than me will take over. I've got them some student union gigs, and they went down very well there. In fact they've been asked back. Oh, and someone with a chain of restaurants . . .'

'Look,' he interrupted again, 'never mind all that. You couldn't sell a white stick to a blind man, if you don't mind me saying so, but I can see you believe in your friends. Me, I can't tell without hearing 'em. You haven't got a demo, have you? No, you wouldn't have.' He rolled his eyes up to the dirty ceiling. 'So, tell you what I'll do, seeing as you don't know the business, I'll give them a try-out. You give me a bell Monday morning and we'll fix up an audition.'

'Well, hey, that's awfully kind of you,' Anna said, going limp with gratitude. 'You won't regret it.'

'And another thing,' he said casually, 'I'm not just Entertainment Manager here. I also represent Handle Enterprises. So if, whatsit, Smooth Talk is as good as you say, we might be able to give them a bit of a push, know what I mean?'

'Really?' Anna said, genuinely interested. 'How's that?'

'No promises, mind,' he went on, 'but now and then we come across an act with talent and we don't mind helping, see. Find 'em a little work, better equipment, that sort of thing. Do they write any of their own material?'

'Yes.'

'Well, I don't suppose you know much about music publishing, do you?' He arched his sandy eyebrows and looked wise. Anna dutifully shook her head.

'You see, the music business is a bleeding minefield,' he said. 'Your heart's in the right place, I can see that. But you don't have the know-how. I'm telling you this as a favour because I can see you're a serious girl. You wouldn't believe in your friends if they was rubbish. But if they're really talented they're going to want more help than you can give. No disrespect, mind.'

'None taken,' she said, doing her utmost to look like a serious girl. 'It'd be a weight off my mind if I could get them decent representation. The thing is, though, they're young, not very worldly. So if Handle Enterprises was interested, I'd like to think there'd be some safeguards. Would there be a proper contract?'

'Plenty of time for that,' he said. 'I don't know as I'm interested yet. But if I was – if – then I'd see if I could get them some work, and *if* I could, that'd be the time to sign them up. That's fair enough, ennit?'

'Very.' Anna looked impressed. 'Is there any chance I could see a sample contract?'

'Not so green as you're cabbage-looking.' He laughed. 'Let's look at the goods first, eh? I'm not a bad judge, though I says it myself as shouldn't. Naming no names, but one of my finds is in the charts as we speak.'

'Really! Who?'

He scowled. 'I said, "naming no names". But I can tell you I've got a nice little network of . . . what's that?' He cocked his head, still scowling. The sound of running feet pounded up the corridor. He got up. The phone on his desk jangled. He picked up the receiver. 'What?' he said abruptly. 'No tip-off? Farkinell!' He threw the receiver down, bent, and opened a drawer under his desk.

'Hop it!' he said to Anna without looking up. 'There's trouble downstairs.' He scrabbled in the drawer and came up with an orange folder. His face was flushed with rage. He came round the desk fast, and grabbed her arm.

'I said, hop it! The filth're downstairs.' He dragged her into the corridor and slammed the door. Then he ran, the orange folder clamped under one arm, and disappeared into another doorway. Doors banged. A man and a girl emerged from another room. The girl sprinted for the stairs. The man hopped on one foot while he put his shoe on.

Anna quietly re-opened Mr Graef's door and slipped back into his office. She started with the drawer he had taken the orange file from. It was empty. In the next drawer up she found some printed sheets headed MANAGEMENT AGREEMENT. She took one. Notepaper with HANDLE EN-TERPRISES on it was in the middle drawer. She switched on the typewriter and tapped out, "If you ignore this or think we're kidding . . . . Honour your contract." She ripped it out of the machine, folded it, and tucked it, with the Agreement, into her bag.

More feet sounded in the corridor. She waited, tense, but they went by. She looked round. There were three filing cabinets. She pulled one open and saw row upon row of files. She started with I, In Hock. Nothing. Then H for Howe and Hock. Then S for Simpson and Shona Una. Nothing.

There was silence in the corridor now. She shut all the drawers she had opened and switched off the light. For a couple of seconds she stood still and listened. Then she went out. She walked quickly to the top of the stairs. There was pandemonium at the bottom. She went back to where Mr Graef had disappeared.

The room was in darkness but an icy breeze told her the window was open. She went to it and looked out. An iron fire escape went down three floors to the ground. At the bottom torch beams waved like fireflies.

Chapter 44

She climbed out of the window and went up the fire escape to the roof. Rain teemed down. At the top was a narrow walkway between the slates and the parapet. She edged along it. Below, the police called to each other and signalled with their torches.

She got to the corner and looked cautiously over the edge. In the street were three mobiles, blue lights winking, and a police van. Dogs barked.

Rain streamed off her hair and face. She went back the way she had come, along the side of the building, to the back. It was darker here, but watery light reflected off the river.

The walkway was awash with roof water. She trod warily, and suddenly remembered it was a condemned building. She stopped dead. She didn't even know if there was a way off the roof. She assumed there was. Why else would Mr Graef have used the fire escape with the police outside when he could just as easily have met them by using the stairs? And was it really worth breaking her neck to avoid an embarrassing interview with them herself?

She was soaked to the skin and very cold. She turned back.

Just as she reached the top of the fire escape she heard someone panting. A head came up over the edge of the parapet. The mouth gaped for air and wheezed, 'Give us a hand for chrissake.' A bare, fat arm waved helplessly. Anna held out her hand. It was grasped eagerly and an enormous woman in a sopping nightgown hauled herself up and on to the walkway. She sat on the parapet and clutched her heart, gasping for breath. Wet hair streamed down her back. Mascara coursed down her face.

She heaved herself to her feet and said, 'Come on. Bill ain't far behind.' She proceeded crabwise. Anna followed. Any surface which could support this woman would be strong enough for her.

They inched along the Thames side of the roof and round the corner. The woman whispered, 'There's a catwalk somewhere.' She felt around in the dark.

Anna rested against the slates and watched the shadowy blob as it groped along. Then the big woman sighed and said, 'Here we are.'

Anna moved closer and peered into the dark. About five yards away was another building. The catwalk was a narrow metal bridge with a single handrail. Below that was too dark to see.

'What's over there?' Anna asked. Her mouth was dry. The catwalk looked very frail.

'Ain't you been this way before?' said the big woman. 'Empty warehouse, ducks. Through that, down some stairs, and we're out. Piece of cake.'

'Well, good,' Anna cleared her throat. 'Lead on.' The last thing she wanted to do was share a narrow strand of metal with such a heavy woman.

The woman caught hold of the handrail. 'Give us a bunkup,' she said. Anna applied all her strength and the woman hoisted herself up. 'Bugger this for a game of tin soldiers,' she gasped. 'I'm too old for this lark. Still, never say die.' It looked as if she was stepping into thin air. The metal groaned and shuddered. Anna climbed on to the parapet. She had no idea what she could do if the catwalk gave way. She could do nothing but bite her lip and watch. Wind caught the sodden nightgown and it billowed like a sheet on a line. The huge dim shape seemed suspended in space. Gradually it disappeared into the dark. The handrail gave a final heave. Then there was silence.

'Are you okay?' Anna called softly.

'Piece of cake,' came floating back across the gulf.

Anna took a deep breath and took her shoes off. She slipped them in her pockets and grasped the handrail firmly. It was not as hard as it looked. She had used up most of her anxiety on the big woman and now that it was her turn she crossed over quite quickly. On the other side she paused to wipe the rain out of her eyes.

She was standing on a wooden gallery that ran round what seemed to be the shell of a warehouse. And, floating away from her along the gallery, was the vast ghost-like figure.

When Anna caught up the woman said, 'You're not one of Mickey's girls, are you?'

'Who's Mickey?'

'Thought not. What were you doing on the bleedin' roof, then?'

'I was talking to Mr Graef about a band. When the Bill came he ran and I followed.'

'Not your lucky night, eh?' The big woman chuckled. They padded along almost silently. Anna had not put her shoes back on, and the big woman had been barefoot to start with.

At the end of the gallery was a rough hole in the wall. They squeezed through into a loft on the other side. Across that a crumbling door frame led on to a flight of stairs that twisted down four storeys before reaching the ground. Just before they reached the bottom the big woman stopped. She was breathing hard, but she held her breath a minute, istening. Far away, they heard the yelp of a police siren.

Anna whispered, 'What're you going to do now? You an't go out on the street like that.'

The woman giggled richly. 'Don't worry about me, lucky. Charlie'll send a car. He always does. I'd've been nicked a dozen times if I hadn't a head for heights.' She glided across a debris-strewn floor to a boarded-up door and out her eye to a crack. 'Good old Charlie,' she said, satisfied. 'Never misses, does he?' She heaved with one shoulder and the boards parted before her weight.

Outside a black Mercedes waited, engine humming. She stalked towards it like Boadicea triumphant, and opened the door. 'Need a lift, ducky?' she asked graciously.

'No, thanks all the same,' Anna said.

The big woman swung her huge shapely legs into the car. 'Well, be good,' she said, 'and if you can't be good make sure you've got a strong fire escape.' The door slammed and the Mercedes accelerated away.

Anna stood dumbfounded in the rain and watched it go. Then she stooped and put her shoes on. Her stockings were torn, her clothes drenched, and her shoulder throbbed wickedly. But at least she was fully dressed and did not look as if she had spent the evening at Dockers.

Thankful for the small advantages fate had put her way, she walked to the corner of Narrow Road and looked down it. There was a crowd outside the club. She crossed the road and walked past. Police were now bringing men and women out and ushering them into mobiles and vans. She looked at them with the right amount of curiosity and went on.

At the next corner she found Johnny's Cortina where he had left it. Johnny leaned over and opened the nearside door. He greeted her with a stream of curses only an ex-soldier could string together. He banged the car into gear and shot off, saying furiously, 'Where the fuck've you been, you stupid bloody cretin? Are you out of your poxy mind? I've been doing my nut. Judas sodding Priest! When I saw you up there with that toe-rag Graef I thought you'd been tumbled, you silly, twatty – '

'Tumbled's what you were with Odette,' Anna interrupted sweetly. 'Don't talk to me about tumbled.'

'Don't talk to me about . . . *listen*, you . . . I left you

'. . . we were only . . .' He raged incoherently. 'And look at you, you've ruined my upholstery.'

'Be quiet!' Anna yelled. 'Graef thought I was promoting a band. That's all. I'd've been down in ten minutes if the bloody troops hadn't come.'

'How was I to know that?' Johnny shouted back. 'You moronic harbrained imbecile, how the *hell* was I supposed to know that?'

'Because you're supposed to know I'm not daft!'

'No-one knows that!' he shouted. 'I had to think of some way to get you out.'

'Johnny Crocker! You didn't call the cops!' she cried, quite shocked.

'What else was I supposed to do? My one-man cavalry act?'

'Johnny,' Anna said slowly and clearly, 'if I'd broken my neck . . . if I get pneumonia, it's all your bleeding fault.'

He turned the car into Houndsditch and said, 'I knew you'd say that, I bloody knew it.'

Chapter 45

Her skin glowed from the heat of the bath, and she sat cross-legged before the fire with the Management Agreement on the floor in front of her. Johnny paced restlessly about the room. The atmosphere between them had calmed but he seemed unable to go home to bed.

The agreement was a three-page document. It would be useless to look for the small print. As far as Anna could see it was all small print. She was still too tired and overwrought to study it properly, but already she had gathered that the contract bound whoever signed it to Handle Enterprises "in perpetuity".

Johnny said, 'I don't understand why you didn't simply come downstairs.'

The phrase "from gross earnings and revenues of whatever nature" caught her eye, but she looked up and said, 'Well, the only women going downstairs were Mickey's girls. They'd've all been picked up for prostitution. I was busted for drugs only three days ago. Can you imagine what Beryl would've said if I got nicked for tarting too?' Johnny snorted with laughter.

The clause she had her finger on appeared to give Handle the right to retain 30 per cent of whatever the signatory earned. There were subclauses referring to performance, performing rights, music publishing, mechanical rights, recording and so on. But even that didn't seem to cover what Handle Enterprises required. "Of whatever nature" looked as though, even if the signatory failed as an entertainer and became a shop assistant, Handle could take thirty per cent of his wages.

'What're we going to tell Bern?' Johnny asked. 'He's not going to be too chuffed, is he?'

'Listen to this,' Anna said. '"All expenses incurred by Handle Enterprises in the development, promotion, exploitation, and management of the undersigned shall be deducted from the net revenues of the undersigned." Sounds a bit steep to me.'

'He'll blame me,' Johnny said, still keyed up.

'Give over,' she said, turning a page. 'We've come away with this, and a sample of typed notepaper. We've made the connection between Lena, Odette, and Mr Hard with Dockers. And there must be a link between Ferdo Howe and Mr Graef. We're laughing.'

The last page revealed a very big space for signatures preceded by the words, "All signatories, individually and collectively, are bound by the terms and conditions of this agreement."

Johnny sighed. 'I suppose we don't have to put the raid and your rooftop caper in the report, do we?'

Anna waved the contract at him. 'If Shona signed one of these,' she said glumly, 'and if it's legal, she'll owe Handle thirty per cent of her old age pension, should she live so long. Danny Darling's going to go spare.'

'So we won't mention me calling the Bill, right?' Johnny asked.

The phone rang and he went to answer it. Anna shook her hair. It was nearly dry. She eased her arm into its sling and listened to Johnny's murmured comments. After a while he put the phone down with an exasperated click and said, 'We're going to have to change our story. The old fox knows about the raid already.' He shook his head crossly. 'Chummy we followed wasn't Mickey Stone. Mickey Stone went to Norwich, and Tim followed him back to Dockers which, surprise, surprise, was closed, with Bill crawling all over it.'

'Then who did we follow?' she asked, mystified.

'God knows.' He looked thoroughly out of sorts. 'Anyway, we've all got to go to the office tomorrow morning. So what're we going to say?'

'So what did you say?' Anna asked. She sat on Mr Horowitz's exercise bike and idly pushed the pedals. Soho and Horowitz Management were like anywhere else at Sunday lunch-time in London: dead.

'I told her I had to talk to her about a contract.' Mr Horowitz switched on the video and went back to his desk. 'She didn't want to come. But she's coming.'

A quartet of black women singing in close harmony appeared on the screen. He leaned forward to watch. Anna stopped pedalling and watched too. They sounded wonderful.

'Mmm,' he said.

'Mmm,' she agreed.

'They look like hell,' he said. 'But, maybe.' He shifted his buttocks restlessly in the chair. He was unable to keep his eyes off the Handle contract. Finally he picked it up and started to read it again. Then he threw it down.

'Well?' Anna asked.

'At least I know the worst.' He flicked the document contemptuously. 'This, I know how to fight. I'll shunt it on to the legal department tomorrow.'

'Is it legal?'

'Outrageous, yes,' he said moodily. 'Legal, perhaps. We'll see. Such a piece of garbage, Anna darling. So many stupid children to sign it.'

A ray of timid sunshine forked across his desk top. Outside the streets were still wet from last night's rain. A taxi drew up. From her position on the exercise bike Anna saw Shona's light furry head as she bent to pay the driver.

'She's here.'

He jumped to his feet and went down to let her in. The video played on, four women with the blues against a plunging background of bass and drums.

Shona stopped in the doorway when she saw Anna. She said, 'Hi, Snoopy. What you doing here?'

'Still watching your tail,' Anna said flippantly.

Shona threw her fur coat on the desk and flopped down in Mr Horowitz's seat. He went over to turn the set off.

'Leave it on,' Shona said. 'They're good. Give them to Lena. She'd make 'em look all right.'

'God forbid,' he muttered. 'Roz darling, listen. Anna here has brought me a curious thing.' He fumbled under the fur coat and pulled out the Handle contract which he placed tidily in front of her. She glanced at it briefly and looked up at Anna.

'Where did you get it?' she asked coldly.

'Mr Graef's office.'

'So?'

'Roz darling,' Mr Horowitz said, 'did you sign such a thing?'

'Danny Darling!' Shona sighed. 'If I had, what could you do about it?'

'Fight,' he said. 'Get you out of it.'

'In court?'

'However.'

She sighed deeply again. 'You and your pretty pink lawyers,' she said. 'Well, jolly good luck.'

'What're you talking about?'

'She means,' Anna said from the window, 'she doesn't think much of your chances with legal remedies when it's far from legal penalties being threatened.'

'We'll handle it,' he said stoutly.

Shona laughed. 'You'll handle Handle, will you?' she asked with heavy sarcasm. 'Goody gumdrops. And will you bring back Barbarella and raise poor Ferdo from the slab? Clever Danny.'

He looked at Anna in dismay. She said, 'You think Ferdo was another warning?' Shona didn't reply.

'I don't think so,' Anna said. 'It might've been very

convenient for them, but that's not all there was to it.'

The tape ran out and the screen exploded with electric snow. Mr Horowitz started nervously and went to switch it off. 'The Handle people killed poor Ferdo?' he asked Anna. 'You didn't tell me that.'

'I don't *know* that,' she replied. 'And it can't be proved yet. But Shona's certainly meant to think so. We've had various results through this morning. One of them was the autopsy which showed that Ferdo OD'd on uncut morphine and uncut morphine was among the things found at Dockers by the police last night. And Mickey Stone was also picked up carrying some of the same batch –'

'They raided Dockers?' Shona interrupted, expressionless.

'Sound familiar?' Anna asked back.

Shona said nothing. Mr Horowitz sat down on a hard chair and got his cigarettes out. 'So it sounds as if you think they did kill Ferdo.'

Anna shrugged and shook her head. 'Thinking's cheap, but the connections are there if anyone wants to make them.'

'But why – if not to frighten Roz?'

'Probably because they thought he'd try to milk their cow.' She looked at Shona. She was staring out of the window and didn't even seem to be listening. 'He had a picture of In Hock in his pocket when I saw him,' Anna went on. 'Later he had a wad of fivers and no picture. When he was dying he told me he'd sold his history. Maybe they gave him the morphine as part payment.'

'Maybe they forgot to tell him it was uncut,' Shona said coolly.

Mr Horowitz looked from one to the other like a man at a tennis match. He tapped a cigarette on his thumbnail. 'Counter-pressure!' he said suddenly, and stuck the cigarette in his mouth. 'The police don't know poor Ferdo came to Clarkestead with . . . whatsisname, do they?'

'Mickey Stone, Mr Hard,' Anna told him.

'So they get told. Yes? That should keep them busy for a while.'

'Unfortunately, it wasn't me saw them together,' Anna said. 'It was Porky.'

'That schlemihl!' he exclaimed. 'Roz darling, you must tell him to talk to the police.'

'All right,' Shona said. 'And while I'm at it I'll tell him to get his legs broken. Save everybody's time.'

He stared at her sadly and lit his cigarette. 'You don't trust us, do you, Roz?' he said. 'After all this time you don't trust me.'

She leaned over and snatched a cigarette from his pack. 'You still don't get it, do you?' she said and lit up with his desk lighter.

'You shouldn't smoke,' he said automatically. 'It's bad for your voice.'

Anna said, 'What she means is . . .'

'I know what she means,' he snapped. 'Listen, darling, I can get you all the protection you need. Porky too. You mustn't worry about that. Whatever you need to get these animals off your back – lawyers, bodyguards – you'll have them.'

'Okay,' Shona said brightly.

'But you mustn't pay them another penny.' He wagged a finger at her. 'And Lena has to go.'

'Ah.' She nodded and blew a ribbon of smoke across the desk. 'Poor Lena. Has to go, does she?'

'Roz darling, she's one of them!'

'No, she isn't,' Shona said clearly. 'Or has Snoopy told you different? Snoopy's seen her paying off the naughty men, right? Two and two make five, right?'

'Where's Lena now?' he asked. 'I thought you never went out without her. So where is she?'

'Don't be bitchy, Danny,' Shona warned. 'She got a call early this morning and she went out. I didn't ask. She didn't say. Some of us don't spend our lives prying.'

'I know where she went,' Anna said cheerfully. She gave the pedals a couple of turns.

'You would!'

'Want to know?'

'No!' Shona got up quickly and grabbed her coat. The tip of her cigarette brushed against it and there was a sudden whiff of burnt fur. 'You neither of you like her, do you? You don't like our friendship. Unnatural, right!'

'It's got nothing to do with that,' Mr Horowitz said patiently. 'Sit down. Don't be so childish. So you give money to Lena. Who does she give it to?'

'Ask Snoopy. She's had her little beadies open.'

'Why're you doing this?' he asked. 'Don't you recognize help when it's offered?'

'By poisoning my friend for me?' Shona said. She draped her coat over her shoulders. 'Yeah. Well, tell me one thing, Danny Darling. If little Roz Greenwood had come to you five years ago with Mr Graef's contract in her little hand, and she'd said to you, "Take me on, Mr Horowitz, sir. I've just signed this piece of shit and I need help. I need a kosher career." Tell me, would you've taken me on?'

He opened his mouth and for a couple of seconds no sound came out. Then he said, 'But, darling, you were with de Blank when I first met you.'

'And de Blank was with you. And you wrote him off. And he died.' She walked to the door. 'Ask him, Snoopy, what he did for de Blank, apart from the minimum – too late. And another thing,' she said, turning back. 'Guess what's Number One in the charts this week? And guess what just entered the charts at thirty-seven? Ask him if he'd take the same trouble for Roz Greenwood.' She waved her hand airily and walked through the door. Mr Horowitz still had his mouth open.

'Christ,' Anna said, 'she's impossible. What's the use?'

'She's wrong,' he said into his hands. 'I did everything I could for de Blank. Everything. But he was harder to help than she is even.'

'How wrong is she?' Anna asked curiously.

'She's not wrong about the Handle agreement. If I'd seen that four years ago I wouldn't have touched her with a barge pole.' He lifted his head and looked at her with mournful eyes. 'Go after her, darling. Please.'

'One more time,' Anna got slowly off the exercise bike. 'After that, *finito*. I've done what you wanted. Enough's enough.'

Chapter 46

The few people out that Sunday only glanced briefly at the sight of two young women quarrelling in the pallid sunlight. It was too cold for more than a casual turn of the head towards the flushed cheeks and raised voices.

Anna had completely lost her temper. 'You're so wrapped up in yourself and your banal little image. You think you're such a tough, lonely little superstar – all alone against the world,' she shouted at one point. And Shona who had begun with cold indifference warmed to the fight. 'You're no more than a bloodsucker yourself, you silly priggish bitch. I never asked you to go ferreting around.'

But after a while they ran out of insults to wound each other with and the wrangle became less personal. 'They're all bloodsuckers,' Shona said more quietly. 'What's the difference?'

'Well, maybe you're right,' Anna conceded. 'In your position someone's always going to take a percentage. Of course they are. But has Danny ever taken more than his due? Has he? Has he ever ballsed up his side of the bargain? Doesn't he work for his cut? They may both be bloodsuckers, but would you really rather pay Mr Graef thirty per cent for sitting on his fat arse and sending you demands and having your cat snuffed? That's stupid.'

'Okay, okay,' Shona shouted. And then more calmly. 'Okay, tell Danny he can wheel in the army if he thinks it'll work. You win, we'll do it your way. But I'm not having anyone put any pressure on Porky if he doesn't want to talk to the cops. Understand?'

They walked slowly towards Oxford Circus. On either side of them shops empty of lights and customers to breathe life into them looked like tombs. They moved tiredly as if they had just finished a strenuous race. At length Shona said, 'You don't like me much, do you?'

185

'So what?' Anna said. 'You aren't crazy about me either. But at least you're consistent, in your way.'

'Same to you. So what was that crack about the cops raiding Dockers? I suppose you think I had In Hock busted. That was the story that went round, wasn't it?'

'That's what I mean by consistent,' Anna said. 'I can't for the life of me see you doing that. But Ferdo could.'

'Yeah, Ferdo. Poor fucked-up Ferdo.'

'And Mr Graef. He's Will Graef's cousin, you know. That letter I found came off his typewriter. He's a bad enemy. I think this mess is as much revenge as extortion.'

'Well, tough titty.' Shona grimaced impatiently.

'So who pulled the rug?' Anna asked. 'Do you know?'

'You're at it again,' Shona said wearily. 'Can't leave things lay, can you?' She thrust her hands deep into her pockets and walked along, head bent. They crossed Oxford Circus and went on towards Marble Arch. A splattering of taxis passed but she ignored them. Eventually she said gruffly, 'All right, I know you're dying to tell me. Where is she?'

'Lena?' Anna asked, surprised. 'She's bailing her cousin out of chokey. Your Mr Hard isn't just a merry supplier of joy-dust to people like Van, or a collector of your pay-offs to Mr Graef. He also runs a string of business girls. Talk about bloodsuckers. I wonder what percentage he takes off them.'

'What's that got to do with Lena?'

'Her cousin, Janine, is one of Mr Hard's women. She was nicked for tarting last night at Dockers. Does that interest you at all?'

Shona stopped and swung to face Anna. 'What're you trying to tell me?' she asked, her face pale and fierce. 'That I shouldn't associate with Lena because her cousin's a whore? Or are you saying that because her cousin works indirectly for the Handles, Lena automatically does too?'

'Oh hell!' Anna exclaimed impatiently. 'Lena gives your money to her cousin. Her cousin either keeps it for herself, or acts as another channel to Mr Graef. She has to be involved.'

'Lena does what I tell her to,' Shona said, enraged. 'I asked her to do the dirty work, and she did. I didn't want those bastards fucking with my career, that's all. I thought money would satisfy them. I told Lena and she made all the deliveries. How she did it is her own concern.'

'How much bloody coincidence can you take?' Anna was getting angry all over again. 'Lena's a bloody plant. Who do you think delivers Mr Graef's demands? She probably killed your cat. Oh, I know I can't prove it. But I've watched her. She's clever and ruthless. She wants to isolate you, and she sets up tensions and quarrels which leave you with no-one but her to turn to. It's quite deliberate. She's using you and you don't know a damn thing about her. Go on, tell me how and where you met her.'

'Piss off. Everyone's using me,' Shona cried. 'I know all about Lena, which is more than you do. Okay, so her background's pretty naff. But she's got guts. She's ambitious. She got herself to art school. She's crawled out of the heap – which is what we're all trying to do, even you. Have you anything concrete against her except your suspicious little mind?'

'No.'

'Then shut up about her.' Shona started to walk again, head down into the wind which blew off Hyde Park. The trees were bare even of the first buds but on the ground daffodils were beginning to show a shy wink of yellow.

Anna caught up. 'All right,' she said. 'Lena wins – this time. But you'll see eventually.'

'No,' Shona said without turning her head. 'You will.'

They turned into Park Lane. After a few minutes Anna tried again. 'Do you know who had me busted?'

'In Bristol?' Shona stopped and laughed abruptly. 'Not my scene, Snoopy. You said so yourself.'

'I wasn't suggesting you. Van, Neil, and Lena knew I was out of my room. Lena knew I already had a matchbox full of your Mandies.'

'But you were caught with snow as well. Lena never touches snow. I told you, just leave Lena alone. I won't say it again.'

'Van, then?' Anna persisted. 'Are you saying it was Van?'

'Saying?' Shona began to get furious again. 'I haven't said a blind thing. You're the one making accusations.

You're the one has has to know every fucking detail. Me – I couldn't care less. I wasn't involved.'

'You're all heart,' Anna said quietly.

Shona stared at her for a long minute. Then she moved away and hailed a cab. When it pulled up at the kerb she turned to face Anna and said stiffly, 'Tell Danny it's okay, right? And Snoopy . . .'

'Yes?'

'You can stick around if you want to. But lay off Lena.'

Chapter 47

'You'd need to be a lot smarter than I am to catch that woman,' Anna said as she bent to pick up two wet corners of the Price's duvet cover.

'What woman?' asked Bea from the other end of the duvet. 'We were talking about Selwyn.'

They bundled the cover into an empty tumble-dryer. Bea fed coins into the slot and stood back, rubbing her damp hands down the side of her skirt. 'We've raised the money. You've got the time. What are we going to do about his bloody books?'

Machines hummed, water sloshed, and the warm air was scented with soap powder. Drowsy people slumped in plastic chairs, hypnotized by the sight of revolving socks.

'We buy them, don't we?' Anna said, sitting down beside Bea and stretching out her legs. 'I borrow Johnny's van, go down to Foolscap tomorrow, pay for them, load them on the van, and then I'll invite Selwyn to steal them.'

Bea started to laugh. 'He'll die of fright,' she said. 'He'll have a seizure.'

'That's the idea,' Anna explained. 'I want to make it sound so hairy that he'll leave the whole thing to me.'

'Shouldn't be too difficult.' Bea felt in her pocket for a box of peppermints.

'I hope not,' Anna replied. 'The tour goes north tomorrow and I have to join it on Wednesday.'

When Johnny phoned from Leeds the following night, Selwyn was sprawled in Anna's armchair looking distinctly pale. Johnny gave her a progress report and finished by saying, 'This is the life. That motor's a dream to drive, and you should see the hotel we're staying in – it's a bleeding palace.'

'No trouble?' Anna asked.

'Just a load of kids,' he said nonchalantly. 'They don't bother me. And that's a great organization. J.W.'s got. It's a pleasure to work for people with a bit of the necessary to splash about.'

'How're you getting on with Dave McPhee?'

'He's an ex-Para,' Johnny said respectfully. Anna hung up.

Selwyn poured more wine into his beer mug and said, 'Tonight, Leo? You're suggeting we rescue *Wholes and Corners* tonight? You aren't giving me much time.'

'We haven't got much time. I'm going up north tomorrow.'

'But tonight!'

'Why not?' Anna stabbed her finger on the inaccurate map Selwyn had drawn. She knew it was inaccurate because she had already been to Foolscap House that afternoon with Bea's cheque. She got up and opened the curtains. 'There's no moon tonight. It'll be really dark. It's cold and wet, so the night watchman will be tucked up in his office keeping warm. Bea's staying the night at her sister's, so she won't give you any bother. All you have to do is change into warm dark clothes, hold the crowbar, and keep watch for me.'

'Crowbar?' Selwyn asked nervously. 'I thought you said you could pick the lock.'

'Yes, but what if the night watchman *does* decide to do his rounds?'

'Are you suggesting I bonk him on the head with a crowbar?' Selwyn stuttered.

'You could bonk him on the head with a bottle of your Château Plonker if you prefer,' Anna said airily. 'Just so long as he doesn't catch us *in flagrante delicto* and set off the alarm.'

'Oh God!'

Anna looked at him solicitously. 'Are you sure you're up to this?' she asked. 'You don't look at all well. There's a lot of 'flu around. Maybe you're sickening for something.'

'Now that you mention it . . .' said Selwyn faintly.

When she thought about it later, Anna wished that everything was as easy to manage as Selwyn and his rescued books. With *Bitterness* at number one the crowds at Shona's concerts had swelled, and although the promoters rubbed their hands at every sold-out venue, the fans became more insistent and unruly.

'Look at those cretins, will you, Tiddler,' Dave sighed. They were watching from an emergency door, waiting for the crowds to disperse and allow them to escort Shona safely to her hotel. They had been waiting for over an hour. 'Isn't it enough they pay good money to get their eardrums split? If they knew Superbitch like I knew her they'd stop home and watch telly rather than knock about out here in the cold.'

'Love conquers all, and all that crap,' Lena said. Dave turned, startled. She was everywhere these days. Anna had become accustomed to her silent approach and barbed comments, but Dave still found her manner and appearance unnerving.

'Think it's love, do you?' he sneered, recovering quickly. 'Looks like brain damage to me.'

'Same difference,' Lena said, darting a sly glance at Anna. 'Everyone knows love rots the brain, don't they, Snoops?' It wasn't the first time she had made a knowing reference to her victory over Anna.

'Don't count on it,' Anna replied lamely. But maybe she was right. Maybe it was love. Nothing else explained Shona's blindness. Certainly she was even more isolated than before. Ducks had left one night in a tantrum largely engineered by Lena. And now Lena had sole charge of wigs, wardrobe, and make-up. She guarded the dressing-room with a triumphant jealousy that reminded Anna of a stoat in a rabbit hole. 'Doing your job for you,' she told Anna, eyes bright with sarcasm. 'My girl don't need outsiders telling her what's what.'

Everyone was an outsider now. Lena had made life so uncomfortable for Porky that he hadn't bothered to come north. Even the band rarely saw Shona to talk to except on stage. 'Ber-loody hell,' Van complained, having failed to break through to the dressing-room. 'What's she got in there? King Solomon's Mine?'

'You're not far wrong,' Wes said in a rare moment of insight. 'Lena's got her hands on the goodies now. She won't let the likes of us on board.'

Van wasn't so hyperactive since he had lost his supplier and was forced to buy drugs where and when he could. Luckily he knew nothing of Anna's part in the affair or he would have taken some sort of revenge. But even so she had learned to keep out of his way.

It was easier now because her only responsibility was for Shona's personal security. She stayed backstage throughout the concerts and no longer took orders from Dave.

Shona was settling quite calmly into the life of a celebrity. She lost her frayed tense look and seemed to rely less heavily on uppers and downers to get through her schedule. Anna never found out if her actions were responsible for this new confidence because Shona never mentioned it. She was neither thanked nor blamed. It was as if nothing had happened. In fact they rarely spoke to each other.

Everyone loved the fans, everyone hated them. They came in their thousands and everyone counted them greedily. They were the tour's visible sign of success but everyone hid from them and avoided them like the plague.

Anna spent most of her time helping Shona hide from them. She watched for the pushy ones and kept track of familiar faces. The one who had gatecrashed Clarkstead only turned up again as they zigzagged south of Leicester. She often saw his hungry face at the edge of a crowd. Sometimes she saw his VW outside the hotel they were staying in. Maybe he had to get home to London every night.

Anna wished she could go too. She was never very happy about leaving London for long. It wasn't that she didn't like the North – more a Londoner's feeling that real life was going on without her.

By the time the tour closed in St. Albans *Bitterness* had slipped to number three and *Logodaedaly* risen to fourteen in the UK charts.

Everyone felt they were associated with a success. Dog Records, the promoters, the sponsors, all claimed to be more than satisfied, and after the last concert, representatives from all of them came backstage to add their congratulations. The tour manager was the only one who looked less than ecstatic. He sat alone in a corner, his job finished, and got quietly but completely drunk. Anna thought he had aged considerably in the past few weeks.

Mr Horowitz wore his pleasure at Shona's success for all to see. 'A European tour next,' he said, rubbing his hands in satisfaction. 'What do you think of that, Anna darling? And after that, the States. I knew if we could get her over the bad patch she'd be on her way.'

The 'bad patch' hadn't been referred to lately. Anna had the impression that things were proceeding smoothly on the legal side. There had been plenty of precedents recently where musicians had escaped from extortionate contracts. And since Mr Graef had vanished and the police were still looking for him, he was in no position to make trouble. Certainly there had been no more demands on Shona.

'I guess you could say she's launched,' Avis said. 'She's in the studio next week to start recording the second LP.' Avis sounded a little dry. She had been appearing at gigs less frequently and it must have occurred to her that her days of favour were over now that Shona was established as one of Dog Records's great white hopes.

'Are you going to the party?' Avis asked. As usual, she was quietly doing the rounds with a champagne bottle.

'Yes,' Anna said. 'And you?'

'I suppose so,' Avis said. 'Danny invited me. Not Shona, you'll notice.'

'Never mind, love, she didn't invite me either.' Anna was sorry Avis took it so personally.

'Yes, well, see you later.' Avis moved on to fill another clutch of empty glasses.

Chapter 48

Danny Horowitz had arranged the end of tour party at Sandman's, an after hours club in the West End which catered mainly for the theatre crowd. It boasted Cordon Bleu food as well as dancing and entertainment, and was modelled on American clubs of the 'thirties. It was very popular with insomniacs of the smart set, too.

There were plenty of mirrors with art deco trim, drooping ferns, and pictures of glamorously swathed women who resembled Gloria Swanson. What it needed was soft sophisticated jazz and a clientele as elegant as the decor. But it didn't get them. It got disco music and anyone with enough money to pay the exorbitant prices.

The survivors of Shona Una's UK tour took up several tables to the side of the dance floor. Danny tried to be democratic about where everyone sat, but inevitably the luminaries gathered in the centre. The rowdy element collected around Van and already bread pellets were being flicked in all directions, wine was spilt, and the waiters cast anxious glances at the flambé trolley.

Anna found herself at the outermost table next to the service door along with Avis, Porky, Wes Gardner's wife, and a few of the lesser technicians.

'Definitely below the salt,' Wes's wife remarked, disgruntled because she had been separated from Wes. She was having a hard time with the menu, which was heavily prejudiced in favour of meat-eaters. 'I hope Wes is thinking green,' she said to Avis. 'He has to avoid all fried food and fat too. He had hepatitis five years ago, just after we married. I've had to watch his health for him ever since.'

Avis tried to look interested, but Wes's diet was an overworked topic. To change the subject, Anna asked about her daughter but was treated to a lecture about the difficulties of a vegetarian household in the fast food age. She was a fanatical woman, Anna decided, and wondered what Wes got out of the marriage. Stability, she guessed, which an older woman with a strong sense of purpose could give. She suddenly had the glimmering of an idea. But it was not the time or place to pursue it. Waiters converged on their table and began to take orders.

Danny came over and said, 'Anna darling, I only just remembered. What about Mr McPhee and those two boys outside? Shouldn't we ask them in too? I don't like leaving anyone outside. Would you go and see if they want a drink, at least?'

It was kind of him, Anna thought. No-one else had remembered the security team. The party itself was a generous gesture. It wasn't just for the band and the money-men; everyone had been invited.

As she passed Van's table he lobbed a bread roll at her. She caught it one-handed and took a bite. Further on Shona and Lena sat together like the black and white queens on a chessboard. Shona wore the silver and yellow wig and a robe of white and silver ribbons. She could not sustain the euphoria and was beginning to slump in her seat. Lena, gleaming all over with jet beads, whispered in her ear.

Anna ran up the stairs and went out into the street. The white BMW was empty. She wouldn't drive it again after tonight. She looked for Dave's car. It was empty too. Kevin's was nowhere to be seen. No Dave, no Kevin; so much for J.W. Protection. She wondered where they had found for their celebration drink. It was their last night on duty too. End of term, she thought. Damn.

She went back inside just ahead of a crowd of theatre people. The club was packed and they had to wait at the bar for tables. Anna squeezed between the tables to get to her seat. She avoided Danny's eye.

Just then the club photographer arrived and began to take pictures of Shona and the band. His flashgun was like a signal. A few people left their own tables and came over, either to talk or to ask for autographs. Van, an inveterate clubber himself, knew some of them. But some of the others, Shona included, began to look annoyed.

One of the executives from Dog Records stood up and

started to remonstrate politely with someone who had become a little too insistent. He moved away and as he did so Anna saw the tall fan with the hungry face.

'Hell,' she said and stood up. The waiters turned up with the food. She pushed past them. The fan leaned over Shona's table and said something. Shona replied. Watching her lips move, Anna saw Shona, almost as clearly as if she'd heard her, say, 'Piss off, wally.' The fan reared back as if she'd struck him.

Anna went over fast. Danny got up and stood between the fan and Shona, talking quickly. The fan stepped away, and backed into a waiter who was flaming crêpes suzettes at the table behind.

'It's all right,' Danny said, as Anna came up. 'I've spoken to him. He understands.'

The fan stood uncertainly, dry-washing his hands in a silly, obsessive motion.

'I'll get rid of him,' said the Dog executive, elbowing Anna aside. The waiter lit a taper and touched the surface of the liqueur with the flame. The pan flared.

'Pathetic little man,' Lena said loudly. The fan's face contorted. Dull red stained his cheeks.

'Take it easy,' Anna said softly and moved round the Dog executive towards him.

'No!' he screamed, 'No!'

In freeze-frame, Anna saw: his hand – the bright copper pan – the burning liqueur – the blue flame – his hand.

She threw herself at him. The Dog Record man, misunderstanding, knocked her aside.

The pan flew up and people scattered. Lena ducked behind Shona. The burning sauce hit Shona. Flame spread.

Shona started to scream.

The flashgun went off.

Chapter 49

The picture was in the evening papers the next day. Somehow it looked even more dreadful in black and white. Anna threw the paper down. It made her sick to look at it. She could still hear screams.

'"Pop Star Human Torch,"' Johnny read out loud. '"Fan Charged."'

'Leave it,' Bernie said firmly. They were sitting together in the new report room with the door shut. It smelled of wet paint.

'Could've been worse,' Johnny said, attempting kindness. 'She might've died.'

Once again, Anna saw the blistered skin, the terrified eyes, blackened hair. No brows or eyelashes at all.

'Look on the bright side,' Johnny said. 'They can work wonders with burns nowadays – a good plastic surgeon, and she'll be good as new.'

'Leave it,' Bernie said again.

'At least she can afford the best,' Johnny said. 'She's not short of a bob or two. Anyway, it's none of our business now. I can't see the Handles bothering with her any more.'

He looked up and, seeing Anna's wan face, at last changed the subject. 'Did anyone tell you? – Graef was arrested a couple of nights ago. Another vice squad bust, so we're told. And they're going to tack an extortion charge to the end of a very long list. What do you think of that? We started it off – you and me. A result, Anna, so stop looking like a wet weekend in Tooting.'

'Tragic,' Martin Brierly said, 'but there you are. As I said before, if you recall, Miss Lee, what a revolting world these people make for themselves.' He wiped a speck of dust from his brand-new pen set and turned a page of the report.

'You'll be glad to hear that no-one blames you in the least. Mr Horowitz saw everything, even that damn fool pushing you over. He says, too, that you were more than efficient in the aftermath. He says, quite justly I'm sure, that most of the blame lies with J.W. Protection.'

Martin Brierly smiled gently and turned another page. 'I spoke with Colonel Beamish this morning.' His smile almost developed into a grin. 'And you might like to know that Mr McPhee has been transferred out of their Executive and VIP Division. I'd say that was the least they should have done in the circumstances. We have it on record that you warned him about that fan, you pointed him out, you even gave McPhee the registration number of his car. All in all, Miss Lee, we have emerged from this affair most creditably. You mustn't blame yourself for the outcome. Nobody else does, I assure you.'

'I can't believe it,' Avis said over the phone a few days later. 'I just can't believe it. There's talk in the office of dropping her contract. Isn't that awful? I've had an offer from Virgin, and I think I'll take it. I don't think I could work for Dog if they dropped her.'

'That's pretty hard,' Anna said, depressed.

'Danny's been great, though,' Avis went on more cheerfully. 'He'll fight them tooth and nail. He's talking about the future already. It's nice to know someone cares.'

It was a long time before anyone was allowed in to see Shona. She had a private room at St. Thomas's Hospital, overlooking the river. Anna waited outside, sharing a bench with Wes's wife. 'Only one visitor at a time,' the nurse said, before striding away to find vases.

'I won't go in anyway,' Wes's wife said. 'I can't stand hospitals, can you? I'm surprised Wes wanted to come. He's so squeamish normally.'

'He's an old friend,' Anna said emptily.

'Still, it's an ill wind, as they say.' The woman shrugged. 'Shona lived the wrong sort of life, didn't she? She'd've burnt herself out before long, I shouldn't wonder, and brought Wes down with her. As it is, he's got some session work lined up with someone else. It's much more his thing. He can sleep in his own bed at night and eat proper food. I'll be able to keep an eye on him.'

Anna turned to look at her. A very ordinary-looking woman – straight hair, no make-up. She went on: 'I worry about him when he's on the road. It wouldn't be so bad if I could travel with him, but my daughter needs a settled home-life too. I've got to look after her.' She shrugged again, encouraged by Anna's attention. 'Hotels, you know – bad food, bad influences, groupies. I'll be very glad he won't be seeing Van again.'

Anna said, 'You're very protective.'

'I've got to be,' the woman said. 'Wes is rather easily led, I'm afraid to say. You wouldn't believe the state he was in when we met. I had to clean him up, sort him out, get him healthy again. It's not just for his sake. There's my daughter too. She was only ten at the time. I couldn't let his way of life ruin hers, could I?'

'No,' Anna said bleakly. It was so simple. As clear as light, she could imagine this ordinary woman picking up the phone and calling Market Square police station. All to make life healthier for her new man and her ten-year-old daughter. She couldn't really blame her either. But she could blame her for calling herself Hilary Simpson when she did it.

Had she known what Dockers was really like? Anna wondered. And that people like Ferdo and Mr Graef would hold such bitter grudges? It was possible. She opened her mouth to start asking questions, but Wes came out of Shona's room. He looked pale and nauseated. His wife jumped up and he leaned against her. 'It's ghastly,' he said. 'Let's get out of here.'

Anna closed her mouth. Who did it matter to anyway? Ferdo was dead, and if Shona had cared enough she would have defended herself at the time. Leave it lie.

The couple walked away arm in arm.

It was hot enough in Shona's room to make fresh flowers wilt. She was covered with a single sheet, and the sheet was supported by hoops. Her raw and hideous hands were in polythene bags. She lay motionless, blinded by bandages.

Anna said, 'Hello, Shona.' After a long pause, a weary croak replied, ''Lo, Snoopy.'

Anna was unable to take her eyes off the hands. She said, 'Is there anything you want, anything I can do?'

'Danny . . . brought tapes . . .' Shona whispered. 'Play . . . put on . . . Fats Domino.'

Anna found the tapes on the dresser and put one in the machine. *Blueberry Hill* rolled out of the speakers. She went back to the bed and sat quietly.

After a while Shona said, 'Snoopy? . . . you still there?'

'Yep,' Anna said, trying to sound cheerful.

'Where's . . . Lena?'

Anna's heart sank. 'Hasn't she come to see you?'

Weakly, Shona shook her head. 'You were right, Snoops,' she whispered. 'Everything you said . . . about her.'

'I'm sorry.' Silence followed. Anna wondered why she had been asked for. Fats Domino sang *I'm Walking*.

The husky voice said, 'Find her . . . please.'

'Christ, Shona. She won't come. I can't drag her here.'

'I don't want . . . advice . . . just help.'

At long last, Anna thought sadly, and too bloody late. She said, 'All right, love. I'll find her.' It would be easy enough, but pointless.

Shona was speaking again. Anna had to lean close to hear her over the music. 'I know she won't come . . . it's over for me too . . . but I want to know why . . . why she didn't . . . care. What's wrong with me?'

'It's not what's wrong with you,' Anna said, wanting to comfort her.

'I was on top of the world . . .'

'I know. Calm down.'

'But you will come back? . . . I know we don't get on, but I trust you . . . At the moment it's better than liking you.'

It might have been wiser to refuse, but Anna couldn't do it.

As she left, closing the door gently behind her, Fats Domino began to sing *What a Party*.

ABOUT THE AUTHOR

LIZA CODY is a graphic artist and novelist who lives in Frome, a small English village. She is the author of five Anna Lee novels, the first of which, *Dupe*, won the prestigious John Creasey Award for Best First Mystery and was nominated for an Edgar Award.

THE MYSTERIOUS WORLD OF AGATHA CHRISTIE

Acknowledged as the world's most popular mystery writer of all time, Dame Agatha Christie's books have thrilled millions of readers for generations. With her care and attention to characters, the intriguing situations and the breathtaking final deduction, it's no wonder that Agatha Christie is the world's best-selling mystery writer.

☐ 25678	**SLEEPING MURDER**	$3.95
☐ 26795	**A HOLIDAY FOR MURDER**	$3.50
☐ 27001	**POIROT INVESTIGATES**	$3.50
☐ 26477	**THE SECRET ADVERSARY**	$3.50
☐ 26138	**DEATH ON THE NILE**	$3.50
☐ 26587	**THE MYSTERIOUS AFFAIR AT STYLES**	$3.50
☐ 25493	**THE POSTERN OF FATE**	$3.50
☐ 26896	**THE SEVEN DIALS MYSTERY**	$3.50

Buy them at your local bookstore or use this page to order.

Bantam Books, Dept. AC, 414 East Golf Road, Des Plaines, IL 60016

Please send me the items I have checked above. I am enclosing $_____ (please add $2.00 to cover postage and handling). Send check or money order, no cash or C.O.D.s please.

Mr/Ms_____

Address_____ _____

City/State_____ Zip_____

AC–12/89

Please allow four to six weeks for delivery.
Prices and availability subject to change without notice.